Watching
Fireflies

Watching Fireflies

A LOVE BUG STORY
BOOK ONE

JAYCEE FORD

Watching Fireflies
Copyright © 2014 Jaycee Ford
Published by Jaycee Ford

Published: Jaycee Ford

Cover Design by Michelle at AlexandMe Designs

Interior Design and Formatting by

www.emtippettsbookdesigns.com

My dream turned into a possibility and became a reality because of you.

Chapter
One

JORDAN

The tick of the clock pounded inside my head. My fingers cramped, grasping the ballpoint pen tight within my grip. An eye twitch due to lack of sleep broke my focus, yet the pen scratched across the page in a battle against time. Caffeine pulsed through my body, my heart beating in double time with the ticking of the clock. The professor's eyes were on me, but I dared not look up. A single bead of sweat trickled down the side of my face as I ran out of the lined paper, continuing my final thoughts on the inside of the blue book's back cover. One last scribbled note and I lifted my hands, an exhausted breath escaping my lips as I sat on this side of the classroom for the last time.

"Pens down."

My heart lurched with a final bout of anxiety. Dozens of historical figures fluttered through my mind as I was plagued with the horror from a previous exam regarding the reasons for World War II. I had managed to forget to mention Adolf Hitler anywhere on the eight pages of the reviled blue book. Relief finally graced me as I dropped my pen to the table. I was done. I had completed my master's degree. I was now one step closer to moving back home to Charlotte, one step closer to becoming Mrs. Ryan Gordon.

Chairs scraped against the tiled floor as my classmates vacated the room, leaving the universally despised blue books in their past forever. A strand of brown hair hung in my face as I leaned down to get my bag. I tucked it behind my ear and crossed the bag's strap over my chest as I stood. After following the herd of cattle to the front, I stood before my professor as I placed my final exam on the pile with the rest.

"Good luck at Charlotte Catholic, Jordan."

A smile beamed across my face. I had been offered a position at a prestigious high school in Charlotte as an American history teacher, pending my degree. With my professor's well wishes, I believed I had just earned my dream job.

"Thank you, sir." I reached across the desk and shook his hand. Upon release, I turned toward the door to exit my final.

"And don't take any crap from a bunch of teenagers."

I laughed at his advice and waved as I left the classroom. The hallway was bustling with my classmates' freedom. The buzz swarmed of an afternoon outing. I assumed a massive amount of alcohol consumption was about to occur; however, I had more important things to do, like drive back to Charlotte and surprise my fiancé.

As soon as I stepped outside of the building, the sunlight

reflected off my ring, and I stared at it like I had so often since receiving it on the last day of my Christmas break. One year ago today, we had met, and three months from now, I would have his name. It was crazy and fast, but when we were together, he was perfect. I didn't know how I had gotten so lucky. My phone rang, pulling me out of my daydream, and I reached into my bag. My best friend's name lit up the screen.

"Hey, Katherine!"

"Are you done? Are you done? Do you get to move back home now?" Katherine had graduated with me two years earlier from North Carolina State University, receiving her bachelor's degree in accounting. I'd stayed to pursue my master's degree, and she had left to become a pencil pusher in the accounting department of a law firm back home in Charlotte. We had been inseparable throughout high school and college, a prequel to the rest of our lives.

"I'm done! Leaving now!" I hopped into my car. The excitement of finally being finished with school surged through me. I started my little four door, rolled down the windows to air out the May heat of Raleigh, and then adjusted the rearview mirror. The dark circles of exhaustion beneath my blue eyes beckoned me to question driving straight to Charlotte immediately after my final exam, but the decision had been made. I couldn't wait to see my fiancé.

"And… what are y'all's plans for tonight?" I switched to Bluetooth as I eased out of my parking spot, looking over the boxes piled up in the back seat. Anything that couldn't fit or wouldn't be needed within the next week was already in the mail to my parents' house.

"I'm going to surprise him. He thinks I'm coming home

tomorrow."

"Need to release some of the stress there?"

The air conditioner kicked in, and I rolled the windows up, laughing at her antics. "Yes. Yes, I do. Two weeks has been long enough."

"Just don't ruin his suit when you claw at him," she joked at his constant attire. A suit made the man, but he definitely looked better without the suit.

"As soon as I knock on the door, I'm stripping him of all three pieces." I gripped the steering wheel tighter. Two weeks had been too long.

"Don't knock. Use the key! He gave you a key! You're supposed to be moving in tomorrow anyway. Just use the key!"

"Should I? I mean, I should. It's practically my apartment now."

"Yes! Do it! Okay, just text me when you get home. Maybe we can all go out tomorrow for ladies' night," she said, piquing my interest.

"So, which suit of Ryan's coworkers do you want to ruin?"

"I didn't think he'd let you go alone, so if that's the case, I'm not picky!" She laughed over the phone.

"You are *so* picky, Katherine." I slid on my sunglasses to block the sun's rays while ignoring her jab about Ryan not letting me go out alone. He was just protective, but she wasn't the one marrying him. I was. She would just have to deal with it. Besides, he hadn't seen me for two weeks. I didn't think he'd let me go alone, either. "I'm merging into traffic, Katherine. I'll text you later."

"Okay. Be careful."

"Love you. Bye." The phone powered off as I turned up the new country crooning on the radio.

After the two-hour-plus drive to Charlotte, I stopped at a convenience store and picked up a six pack of Ryan's favorite beer. A few signal lights and a right turn later, I idled in a parking spot as I stared at his apartment complex—our apartment complex. I couldn't believe I was finally going to be with the most perfect man.

Excitement pulsed through me as I got out of the car, lugging my bag and the six pack of beer along with me. I climbed the flight of stairs to his door with the key clutched tight within my grip. This was my home now, too. There was no reason why I shouldn't use it. I stared at the lock, the key resting just inside, but I couldn't push it in. Ryan preferred structure and an organized schedule. Very early in our relationship, I decided to go away for the weekend with Katherine. She needed a breather from work and I needed one from grad school. He went over the edge when I didn't go visit him that weekend and went to Myrtle Beach instead. The texts and phone calls were crazy. That just proved how much I meant to him so early on. He still called and texted like crazy; I never understood his constant need for reassurance. But barging in on him was something I didn't think he would appreciate. I pulled the key away from the door, stuffed it back into my bag, and assured myself that tomorrow I could come over unannounced, but doing so today wasn't the brightest move, I raised my hand up and let my fist rap on the door. I couldn't wait to throw my arms around him. I hadn't seen him for two weeks due to finals, and now, we would never have to be apart again.

I stood still as I waited, but there was no answer. I walked over to the railing and peered out into the parking lot. His car was parked a few spots away from mine, so I knew he was here. I knocked once more and waited again. The element of surprise lurked around me, tempting me, and I pulled out my keys as I walked back to the door and quietly let myself into the silent apartment.

A smile inched up my face at the sound of the running shower. Images of his body drenched by water and lathered up with soap filtered through my mind as I emptied my hands of my bag and the six pack of beer. I walked toward the bathroom, tossing my jacket on the ground, taking down my hair, and then pulling the shirt over my head. As I slowly opened the bathroom door, I smirked at the sounds of his quiet grunts emerging over the showering water.

Knowing a man had needs, I slowly grabbed the shower curtain. Throwing it open, I purred, "Need a hand, sexy?"

My breath hitched.

My feet froze in place.

I stared at my fiancé as he continued to thrust. His eyes slowly opened and he did not stop fast enough at the sight of his fiancé standing in front of his apparent conquest. My heart plummeted into the pit of my stomach, bile rising up my throat.

"Oh… my … God…"

His eyes widened when they settled on me. "Jordan!"

My gaze drifted down at some bleached blonde bitch with Ryan… in her mouth.

"Oh, my God!" My eyes flickered back up to his, which were filled with shock. Was this my fiancé? Was this the kind of man I intended to marry? How could I have been so oblivious?

"Jordan, it's not what you think!" The words echoed in the bathroom while he freed himself from my replacement's mouth. That phrase alone snapped me out of my incoherent stupor. He struggled to step out of the shower while my stand-in knelt with her head down, resuming her position.

"Ryan, how stupid do you think I am? Your dick was just in someone's mouth!" A whirlwind of emotions flared through me. My vision blurred with a mix of rage and tears. I couldn't believe this was happening. A year! I had been with him for a year! Ice seeped through my veins, freezing me into this spot. My chest hollowed with despair, regret lodging with the toxins creeping up my throat. He stepped toward me as disgust riddled me. All that I had done with him was a lie. Our whole future was a failure before it even began.

I was so appalled at myself and the unsettling sight. My feet finally willed themselves to move and I stormed back into the living room, putting distance between me and my fiancé as I yanked my discarded clothing back on. A naked and dripping wet Ryan followed me. I turned around and found no shame reflected in his distrusting brown eyes as they widened. I turned my back on him and started for the door, not wanting to deal with the horrid memories that would forever seep into my brain.

"Please, sweetheart. I can explain." He grabbed my arm and spun me around, keeping me from fleeing his life. A hand snaked around my other arm and clamped down to grip me so tightly in place I couldn't wriggle out of his hold. I twisted my arms within his constricting hands. A sob escaped my mouth. I just wanted to go.

"Let go of me…" I begged through heart-wrenching tears, the air catching in my throat. I couldn't breathe. He shook me in place, his fingers digging painfully into my arms.

"No, God dammit! Stop trying to run away from me!"

I flinched at his barking order while wincing from the pain.

"Let me go, fucking bastard!" The vile sight of that man gave me the strength to put as much distance as possible between me and this place. I yanked one arm from his grip, and my opened hand slapped his cheek. His head turned to the side, following the force of the blow. The room became eerily still as the man I had loved so much inflamed with anger. His head creaked slowly back toward me; his nostrils flared as he clenched his jaw and focused on me with a glaring shock. Disapproval crossed his face and, for a moment, I feared I had wronged him. I covered my mouth with a shaking hand, but then the sight of a robe-covered imposer caught my eye from the bathroom doorway. He'd wronged me! He did this to us; to the future I thought we would have. I raised my hand again and slapped him harder than the first time, glaring back at him the way he'd done to me.

I ripped my other hand from his clutch, my chest heaving for breath. Fire spread across my skin as my lungs ached from the sobbing pain. I grabbed my bag and ran for the exit. When I reached the door, I glanced back at the man I thought I knew. He stood completely still in utter silence. His hands clenched into fists and his narrowed stare never wavered.

I wouldn't let him control me anymore. I wiggled the ring off my finger–the ring I had not once removed since he'd asked me to marry him. I chucked it at him. It bounced off his naked stomach and fell to the floor with finality.

"You can pay your whore with that," I fumed through heartbreaking sobs. Closing my eyes, I twisted the knob and opened the door to a better life, a life where I never had to see his face again.

When I reached my car, I fell into the driver's seat, slamming the door shut behind me. My hands rested on the steering wheel, and I gripped it tighter to ease their shaking. I stared at my bare finger, noticing the faintest tan line where the ring had been for so many months, now void of the weight. The tears streamed down my face. I heard my name being yelled outside. I saw a barefoot, bare-chested ex-fiancé running toward me. I ignited the car into life, slammed my foot down on the gas, and sped away. I never looked back. I promised myself that I never would.

Chapter Two

JORDAN

The wheels of a rolling suitcase echoed down the hardwood floor of Katherine's building. I adjusted the duffle bag that was dislocating my shoulder, shifting the strap away from the still-sensitive spots on my upper arms. It had taken weeks for the deep bruises to heal; bruises in the shape of Ryan's broad fingertips. The skin was still tender to the touch, or maybe I was just raw all over. I heaved another sigh as I continued down the long corridor. Sighs were my only form of communication of late. I had hibernated my summer behind the door of my childhood home, listening to hundreds of unanswered calls going straight to voicemail. I didn't want to leave the house, not when I knew he was somewhere on the outside. The cutthroat financial advisor knew all about money and had a lot of it; he wanted to climb the corporate ladder with some sort of trophy wife on his arm. A reflection caught my eye as I passed by a mirror in the hallway. My hair was haphazardly thrown into a ponytail as I modeled a NC State T-shirt and running shorts. My cheeks sunk in as I sported a winter's tan. My eyes grayed like the inside of my soul. I was so far from lost. Yep. I was some trophy all right.

And this was all my fault.

I turned away from the unsettling sight and continued down a few more doorways until I reached Katherine's condo. Inconvenience was something I would rather not bestow upon my friends, but my parents had left for a well-deserved vacation and I couldn't stand to stay alone. The suitcase rolled to a stop behind me and I adjusted the strap on my shoulder once more. As I raised my hand up to knock, I exhaled in an attempt to rid the toxic past from my being. I didn't bother trying to smile. I knew it wouldn't work. The door flew open and my best friend stood in front of me with a bittersweet happiness etched across her face. Auburn hair softened her features, but in her narrowing brown eyes I detected a certain amount of pissed-off-ness.

"Thanks for letting me stay?" I shrugged my shoulders in question and winced away from her glare.

"I barely get any texts much less a call from you since you've been back." She opened the door for me to pass, but didn't bury her frustrations. "You could have called me, you know." She closed the door behind her as I wheeled my suitcase into the middle of her expansive condo. "I know what he did was shitty—so ungodly shitty—but you can't be a hermit. You can't let him win."

The view out of her picture window drew me. I stood

before the wide expanse of glass and got lost in overlooking Center City Charlotte, watching the line of cars weave down North Tryon. The morning sun beat down on the pavement, summer stretching on for what seemed like an eternity. I turned away from the sun, wanting to hide from the light. Her welcoming palette of colors soothed me to an extent, but I hadn't healed in these past few weeks.

"I don't have to let him win. He already won." I dropped my bag to the floor as my best friend's eyes softened from the glare of anger to sympathy and sorrow.

"Honey, *he* lost *you*. He didn't win." She unfolded her arms and walked over to me. She tried to pull me into a hug, but I pushed away. I couldn't handle being coddled. I wanted to live in my misery alone. But I just couldn't *be* alone.

"But look at me. I'm a wreck! If I hadn't gone home a day early, nothing would have happened! I would be getting married in a few weeks. I would be happy." The tears reappeared as they had so often this summer. "Does this look happy?"

"It looks like a damn fool. Who would accept her fiancé's dicking around? That's what he did, Jordan. He dicked around on you. Do you want that? For even the possibility of happiness?"

"But I didn't—"

"And now you know. It's better that you know." She wrapped her arms around me. "I swear. You don't want that. You don't want a guy who needs to go somewhere else."

As if on cue, my phone started to ring. His song played over and over, not letting up. She pulled out of our hug with her face wrinkled in annoyed confusion.

"Why is he calling you?"

I released a sigh.

"Because he calls every day."

"Why haven't you changed your number?"

I shrugged my shoulders in reply, but I knew that a part of me needed the constant reminder to never trust someone that much again. No man was worth all of this pain.

"Tell him to stop."

I shook my head. "I've tried that. It doesn't—"

"You tell him to fucking stop, or I'm going to."

I nodded as I pulled out my phone before dropping my bag back to the floor. I stared at the screen lighting up with Ryan's name across it. It continued to ring, reconnection within my grasp. I didn't move fast enough and Katherine snatched it from my hand. She swiped her finger across the surface. As soon as she placed it up to her ear, I grew a pair and snatched it back.

"Ryan, I've asked you to stop calling me."

Before I could exhale, Katherine showed her distaste.

"Tell him to stop. *Tell!*" He could hear her clearly through the phone, but what did it matter anymore.

"Ryan, stop calling me."

He breathed heavily into the phone, and with a scratchy voice, he said, "Sweetheart, you know I won't stop until you come back home."

Katherine's constant encouraging glare gave me the sort of confidence I needed.

"Well, I hate to break it to ya, but that ain't happening."

"Well, I hate to break it to you, sweetheart, but you're going to have a little trouble stopping me." His voice made me cringe; a mix of emotions I couldn't place. He laughed and continued, "And I always get what I want."

"You know what, Ryan? Whatever." I hung up and looked to Katherine, holding the tears back as best as I could.

"I never did like him. A year ago, you would have never allowed yourself to turn into what you've turned into now. And all because of a guy like him?"

My chest hollowed at her words. "I was going to marry him."

"Well, I should have spoken up sooner then, and that's my fault, but he was obsessive and controlling. You just let him get away with it time and time again. I never knew why, and I never approved."

I grabbed my bags and, without saying a word, marched to the second bedroom where I usually stayed after nights of partying—where I had been staying when I met Ryan out with his coworkers at the beginning of last summer. I wished I had never gone into that bar and let him buy me drink after drink. I was putty in his hands from that point on, and I was still a mess.

My best friend, out of all people, couldn't tell me what kind of man I was marrying? Was I that blind? How could he have brainwashed me so much into thinking he was so perfect? Why did I believe him to be so perfect?

The sun beamed against the mocha-colored walls, and my eyes winced from the glare. I dropped my bags in the middle of the floor and immediately went to the window, shutting the curtains. I huddled within the darkness. I went for my bags and the one I needed most. The *zip* echoed in the empty space as I heard the front door close behind Katherine's departure for work. The welcoming sight of six bottles of red grinned at me. Once I found my corkscrew, the first smile in weeks eased up my face.

THE THICK GLASS of an empty wine bottle hit the carpeted floor with a *thud*. I stared off into the distance of vast nothingness, my gaze settling on the plaster ceiling. I had given that man a year that ended with me being sucked into a black hole. I was scared it would never allow me to escape. What did it matter anymore? The phone rang again as it had over and over while I had been holed up in Katherine's guest room for the past three days. How could he want me so badly, yet go to someone else when I couldn't be there? Was I that awful of a person?

I reached over to the nightstand only to find nothing there. I peeked over the bed and counted nine empty wine bottles, six of mine and three of Katherine's that I had stolen yesterday. Her stash of wine was vast. I doubted she would even notice. As if on cue, Katherine burst into my room, slamming the door back against the wall.

"That's it! You're out!"

"What…" I garbled, hearing her clearly, yet barely comprehending.

"I can't take your self-pity. Get up. I can't deal with babying your ass anymore. You have the strength to deal with this, even if you don't believe you do." She glared at me, crossing her arms over her chest. I shot up into a sitting position and winced from the alcohol-induced head rush. When my eyes focused after a momentary lapse, I glared right back at my supposed best friend.

"Katherine!"

"Oh, don't Katherine me! You are getting a dose of tough love! Get up!" Katherine pulled me to my feet and pushed me out into the hallway and toward the bathroom.

"You stink! Take a bath!" She slammed the door behind her, but continued to yell, "We're going out tonight or I am seriously shipping you off to Vegas to meet your parents. And you *know* I have the means to do so!"

The slam of the door awoke something inside of me and pulled me out of the trance that had taken over my mind for the past few weeks without Ryan. Turning the water to a scalding temperature, I undressed and tossed my clothes into the trash can, solidifying my first step toward a life without him. As I stepped underneath the cleansing water, the heat tingled across my skin. I slowly scrubbed the grime, washing it all away.

I emerged from the bathroom in a robe with a towel wrapped around my hair. Katherine's tough love seemed to help – or maybe it was the not smelling like a hyena that helped. Either way, I actually felt like getting out and doing something for the first time in weeks. When I walked into the living room, I noticed Katherine was wearing a jean skirt with a tank top and a pair of cowboy boots.

"Cowboy boots? What's the occasion?" I asked as I helped myself to more wine.

"We, my dear friend, are going to Whisky River."

I instantly perked up with the knowledge of my Friday night.

"I love Whisky River." I took a long sip of white, but it was stolen from me. I gasped as a little wine sloshed out of the glass.

"I know. Go get ready so we can have a girls' night."

I snatched my wine glass back.

"I need this to get ready."

A PAIR OF hip-hugging jeans with a tight, plaid-button up shirt covered my body as my trusty cowboy boots clicked against the floor into Whisky River. The bar was packed with weekend revelers. We waited in line for a drink as Katherine gasped beside me.

"What?" I hollered over the crooning of Luke Bryan.

"Hot attorney, hot attorney." Katherine worked at a law firm in the city. She definitely had a thing for men in suits; however, when I followed her eyes, they landed on a blond in jeans and a buttoned-up shirt with the sleeves rolled up. I nudged her in the middle of her gawking.

"Go tell him hi."

She shook her head and looked back toward me.

"Way out of my league."

"Oh, please."

She placed her hands on my shoulders, and her brown eyes widened with determination.

"Tonight is about you, and we're about to have fun, chick." We moved up in line and Katherine ordered. "I need two drafts and two shots of whiskey."

"Whiskey, huh?"

"Yep. Now, what do you want?"

A MIXTURE OF wine, beer, and whiskey filtered through my body with no best friend in sight, but I owned the dance floor like no one had before. At least, I felt that way. It was more than likely the whiskey owning it, but I didn't care. I swayed my hips to the beat of Trace Adkins as strong arms weaved around my waist. Hips massaged into me as I let the beat lead the way. I was single and free. I aimed to do whatever I wanted without the responsibility of being a controlled wife, and right now, it felt damn good. A hand pushed the hair off my neck and light kisses peppered up to my ear.

"I told you I always get what I want." I froze at the sound of his voice. "Why are you dancing like a slut and letting any and every bastard grind up on you?"

He pressed himself harder against me and I tried to pull away, searching for anyone's attention for help. His arm yanked me closer as his fingers threaded through my hair and pulled my head to the side. He nibbled my ear lobe, an act that used to make me willingly fall to my knees, but all I could do now was tremble in terror.

"Ryan, let me go!" I yelled over the music. My hair was pulled back, and then his grip released. Katherine's hot attorney pulled him away from me as she grabbed my hand. We ran straight for the exit, his words chasing after me.

"I will find you, Jordan!"

The tears I had kept bottled up during the evening blurred my vision as we hopped into a cab. Katherine pulled me into a hug, telling the driver to go. I wept on her shoulder, not for the man I had lost, but for the man he had become. Or maybe it was the man he'd always been, but I had been too stupid to see it. I continued to cry as Katherine rubbed my back all the way back to her condo.

AFTER THAT NIGHT, his ringtone hadn't blared from my phone for a few days. Peace consumed me, a foreign concept this summer. The school year was approaching soon and I looked forward to my new job and the new possibilities.

A knock came from Katherine's door. I glanced at the clock to see it was just after five. Maybe she'd forgotten her keys. I rose from the kitchen table and walked to the door. As I opened it, I gasped, a chill rising up my spine. I tried to slam the door shut, but he wedged his foot inside and pried it open.

"Sweetheart, why do you keep pushing me away? I just want to talk to you. It's been weeks already. Can't we talk?" He stood inside the open door. His disheveled hair edged his menacing eyes, his body strumming with fury.

"I have nothing to say to you, Ryan. You need to leave." I feigned confidence and stumbled backward, putting distance between us.

"Baby, you know I can't leave you, and you know you can't live without me." He moved closer to me. His eyes looked so cold… so haunting. The confidence I needed was nowhere to be found, but I stuck my chin up in the air and steeled my face anyway.

"Ryan, what you did is unforgivable. I don't want you near me."

He grabbed my shoulders at my last word, and kept me from pulling away.

"Jordan. I'm not going anywhere. You belong to me."

My body slammed against the wall, but I didn't fall. I kept my eyes firm on his even though my whole body trembled. He slithered closer to me, my stomach turning with each step.

"Ryan, you have to leave."

His body pressed against mine. He nuzzled his face against my neck and inhaled the scent of my hair. My body cringed with disgust. The warmth of his breath seared my ear as he seethed with dominance.

"You. Are. Mine."

My body trembled as tears rolled down my cheeks. How could I have ever been with someone like him? How did I manage not to see who he really was all those months I spent with him? A whole year of my life?

The front door slowly pushed open, and then slammed back against the wall.

"What the fuck are you doing here? Get your hands off her or I'm calling the cops! Now!" Katherine barged in as Ryan turned back to look at me with his evil grin and a laugh to match it.

"Another time, sweetheart." He kissed my cheek, brushing passed Katherine on his way out.

The floodgates opened as I slid down the wall. I had made the decision. I was leaving this city and getting as far away from my ex fiancé as I could.

Chapter Three

JORDAN

The car silenced with the turn of the key. I stared at what was to be my home for the next few months as I sat motionless in the silence of the countryside. I had to get away. Three months of hell would push anyone out of the city. I just couldn't do it anymore, and I had to get away before anything worse happened. I had accepted a position as a world history instructor at a community college in the middle of the foothills after relinquishing the highly sought after position at Charlotte Catholic, an opportunity I had desperately wanted. Three months ago, I left my last exam excited for the promising life that stood in front of me, all to have it taken away within moments. I exhaled one last breath and hugged my purse to me as I got out of the car.

"What is that smell?" I slammed the car door closed behind me and stood in front of an old country inn. The beauty of the weathered, three-story house didn't match the horrendous odor surrounding it. While I admired the long wrap-around porch, the smell of the cow manure in the heat of the southern summer assaulted my senses, making me gag. I couldn't help but pinch my nose against the stench.

The horrid smell came back in a wave as the breeze picked up. I held my breath as I grabbed my laptop bag out of the back seat, slung it over my shoulder, and slammed the door. In an attempt to get inside the inn as fast as possible and away from the stench, I fumbled with the car keys. Once I reached the trunk, they slipped out of my hand and fell to the ground.

"Damn it!" I inhaled again, followed by the now ever-present gag reflex. It was definitely the smell of a farming town. I held my breath as I grabbed my suitcases out of the trunk and slammed it shut. My heels lodged in between the gravel on the path as I stumbled to the front door of the inn. The moment I was inside, I exhaled to the welcoming sound of country chimes.

The scent of cinnamon and apple pie replaced the smell of the farming town that surrounded the quaint inn. Pristine, antiqued, white walls served as a canvas to the largest display of country living I had ever seen. Lace curtains covering the windows flanked the doorway and muted the afternoon sunlight. Wooden rockers steadied on either side of a fireplace, which, thankfully, wasn't lit. Over the mantel hung a wooden sign simply stating, *Welcome to The Inn*. Presumably, *The* meant "*The One and Only*."

"Good afternoon. Welcome to The Inn," a warm female voice said behind me, taking me away from my adoration of the country atmosphere. An older lady stood behind a counter. She was much shorter than me with curly gray hair cut short and hot pink framed glasses that matched her shirt. She looked like quite a character.

"Good morning," I said while peering down at her name tag, "Ethel." Of course, her name would be Ethel. "My name is Jordan Hawthorne, and I have a room reservation."

Mrs. Ethel turned to the oak bookshelves that lined the wall behind her, pulled out a huge ledger, and placed it on the matching wooden counter in front of her. While she perused the aged sheets through her bifocals, her finger slowly skimmed down the page. She stopped halfway down and replied, "Yes, Ms. Hawthorne, here it is, and it's an open-ended reservation, correct?"

"Yes, ma'am. This will be my home away from home for the time being."

A natural, warming smile lit up her face.

"Well, welcome! I have you set up in the suite. It should be the most comfortable for you. Across the foyer is the dining room, where breakfast is served between 6:30 and 7:30. If you want some biscuits and gravy, you better be down here early. Those, of course, are my husband's favorite, so he naturally cooks them every morning. Everyone calls him Chef Al. Unfortunately, dear, he's not very handy with tools, and there is a slight leak from the sink in your suite. I've been trying to get in touch with my nephew to come fix it, but I haven't got a hold of him today. Would it be all right if he comes by in the morning?" She rattled out the whole thing without taking a breath.

"Oh sure, that won't be an issue." I would be getting settled at the community college anyway. Basking in Mrs.

Ethel's grin, I continued, "This facility wouldn't be equipped with Wi-Fi, would it?"

Her grin turned into a chuckle. "Oh no, dear, I'm sorry, but down the block is Main Street. There's a new coffee shop with that fancy coffee that everyone talks about, and they also have the internet. That might be suited better for your work. No reason to be stuck up there in that room."

Mrs. Ethel continued introducing me to The Inn, and when she finally handed over the key, she instructed me that my suite was number six located on the third floor. With a thankful nod, I picked up my bags, anxious to see where I would be spending the next few months, but before I stepped up the first step, I turned back around.

"For the record, if anyone ever calls looking for me, you've never heard of me."

Her smile faltered for a moment, but she nodded in understanding.

"No problem, dear. I understand."

"Thank you." The tightness eased in my chest as I turned back toward the stairs and hauled my luggage up the three flights. The smell of apple pie followed me all the way to my room. As I opened a door marked with the number six, I mumbled, "Home sweet home."

The afternoon sun hid behind lace curtains, the cool room kept the sweat from dripping down my face. The grip holding the handle of my bag loosened, and it met the floor with a *thud*, breaking the silence in the vacant room. A pale yellow rug matched the patterned quilt adorning a white iron bed. A few framed paintings hung on the neutral colored walls, mirroring the Blue Ridge Mountains that hid behind the lace curtains. I stepped out of the doorway in awe of how my life had changed so vastly within a few weeks. I went from a fiancé to a girl in hiding. How did everything come to this?

The view outside the window beckoned me, and I eased myself away from the open door, rolling a suitcase behind me. The door closed by itself as I left the suitcase in the middle of the floor to eye the view on the other side of the lace curtains. I pushed them open to be graced with rows upon rows of rolling hills, peaking up to the Blue Ridge Mountains in the distance. My shoulders relaxed for the first time in weeks with the sense of calm and peace. Even for just a moment, it eased my aching heart and soothed my bruised ego.

Knowing I had to get the painful moving process over with, I dropped my laptop bag on a little bistro table tucked in the corner of the room. I walked over to my suitcase and lugged it on top of the bed, unzipping it much slower than I should have; reluctant to begin my existence as a runaway, so far from the life I had planned. I could survive this for a semester or two, I assured myself. There would be more opportunities for dream jobs in Charlotte.

I shook my head and squared my shoulders before unpacking my belongings, which consisted of only clothes and a few framed photographs of my parents and Katherine. After emptying the over-sized suitcase, I placed the pictures around the suite, trying (and failing) to make it feel like home.

After adjusting a frame on the dresser, I anchored another slightly in front of it. My smile in the picture was one of hope and optimism as Katherine and I wore our caps and gowns with pride. When we graduated high school, we believed nothing could stop us. I never dreamed that years later a man could make me crumble to my knees.

A shiver ran up my spine as the memory of his hands all over me, pressing me against a wall, vomited up from my brain. His ominous laugh echoed in my ear. *I always get what I want.* I closed my eyes and exhaled a deep breath, reassuring myself that I was far enough away, having left without telling anyone where I was going. Steadying myself with the task at hand, I grabbed another frame. A gasp escaped me when a picture of the man whom I ran away from burned my eyes. Shaking, I chucked the frame encasing the devil across the room. The glass shattered against the floor, and I clenched my chest as I sank down to the bed, straining for breath, my heart racing.

While I tried to retrieve the sense of calm I had earlier, a repetitive drip echoed throughout the room, a quiet hammering in my ears that reinforced the pounding in my chest. I pushed up from the bed and walked over to the bathroom, hoping there would be a way to quiet the annoyance. As I eased open the door, the unpleasant sound of dripping water vanished when my attention was diverted by white claw feet holding up a huge, high back tub, beckoning me to fill it with water and bubbles and sink into a foamy embrace. A smile crawled up my face, until the thought of showers and Ryan seeped back into my brain. My grin faltered.

I walked back to the bed and grabbed my bag of toiletries, my phone with ear buds, and a robe, deciding that I deserved one final cleansing of my former life. After stripping out of my clothes, I sat on the side of the tub running my fingers through the stream of water. As it turned warm, I began to pour in the bubble bath, watching the bubbles foam up. I readied my phone with music while the water continued to rise. When the tub became full, I turned off the water and eased myself into the rolling hills of suds, determined that this would be the last time I ever felt weak over that man – or any man. My phone rang his tune and I pressed decline for the hundredth time. He always got what he wanted, or so he said. Well, not this time.

The heartbreaking music played softly in my ears, and I closed my eyes before they burned with tears. My chest knotted with a sob, but I tried to keep it together. I never expected this of my life. I would forever only be Ms. Jordan Hawthorne. The only thing I could hope for was to let sleep consume me and awaken better than before.

I slid down into the hot, sudsy water and let my eyes close. The sobs rolled out, deep and slow, like a thunderstorm churning up out of the depths of my soul. Eventually the sobbing slowed to just tears and the occasional hiccup, and I began to relax into the sound of the music playing through my ear buds. Suddenly a loud *thump* echoed over the music purring in my ear. I cracked my swollen eyes, slowly until my blurry vision focused on a figure standing in front of me. Ryan! My heart lurched with the thought he'd found me, until the outline of broad muscles hiding under a T-shirt assured me it wasn't him. Piercing blue eyes peered from underneath the bill of a rugged cap. This was no dream. There was a strange man in my bathroom… and I was naked.

"Oh, my God," I said, freezing in place in the water.

"I'm sorry."

"Oh, my God! Get out!" I screamed, leaning up to cover

my chest.

"I'm—I'm sorry, ma'am," he stuttered without shifting his eyes from mine.

"Move it, pervert!" I yelled while reaching for my robe.

My eyes clicked with his again, the breath catching in my throat. He was like nothing I had ever seen. The corners of his mouth curved into the slightest smile as if he could almost hear my thoughts. He slowly walked backward out of the bathroom, cowboy boots clicking on the hardwood floor as his stare held my eyes. He turned away, vanishing from my sight. The sound of the door closing shut confirmed his departure.

Those eyes. There was something about those eyes that made me crave more.

"Oh, my God, what just happened?" My eyes remained bugged in shock, but my body still tingled from his stare.

"Oh, my God, this water's freezing!" I jumped out of the ice bath and pulled the robe tightly around me. I quickly vacated the bathroom and my gaze shifted to the closed door of the suite. Mortified, I plopped on the bed and buried my face in of my hands. Lying back onto the pillows, questions regarding his identity ran through my head, leaving me to wonder. Why did a sexy country boy break into my room?

Chapter Four

TOM

After a long morning taming the farm, I closed up the weathered barn door, and as my cowboy boots crunched over mulch and gravel, I walked back toward the old farm house to get out of the summer heat. With Hampton trotting along by my side, I stooped down and picked up a stick, chucking it toward my two-story farmhouse. The chocolate lab sprinted for it. By the time I caught up with him, my phone was ringing. I stopped as I stared at the front porch, longing to lounge in my rocking chair and sip from a Mason jar filled with sweet tea. I blew out a breath and answered, "Tom McCloud."

"Tommy! I know your grandmother taught you to answer the phone better than that!" The voice of my only living blood relative rang in my ears and I cringed. Thanks to my busy schedule, I had neglected her, my uncle, and The Inn.

My best friend, Lance, had taken over the task of occupying Hampton. As I turned away from them and the house, I stared across the rolling foothills that had always given me such a sense of calm, but they weren't offering it today. I pulled off my cap and wiped the sweat from my forehead, steeling myself for the conversation to come. "Aunt Ethel, I'm sorry. It's already been a long day."

"Yeah, yeah, yeah. Listen," she said, cutting off my apology. "The guest checked into room six already and the faucet is still leaking."

As the strain of work weighed down on me, I lifted off my hat again and scratched my head. "Aunt Et, I'm sorry. We had some runaway cattle to deal with this morning, and a section of the barbed wire fence needed to be replaced. I'll get Hampton and we'll head your way now."

"Thanks, Tommy. See you in a bit." She rushed off the phone without any further conversation. Even though running the farm kept me busy, I always felt responsible for helping out my aunt and uncle. They were all I had left.

As I shoved the phone back into my pocket, I abandoned my plans of going to the house and headed to the tool shed alongside the barn instead. With my tool bag in hand, I strode to my truck and whistled for Hampton. On command, the dog left the game of catch with Lance and darted toward me, hopping inside the truck when I opened the door. I tossed the bag onto the bed of the truck as Lance approached. He was an all-hat-no-cattle kind of man; looked like a cowboy and walked like a cowboy, but he ain't a cowboy.

"So, are we going to Dixie's tonight?" Lance asked as he hung his thumbs from loops of his belt.

"I reckon," I answered, digging for the keys to my truck in my jean pockets.

"Ya think Angela will be there?" His shit eating grin stretched from ear to ear.

I rolled my eyes.

"She's a leech. Don't you usually find leeches in murky waters?"

"And you know what they say about leeches?"

I shook my head at the thought of him and Angela Butler, better known as the thorn in my side from a night of drunken foolishness.

"I know what they say about leeches. I'm the one who told you about leeches."

"And I'm so glad you did!" He punched me on the shoulder.

I stared at the spot he hit and then back at him as he tried to contain his laughter. I shook my head again as I turned away.

"Go look around the fence line so we don't have to do this again tomorrow. Paul's taking care of the area in the back." I hopped into my grandfather's old pickup and settled next to Hampton. I grabbed the handle to close the door.

"You got it, boss." He smirked.

I looked over at him with my hand still clutching the handle.

"Lance."

"What's up... boss?" he replied, egging me on with a smug face. I cocked my brow out of annoyance.

"Cut the crap." I slammed the door, hanging my elbow outside of the open window, and started the truck.

"Whatever you say, boss," he hollered and then turned away to do the job as requested.

I revved the engine and patted Hampton's back. He scooted away from me and poked his head out of the passenger side window. I pulled out of the farm onto the windy roads of the countryside. The sun flickered between the trees that lined the roadsides. The heat beat down on the asphalt, but I swore I caught the hint of fall riding on the breeze. It was probably wishful thinking. It was still August, and I lived in the South. I eased on the brakes at a signal light and turned right, hitting the limits of our small country town. As I drove down Main Street on the way to The Inn, I passed the hardware store and noticed the crew setting up for the End of Summer Festival in Olde Town.

"Well, shit." I grabbed my cell and flipped it open to call Paul. I was too damn busy to do it all.

"Paul Harris."

"Hey, Paul. I forgot about helping with the festival setup. Can you go get us started on Main Street, and I'll come after I help Aunt Et at The Inn? Just have Lance finish up."

"Yeah, no problem. We'll grab a beer afterward."

"Sounds good. Thanks." I flipped my phone shut, ending the call.

My truck slowed as it pulled alongside the old familiar inn, the gravel rocks of the driveway popping underneath the tires. I got out of the truck and grabbed the bag out of the back; Hampton trotted along, following me to the front door. I had walked up those steps thousands of times. The Inn was the closest thing to home besides my farm, and the only family I had lived there. When I opened the door, the chimes announced my entrance. I could hear Uncle Al singing from the kitchen. The lingering scent of apple pie and cinnamon welcomed me as it did every time I crossed the threshold. Glancing around for Aunt Et, I walked up to the counter, where I found a note instead of the woman.

> *Tommy,*
>
> *I tried to call Ms. Hawthorne, the guest in six, and knocked on the door, but she didn't answer. She must be out. Your uncle has a few pies to bring back to Lance and Paul. Some treats for Hampton are also in the kitchen with the pies. I ran to the market. If you need your uncle, you know where to find him.*
>
> *Love, Aunt Et*

With my tool bag in hand, I turned around and found Hampton lying on his blanket in the corner near the fireplace, gnawing on one of his many rawhide bones. As I began the climb up the stairs, I said, "Good boy."

Taking two steps at a time, I made it up to the third floor, turned down the hall, and stood in front of room six.

"Maintenance." I knocked, holding the bag in front of me as the door to the suite next door closed. An older couple emerged from their room. I nodded at them, pulling down the bill of my hat. As they started down the stairs, I was still waiting for a response from room six. When I didn't hear anything, I knocked a second time and repeated the call for maintenance. I dug out my set of keys as I waited for any sign of the guest. When I still didn't get a response, I assumed the guest was out and pushed in the master key to unlock the door. I walked into the shady room, shutting the door behind me.

A mass of clothes covered the bed with half-unpacked bags thrown on top. I glanced at the mound and at a few personal items the guest had already placed inside the room. There was an awful lot of clothing and necessities for someone just passing through our small town. The note did read *Ms*. Maybe there would be fresh meat at Dixie's tonight. Lance could use any excuse to get away from the leech. The loud drip of the plumbing problem got my attention away from the bed, and I turned back toward the bathroom. I dug through my bag of tools, checking that I had all I could possibly need as I followed the sound of the leak to the bathroom door. I nudged the slightly opened door with my elbow, still rummaging in my bag as it swung open. When I looked up, what I saw took the breath away from me.

Only two words formed in my head: beautiful and naked.

The most striking goddess I had ever laid eyes on lay in a tub, holding the remnants of bubbles. Her closed eyes were swollen, a sad commentary on her gorgeous face. *Has she been crying?* Then I eyed a pair of incredible, long legs peeking out from the water and drawing my gaze to two of the most luscious nipples pebbling from the cool of the air conditioner. My body immediately stood at attention. My mouth hung open like a damn fool as my bag of tools fell to the floor with a loud *thump*.

Her eyes popped open. A gasp escaped her parted lips, and my gaze flew up from the glorious view of her chest to her compelling eyes. The most beautiful, blue-eyed bombshell. I couldn't move. I stood in awe, staring into those mesmerizing eyes and trying not to linger on that amazingly wet body, but my gaze wanted to wander. Curves like hers deserved to be lingered on.

"Oh, my God." The words slipped past her soft pink lips.

"I'm sorry," I whispered, but I couldn't move. I couldn't tear myself away from the plumpness of her mouth. Her lips parted as she panted a nervous breath, but I still couldn't move.

"Oh, my God! Get out!" She sat up, pulling out her ear buds and covering her chest with her naked arms.

"I'm—I'm sorry, ma'am," I babbled like an idiot.

"Move it, pervert!" she fumed, eying me intently, but a sparkle in her eyes had me wondering. *What intent would that be, exactly?*

I took the smallest of steps steadily backward and out of the bathroom, trying not to miss the view. A smile crept across my face as I maintained eye contact. Her chest rose and fell rapidly with the heat pulsating between the two of us. There was the slightest hint of an invitation in her eyes and, for the briefest second, my heart surged with hope. This would not be the last time I would see her. It couldn't be. With a smile threatening to to glide further up my cheeks, I unwillingly retreated and lost sight of her.

The image of her still crystalized in my mind, I left her room. I shut the door behind me and let my body slump against it, unable to calm my now racing heart. Sure, I'd seen naked women before, that was nothing new. But this one…

something was different about her. She made something feel different about me. Inside me. What the Hell? As I shook my head in disbelief, the stupid smile spread across my face again, and I thanked God for that damn leaky faucet.

Chapter Five

JORDAN

My eyes flickered open to find a muscular, sweaty cowboy standing in the doorway to the bathroom. Cowboy boots, tight-fitted jeans, and a gray v-neck shirt hugged the broadest chest I had ever seen. I yearned to run my hands over the muscles that hid beneath that shirt, stretching the fabric taut. I thought for sure I was dreaming... until he slowly walked toward me.

With each step, my heart thumped as his blue eyes bore into mine. I scooted up slowly, covering myself with the warm bubbles that danced around me. I tried to speak, but I couldn't manage to make a sound. Being around someone so unbelievably sexy rendered me completely speechless. When he reached the edge of the tub, the nameless cowboy took off his hat and slowly peeled off his sweat-soaked shirt. Not once did his eyes leave mine. He turned slightly and sat on the edge of the porcelain, giving me a full view of the muscles of his arms and back.

The need to touch him was overwhelming. I lifted my hand out of the bubbles and grazed my fingertips slowly down his biceps, leaving a trail of dampness and suds. His chest heaved with anticipation. My fingers glided down to his forearm, lifting his hand away from the edge of the tub. He took control of his own movements and caressed my cheek with his fingertips. His eyes filled with need as his fingers drifted down my neck and across my chest, causing my nipples to pebble. I dropped my hand back into the water, allowing him to linger across my body.

My eyes never broke from his stare. Not even a blink. His fingers traveled down my stomach. My breath hitched. A smile played on his lips as his fingers glided under the water, caressing me gently. The instant contact caused me to tense and my hands balled into fists, having nothing to grab on to. Flicking with slow, yet steady timing, I began to buck against his hand. His expression turned lustful as his finger pushed gently inside. A silent moan escaped me. I blinked, feeling the beginnings of ecstasy. His agile movements became more rapid, and I rode his finger, focused on release. He could feel me tense and slid a second finger inside. I gasped at my dire need to have more of him inside of me. Blinking again, I found those nameless eyes memorizing mine. Warmth pooled in the pit of my stomach, and a panting breath slipped passed my lips, causing him to move his hand even faster. Nearing the brink, I closed my eyes, feeling the imminent release.

My eyes shot open as my breath turned into pants. I glanced around the unfamiliar surroundings and realized that I was in the country now. A drip echoed from the bathroom and as I sat up, my head filled with the memories of my morning bath. I peered over my shoulder into the bathroom and I noticed a bag of tools lying open on the floor. I eyed it with determination and scooted out of bed. Holding my robe securely closed, I walked over to the bag, picked it up, and set it on the counter. My hands rested on my hips while I looked inside, and it was filled with what appeared to be tools. The bag, embroidered with the initials *T.E.M.*, included no other identification of its owner. Embarrassment crept over me with the realization that he had been here to take care of the leaky faucet, which I thought was supposed to be fixed tomorrow. Even through the embarrassment, I kept imagining those piercing blue eyes staring at me.

Finally putting the intrusive cowboy behind me, the need to explore this little town crept upon me. I threw on a pair of jeans and a T-shirt and hiked the strap of my laptop bag over my shoulder, eager to check out the café and the all needed Wi-Fi. I headed downstairs, and as I passed the counter, Mrs. Ethel looked up from her book with her pink frames low on her nose.

"Oh, good afternoon, dear. I thought you were out this afternoon?" Mrs. Ethel's brow scrunched in confusion.

"No, ma'am." A blush flamed my face as I remembered my cowboy encounter. "But I guess you thought I was."

"Did my nephew catch you at a bad time? I'm so sorry about that. Was he able to fix the faucet?" she asked with sincere innocence.

"Um… no, but I'll be out all day tomorrow, so he'll have the whole day to fix it at any time," I muttered, heading toward the door as fast as I could.

"Okay, dear, have a good afternoon!" Mrs. Ethel hollered after me.

I decided to explore down toward Main Street, assuming that direction would be the place of greater population in this small town. Walking toward the little café that Mrs. Ethel told me about, I embraced the slow, simplistic town surrounding me. The aroma of the livestock still lingered, but my sense of smell seemed to numb over time and I was starting to get used to it. As I peered into the storefront windows during my walk, I came across a little boutique with cute sundresses, shoes, and purses arranged behind the glass. Some magnetic force, or a touch of fate, guided me to grab the handle and take a step inside. Barely one second through the door, I was welcomed by a chipper, bubbly redhead behind the sales counter.

"Hi, welcome to Ellie's. My name is Ellie. Are you looking for something in particular today?"

I smiled at her and glanced around the store, attempting to find the first area to conquer.

"Not really. I was just passing by your shop on the way from The Inn, and I saw the shoes in the window. A girl can't pass up shoes."

Shoes seemed like a good place to start.

"Oh, are you vacationing here?" Ellie asked, walking around from behind the counter.

"No, I just moved. I'm currently staying at The Inn, but I'm not sure if it'll be a permanent move." I turned toward her as she approached.

"Well, welcome to the area. My name is Ellie Caldwell.

This is my store... obviously," Ellie said with a cheerful grin. "Did you move here for a job?"

"Yes, I'm Jordan Hawthorne, the new history instructor at the community college." I extended my hand to meet the new acquaintance.

"Oh, that's fabulous!" she replied as she shook my hand in greeting. "Well, let's get you some new clothes for the role, then."

I needed to spend money like I needed a hole in my head, but with all of the drama I had endured these past few months, I deserved some retail therapy. Ellie continued to talk while she showed me various dresses and skirts, and all thought of saving money vanished with no question. They all were adorable. New wardrobe pieces wouldn't hurt at all.

"Okay, so, what size are you?" Ellie asked while she flipped through the clothing racks.

"An eight."

She studied my frame and eyed my attire.

"Honey, if you're wearing an eight now, then you need to go down a size or two. Those clothes are engulfing you."

My eyes shifted downward to look at my clothing choices, and Ellie turned me around before I could question her sizing notion. She proceeded to scoot me in front of a three-paneled mirror, grabbing the back of my jeans right underneath my butt and stretching out the fabric.

"Jordan, you can fit an elephant inside these pants. Haven't you heard of skinny jeans?" She shook her head as I watched her reflection in the mirror.

"Um..." I mumbled, wincing. "These are skinny jeans."

Ellie's eyes rose as she shook her head. "March into the

dressing room, lady. You are getting a new wardrobe, right now!"

She guided me toward the back of the boutique into a changing room. As she shut the door behind me, she ordered, "Now, strip! I'll bring you back some clothes to try on."

On her order, I stripped myself of the not-so-skinny jeans and the navy crewneck T-shirt. In only a bra and a pair of panties, I stood before my reflection and studied my apparent weight loss. I couldn't help but feel hopeless with the images of the past few months looming over me constantly.

"Jordan, open up. I have clothes for you." As I opened the door to the dressing room, she handed me a bundle of clothes with a curious look in her eye and a humorous smile. My brow furrowed in confusion.

"What's wrong?"

"Oh nothing." Beginning to turn away, she added, "Just so you know, there's some underwear in that pile, too. I think you could use it."

I glanced down at my white cotton bra and granny panties. Ellie winked as she pulled the door closed behind her. I shook my head at my lack of fashion sense and hung up the clothes she'd handed me. Excitement began to fuel my senses as I sifted through the dresses, skirts, and shirts. Before I allowed myself to get too worked up, I glanced at the tags to check the prices, but found myself instead gasping at the size numbers.

"Um, Ellie?"

"Yes?" Ellie bubbled from the other side of the door.

"These are a size four," I reasoned.

"And?"

"These are a size four… like one, two, three, FOUR!"

"Jordan, I know sizes. I own a boutique, remember? Now, put them on!" Ellie chimed as her boots echoed across the hardwood floor, leaving the dressing area.

I let out a grunt and grabbed the first dress from the hanger, feeling sure that the clothes wouldn't fit. The dress in my hand was black, straight, and strapless with a zipper on the side. When I pulled it on, I immediately turned away from the mirror, not wanting to witness the inevitable. As my fingers grasped the zipper, I pulled it up slowly and closed my eyes as the teeth of the zipper welded together. For some reason, somehow, the zipper found its way to the top. My eyes flew open in shock as I slowly turned to face the mirror.

"Oh…" I gasped almost silently, staring at my reflection. My hand rested on my chest in disbelief. It was the most beautiful dress I had ever put on, and it looked like it was made just for me. The hem hit my legs roughly at mid-thigh, which made them look supermodel-long. The sleekness of the dress flattered my curves with the dark color hiding any imperfections.

"Let me see! Let me see!"

Taking a final calming breath, I opened the door and stepped out. Slowly, I turned toward Ellie.

"Whoa, you're an effing model!" Ellie bounced up and down.

My head shook in disbelief, and I pulled on the fabric, trying to find some wiggle room. "It seems a little snug."

"A girl can't help it if she has boobs! If you got 'em, flaunt 'em, right? I'll make you a deal. You buy that dress, and I'll give you twenty percent off all of your purchases."

"Twenty percent off? What's the catch?" I said as my eyes remained on the bouncy, bubbly lady.

"The catch is you have to come out to the tavern tonight and show off my design."

My eyebrows arched in amused shock. I glanced down at the dress and then back up at her.

"Your design? Wait, these are yours?"

"Yep! And you're the perfect model to show them off!"

My whole body tensed and my forehead furrowed in worry.

"Jordan, it's just the tavern. Besides, you need to meet some new people in town, and you are officially my new best friend!"

Chapter

Six

TOM

he sun fell behind the mountains as work finished for the day on the setup for the End of Summer Fest.

Paul and I wandered across the street and into Dixie's Tavern as we continued a conversation about my unusual yet welcoming morning. I walked through the doors as I dropped one important piece of information about the event. He stopped midstride, staring at me in envious disbelief.

"Naked?"

I tried to hide my grin and confirmed, "Completely."

He shook his head, took two steps, and stopped again. "Hot?"

"You have no idea." I shook my head, still in utter astonishment. The view I had feasted on earlier today was one that I wouldn't forget in the foreseeable future. It was the absolute hottest thing I had ever seen, and I had seen my fair share of… things.

Paul nudged me out of my vivid memories and pointed toward Lance on the other side of the bar. We approached our dear friend just in time to hear him say, "Betty, I swear, you are the most beautiful woman in this place."

Paul and I looked at one another and shook our heads at this person we called a friend. Lance was the biggest flirt, able to charm anything with two legs and a rack.

"Lance, leave Mrs. Betty alone," Paul said as we took our regular seats at the bar.

"Lance, I'm old enough to be your grandmother." Betty chuckled. She was at least old enough to be our mothers, but she definitely was no grandmother. She was pretty slender with short, jet-black hair. Betty was the kind of woman who didn't take crap from anybody.

"And a hot one!" Lance said with a wink, attempting to charm the pants off anyone within earshot.

Still laughing, Betty turned to Paul and me. "What'll it be, boys?"

"Whatever's on tap, ma'am," I said, nodding my respect, even if Lance showed little to none.

"Coming right up."

Betty grabbed two glass beer mugs and turned toward the row of taps standing tall in front of the bottles of spirits behind the bar. The tavern was your typical hole in the wall with beat-up hardwood floors covering the space and sports paraphernalia littering one wall; the adjoining one behind the small stage was papered with license plates from every state. A few dart boards and a pool table in the back decorated the rest of the bar. It was kind of crowded for a Monday.

Classes at the local community college would be starting on Wednesday, which meant tonight was everyone's last hurrah.

"Fellas, the first round's on the house, and ya better keep your eye on that one." She placed the beers in front of us and pointed at Lance as she departed for the other side of the bar.

"So, Tom, are you going to fill in Lance about what you saw today?" Paul said, smirking into his beer.

After taking a sip of beer, I said, "You know how I went to The Inn today to help my aunt?"

"Yeah," Lance answered as he glanced around at the women in the bar.

"Apparently, a guest had a plumbing issue in their suite."

"Uh-huh," he replied, his eyes locked on some blonde chick.

"I knocked on the door. There was no answer so I assumed the guest was gone, and when I walked into the bathroom to fix the sink, the guest was in there." I tried to divert his attention from the blonde chick.

"Oh shit! Was it some old guy on the crapper? That'd be hilarious." Lance's eyes popped in amused shock, tearing his concentration away from the blonde and back to me.

"Nope." The vivid memories filled my mind, and I couldn't help getting lost.

"Who was it then?" Lance still chuckled to himself as he raised his mug to take a sip of beer.

"I don't know who she was." I rubbed my hand over my chest, feeling an indescribable ache.

"What was she doing in the bathroom, Tom?" Lance eyed me with that stupid grin of his rising up his face. As Lance took a gulp of his beer, I smirked, reaching for my mug.

"Taking a bath."

Lance spewed his beer all over the bar.

"Holy fuck, you're kidding!"

"Nope." I grabbed a few napkins to wipe up his mess. Even though the bar was now covered with beer, I couldn't help but laugh at his antics.

"Hot?" Lance asked the same as Paul had.

"Unbelievable." The visions of her curves continued to blind me.

"Holy shit," Paul mumbled under his breath. I looked at him, followed his eyes over to the corner booth, and noticed my good friend Ellie talking to someone I couldn't see due to the crowd between us. Paul had always been hooked on Ellie, though she and Lance had dated back in high school and left Paul to harbor his feelings all these years.

"Oh, it's Lance's ex."

"Shit, which one?" Lance ducked.

I laughed at his hysterics and said, "Calm down, Lance. It's just Ellie."

"Tom," Paul whispered, still staring in Ellie's direction. "Who's the chick with her?"

I leaned back and forth to get a look around the swarm of people who stood in between the bar and the corner booth.

My whole body froze when I laid eyes on Ellie's friend, and I lost my breath once again. In the sexiest black dress, my water goddess was talking with my friend while she ran her finger along the rim of her wine glass. My blood instantly flooded south with the fantasy of her straddling me, doing to me exactly what she was doing to her wine glass. I was in agony. The desperate desire to pounce on a woman had never been a factor in my life before. I didn't want to just fuck her. I wanted her... every bit of her.

As if she could feel my stare on her, her eyes flickered up, and they connected with mine with such a force. I had never felt such a pull to any woman before, especially one I'd never met. I needed to get close to her. I rose from my bar stool, and headed straight for her. She leaned in close to Ellie and whispered something in her ear. Without a second glance, she rose from the table in haste, and she hurried out the door.

My heart dropped as she exited the bar. I needed to catch her before I lost her again. Moving quickly toward the door, I was stopped by a firm tug on my arm. I turned around, coming face to face with the most unpleasant thing ever imaginable... Angela Butler.

"Hey, sexy baby! What's the rush?" Angela purred near my ear, and I held back a cringe.

Angela was a drunken mistake two years ago. Bachelor party... lots of shots... horrible hangover due to the mess of a beast lying next to me in the morning. She was pretty, with long blonde hair and muted blue eyes. Not the sharpest tool in the shed, though. She had a bad reputation in high school, and it still suited her today. She possibly welcomed it, which wasn't very flattering.

After the drunken night of misguided passion, she followed me around all the time. I sat her down once and explained, sincerely, that she could do better than me, reinforcing that I didn't have time for a girlfriend. I tried to be nice, but she wouldn't have any of it. Being a jerk wasn't my nature, but I got really tired of being relentlessly harassed.

"Hey, Angela. Sorry, I thought I saw someone," I said,

trying not to make eye contact. As I turned to walk away, I added, "It was good to see you. I'm going to head back to my friends."

"Dude, was that Angela?" Lance asked as I sat back on my stool by the bar.

"Yep."

"Awesome! See y'all later!" Lance said with a punch on my arm, and he headed over to the leech. Nothing surprised me with Lance.

As I turned my head and glanced at Paul, he was leaning over and talking up close with Ellie, who followed him over from her table. Both of them had that unmistakable horniness in their eyes, confirming what I already knew: they just needed to get it over with already.

"Hey, Ellie," I said, smiling at my dear friend. She had only ever been a friend to me, nothing more.

"Hey, Tommy! How are you?" Ellie said, ducking under my arm to wrap hers around my waist. There was only one other person who could get away with calling me Tommy besides my Aunt, and that was Ellie.

"Oh, good. Good." I continued, "So, who was the friend you were with? I've never seen her around before."

"Oh, I just met her today. She came into the boutique and bought a few things from me. She's pretty cute, huh." She winked for good measure.

"What's her name, El?" I inched forward on the seat of desperation.

"Oh, Jordan Hawthorne," she replied with a hint of a smirk, knowing good and well I wanted every last detail.

"And what is she doing in town, Ellie?" I asked impatiently.

"She's the new history instructor at the college. Oh, hey! I bet you'll have her since you're starting class Wednesday!"

My heart skipped a beat, causing that ache to return, but it accompanied some other feeling I couldn't identify, making me feel really uneasy.

"Tom?" Paul asked. "Are you okay?"

When Ellie picked up a conversation with Betty, I leaned over to Paul, whispering over the music, "It's her."

"Who's her?" Paul asked, turning his head and looking around the bar.

Shaking my head, I said, "Naked tub girl. She's Ellie's friend."

A shit eating grin rose up his face, and he said, "Dude, if that's her, then you better mark your territory. She'll get picked up real quick. You know what happens if Lance sees her."

Paul leaned in closer to me, taking a look back at Ellie to make sure she wasn't listening, and he continued, "I mean that chick was pretty hot."

As I lifted my mug, I smirked. "Can a student get with a teacher?"

Paul laughed, patting me on the back. "Well, if anyone can, it's you!"

After sharing another laugh, we clicked our mugs and downed our beers in one long pull.

Chapter Seven

JORDAN

While my newfound friend strutted down the sidewalk, my heels clamored with no grace as we made the pilgrimage down to Dixie's Tavern. Bouncing red hair and a bubbly smile, she exuded the natural country charm embedded within her. The outfit she'd chosen for me was a sleeveless little black dress she had designed, and a pair of killer heels that would surely kill me if she didn't slow the hell down.

"Ellie, are you sure this looks okay? I don't want to look like a slut." I tugged at the hem of the dress that seemed to be shrinking every second.

She stopped in her tracks and I almost ran into her. Her hands fisted as she slowly turned around and glared at me like the fire of hell. Maybe she wasn't full of country charm after all.

"Are you saying my clothes are slutty?"

"No, of course not!" I retracted with almost a stuttering babble. "I just didn't want to look out of place at a corner bar."

And just like that, the country girl full of charm returned with a shrug of her shoulders, and she started walking again.

"Well, I can't help you there, because you look pretty hot." While glancing at me mid stride, she waved her hand and continued, "Don't get me wrong, I'm straight and all, but you look fucking awesome."

We arrived at the corner, and I peeked through the beveled glass panes of the double wooden doors. The young adults of the town filled Dixie's Tavern. My stomach flipped with nerves as I looked in on them. My hand reached out for the brass handle, and with one last silent exhale, I said, "Okay, then. It's showtime."

The door swooshed open. The sound of country rock blared, the watchful eyes of the little town landed on me. Being face to face with plaid, jeans, and cowboy boots in every direction, I froze immediately. The guys ogled and the girls sneered. I was definitely overdressed. Feeling like fresh meat, I gently wrapped my hand around Ellie's arm and asked over the noise, "Ellie, how about the booth in the corner?"

Ellie looked at me with slight pity at my lack of confidence. She rolled her eyes and said, "Whatever you say. Go grab the booth, and I'll get us a bottle of wine. White or red?"

"White, please," I replied as I sat down, trying to blend in like a wallflower. In order to avoid the ogles and sneers, I pulled out my cell phone and scrolled through my recent texts. My smile instantly reappeared when I saw one from Katherine.

Miss you bunches! Tell me how the move went when you get a chance.

My fingers flew as I typed a reply, the knowing smile blazing my cheeks.

It went okay. Miss you, too! I'll give you a call tomorrow and fill you in on an embarrassment already. At least it was a hot embarrassment. ;-) Love you!

The next message caused the breath to catch in my throat.

Where are you?

The words sent the coldest shiver up my spine. Ryan must have figured out that I was no longer in Charlotte. I just hoped he hadn't figured out where I fled. I deleted the message, poking the screen harder than I really needed to. Ellie arrived at our corner booth, holding a bottle of wine and two glasses.

"I hope Pinot Grigio is okay. I figured that was kind of middle of the road with whites." Ellie set down two glasses on our table and poured wine into each one.

"Perfect!" She handed me a glass, and I took the smallest sip of the glorious fermented grapes. The tingle spread across my lips, and a sense of calm washed over me.

Ellie let the wine talk as she informed me about the town and the people. An owner of a women's boutique apparently hears a lot of gossip, and even though I didn't really know any of these people on the dance floor, she was pointing them all out to me, telling me who to stay away from and who to befriend. Being that she was so nice and outgoing, I was thankful to be friends with her. It would be good to get to know people. A fresh start. I needed that. I needed to move on.

"So, what brought you out of Charlotte, anyway? It's not like we get that many straight-out-of-college single adults rolling through town."

Did I feel comfortable enough opening up to someone I had just met?

"You don't sound like you come out of the country, either." She smiled.

"I was born here, then moved to New York with my mother, then moved back here in high school to live with my dad. After graduation, I went back to New York for fashion design, and just moved back a few months ago." She smiled as if the back and forth was common.

"So, why here and not New York?"

She shrugged her shoulders while taking a sip of wine.

"I just always liked it here." It seemed as if there was more to the story, but I understood how it was, getting to know someone new. "Now, what about you?"

"Bad breakup. Just wanted to clear my head for a while." She nodded.

"I know all about moving just to try to get away from your own thoughts."

We both sipped at our wine as I glanced around the bar. I did feel like I had gotten a good read on Ellie. It almost seemed as if she needed a friend as much as I did.

"Oh my God, there's Paul..." she stated suddenly.

My eyes shot around the tavern, but there were so many cowboy hats in this place, I couldn't tell who she was looking at.

"Why don't you quit staring and go talk to him?"

She shook her head solemnly.

"No, I've always liked him, but he's friends with my ex, Lance. So, you know… awkward."

"Do you not get along with Lance?" I asked in hopes of getting to know my new friend better.

"Oh, I'm sure we'd get along fine. We dated in high school. I just feel weird about trying to pursue his friend." Her sights on him were strong, a little too strong for only a high school infatuation.

"Which one is Paul?"

She scooted over toward me and arranged herself so she could point without anyone else seeing.

"Paul is the one in the plaid shirt at the end of the bar, and Lance is to his left with their friend Tom, who's sitting to his right."

"Oh, I see him. He is pretty cute. I like his…" The words stopped flowing when I saw the friend on the right, looking at directly me.

Piercing blue eyes.

My breath started to quicken. *Just look away, Jordan. Look away!* I begged myself, but I couldn't. He was… beautiful.

He jumped off the stool, startling me. His eyes bored into mine; my heart banged against my chest and panic rose as he took a step toward me. My only instinct was to flee as fast as these heels would take me.

I grabbed my purse, leaned over to Ellie and said, "Ellie, I have to run. I am so sorry. Can we do this another time?"

Ellie looked up at me with her face scrunched in confusion and replied with a questioning voice, "Sure, we can do that. The festival is Friday. Stop by the store this week for lunch."

"Awesome, thanks Ellie! See you!" I darted straight out

of the door.

The vision of those blue eyes clouded my thoughts. His stare felt like an eternity. I lost myself in the lust that I felt for him. Reprimanding myself as I walked faster toward The Inn, I put a stop to those thoughts. I was never going to put myself in that situation again. Love was not worth it. For all I knew, he was just as bad as Ryan. No sense risking it.

As the heels I had worn dangled from my fingertips, my bare feet carried my hollow heart up the stairs. I walked into my room, dropped the shoes to the floor, and stripped off my dress, letting it fall recklessly beside the shoes. Not bothering with pajamas, I slid beneath the quilt, trying to find a sense of security as the memories of Ryan continued to haunt me. The tears that I had learned to hold in started to fall. My eyes closed, heavy with despair, and it felt as if his cold ones were looming in the darkness.

The creak of the tavern door echoed into the shadows. The only light came from the jukebox in the corner. The heels of my shoes made a haunting echo in the vast space. I didn't know why I was here. I wanted to turn and run away, but something kept me going forward.

"Hello?" My voice echoed from the rafters as I noticed a body perched on a stool. I took another step. "Hello?"

He turned around, peeking at me from under the brim of a cowboy hat. I only saw the glimmer of blue eyes. My heart raced as he turned completely around, resting his elbows on the back of the bar.

"Tom, right?"

In an instant, he vanished. I stepped forward again.

"Tom?"

A hand pushed the hair off my neck as my heart raced. The jukebox came to life, playing an old country tune. Hands pressed on my hips as a body swayed me side to side to the beat of the song. I wanted to feel safe, to relax into those hands, but some primal instinct kept me on alert, telling me to beware. A hum came from behind me. The breath stuck in my throat.

"Why are you dancing like a slut and letting any and every bastard grind up on you?"

I gasped when he yanked my hair, pulling my head to the side.

"I told you I always get what I want."

Tears streamed down my face. This isn't happening. This can't be happening. *I pressed my eyes closed, praying that someone would help.*

All traces of Ryan had vanished. I stood alone in the middle of the dance floor. The echo of the door startled me and I turned around. I wiped the tears from my eyes. The cowboy from the bar stared at me from just inside the doorway. He tilted his head down, pulled the brim of his hat, and then walked away.

A jolt awoke me from the nightmare. I cringed, remembering the touch of his hands on me. Calm eased through me when I realized I was in my bed at The Inn, far away from Ryan. At least I had the nightmares. I didn't want to dream of happier times with Ryan. They were all lies. It was a new day with new opportunities, and I was going to make the most of my new life.

"GOOD MORNING, Ms. Hawthorne."

"Good morning, sir. I'm very thankful for the opportunity," I said, sitting straight in my chair. Hope painted my face as I sat across from my new boss, the head of the history department.

"We're glad to have you." He leaned forward behind his desk, pulling out a stack of paper and began, "First things first. You'll be instructing four classes this semester. Two will be on Mondays and Wednesdays, and the other two will be on Tuesdays and Thursdays. Monday and Wednesday classes are from 9:00 to 10:30 and 6:30 to 8:00. Sorry about the night class, but we have to accommodate the working crowd. Tuesdays and Thursdays will be back to back, 9:00 to 10:30 and then 10:45 to 12:15. The rest of the time is yours. Pretty simple, right?"

After my hopeful nod, he stood. I followed his lead.

"Very good, Ms. Hawthorne. Let me show you to your office."

A breath of relief escaped me as we strolled down the hall to the end. He unlocked a door and handed over the key. "Not much of an office, but make yourself at home! Good Luck, Ms. Hawthorne, and welcome again."

With a final handshake, he departed, leaving me to my new surroundings. The tiny office was no bigger than a closet, but the biggest smile crossed my face and I got to work right away. This was something to be proud of. While I was going through my belongings, my cell rang. Always checking the ID, I answered the call of my beloved friend.

"Hey, Katherine!"

"Hey, chick! How's life in the sticks?" Her smug sarcasm oozed through the phone. After I replied with a sarcastic laugh, she added, "So, tell me about this hot embarrassment you texted me about."

The retelling of yesterday's events made my cheeks blush. My body tingled once again just from the mere thought of that cowboy.

"Oh, my God, and you were still naked in the tub?"

"Yep," I said plainly.

"And you didn't start screaming and throwing things?"

"Nope. I couldn't move! But believe me, he was definitely hot. And I saw him again last night at the bar in town." A smile rose up my face. Since that cowboy walked into my life, I couldn't stop thinking about him. It was almost weird to smile again. It was weird that my heart fluttered. It shouldn't do that, not after what brought me to this point. But maybe it was safe here. Maybe I could let my guard down some.

"Oh my God, did you talk to him?"

"I ran out of there as soon as I saw him. I didn't know what to do. I freaked out." I hid my face inside of my palm, reliving yesterday again.

"Jordan, it's a small town. You're going to run into Mr. Cowboy soon enough."

She was right. The words caused my smile to grow even more. *Oh, I hope so. I need to see him again.*

Chapter Eight

TOM

The chimes banged against the wooden door as I walked inside the old, familiar inn. I breathed in, getting a whiff of ham from the kitchen. As I closed the door behind me, my aunt's eyes peered over her glasses as she bent the newspaper down with an annoyed exaggeration. She folded the paper bit by bit, keeping a stern glare on me.

"Hi, Aunt Ethel."

Her lips pursed. She wasn't happy.

"Tommy! You said you were coming yesterday, as in Tuesday. Do I need to buy you an appointment book?" Oh, she looked pissed.

"Aunt Et, I'm sorry. I went down to the college to register for my classes, and I didn't think it would take up so much time. And I didn't want to… *intrude* on your guest again." My shoulders hung down with the weight of the world resting on them, although, her eyes lit up with the knowledge that I was finally going to college. When I saw a smile to match the pride in her eyes, I knew I was still on her good side.

"Well, if that was the reason, then okay. I'll let it slide." Her easy going smile changed into her pointing a finger at me with an order. "But get up to the suite and fix the leak. Ms. Hawthorne didn't say anything this morning about the leak when she left, but I don't want to cause any further inconvenience for my guests."

"Yes, ma'am." I tugged the bill on my baseball cap, pairing it with a curt nod, as I tried to be the gentleman she helped raise me to be. Aunt Ethel gave me her natural, heart-warming smile, and I knew I was forgiven.

"Well, what classes did you register for, Tommy?" She leaned forward, her pride beaming.

"I'm going to take a few core classes which shouldn't be too difficult since this fall will be a little busy at the farm. So, I'm taking Intro to Business, English, and history." The corners of my mouth quirked up. One night class taught by one water goddess that I might have seen a time or two.

"Good. I'm glad. Now, go fix the sink," she ordered, yet again, and went back to reading.

Withholding a laugh at my crazy aunt, I jogged up the stairs, taking two at a time. I walked down the hall to room six. I knew Aunt Et had assured me that she was out, but I couldn't help wishing she was wrong. The thought of Ms. Hawthorne in the tub, wearing nothing but bubbles, sent my blood heading south once again.

After unlocking the door, I held it open with my foot and listened carefully. I heard nothing except the drip from the faucet. My eyes shifted about the room, stopping when something red caught my eye—something made of red lace—lying on the edge of the bed. I really wasn't planning on snooping, but I couldn't help it. My foot moved away from the door as I closed the distance between it and the bed. When I reached the edge of the mattress, I planted my feet and stared at the sexy lace cups. My hands began to twitch unconsciously so I shoved them in my pockets to make sure all I did was look at it. Oh, to have been where it had been.

This girl did things to me that I didn't know were even possible. My thoughts lingered on the image of her taking off the red lace bra and staring at me longingly with those blue eyes, her finger beckoning me toward her. I longed to touch her. I needed to taste her.

Shaking the thoughts out of my head, I turned away from the amazing red lace before my jeans became too unbearable. As I took a step toward the bathroom, the afternoon light bounced off what appeared to be shards of shattered glass lying on the floor in front of the waste basket. I turned back and walked around the bed to the other side of the suite. After studying the mess momentarily, I bent over to pick the pieces up and noticed the source of the glass shards. A picture frame had once encased my water goddess and some guy that I quickly named *douche bag*, because his arm was draped around my girl. I would properly dispose of this when I finished fixing the faucet. She didn't need trash like this lying around.

AFTER I HAD finished fixing the sink, I decided to walk down to Main Street to help Paul with the festival setup. He had been down there all morning while Lance looked after the farm. The festival was Friday night, and I looked forward to all of the possibilities that could occur.

As the late summer sun beat down, I neared Ellie's Boutique and decided I would stop by to say hello. Just as my fingertips touched the door handle, I looked through the window and saw my girl sitting on a stool next to Ellie. My eyes didn't register what she was actually wearing. I could only envision her in that red lace bra. Her skirt hiked up just a little as she crossed her legs—her long, luscious legs. She and Ellie laughed in near hysterics. I backed away from the door – from perfection. She was just so… beautiful.

My hand dropped from the handle. The need to see her reaction when I walked into her classroom later this evening helped me find the strength to turn away with a smile on my face. The mere thought of her had me doing that a lot lately. I wasn't one to get into deep relationships; I usually just had random hook-ups after a night at the tavern. Girls around here knew that I couldn't settle down. The farm always came first. It wouldn't run itself. I had become content with my life until I found Ms. Hawthorne asleep in the bath. This contentment of bachelordom was starting to fade as Ms. Hawthorne had me rethinking my single strategy.

My brain willed my body to continue walking away from Ellie's and toward the intersection of Main Street where the festival was to be held. The booths along either side of the street were ready for the different vendors to sell their food, booze, crafts, and clothing. I headed toward the middle of the square where the dance floor was to be laid, several stringed lights hanging overhead. I found Paul near the stage area trying to untangle the lights. From the looks of it, he needed help untangling himself.

The bulbs were huge, not like small Christmas tree lights. As Paul tried to untangle the wires, one bulb slipped from his grasp and fell to the cobblestone street. He cussed. I shook my head in disbelief. That was more broken glass I would have to pick up today.

"Do you need a hand there, Paul?" I asked as I approached him.

His gaze shifted up from the wadded mass of wires and toward me, annoyed tension clouding his face. He clenched his hands around the cords, frozen in place by the building frustration. "What do you think?"

"I think you've got it all under control," I said, hanging my thumbs through the belt loops of my jeans.

His glare never wavered. "There's more in the box over there, dipshit."

"But you seem like you're all over it… dipshit." I tried my damnedest to hold in my laughter.

He gave me a *go-to-hell* look, dropped the whole string, bulbs and all, and folded his arms across his chest. The lights hit the ground, and I heard at least three more bulbs break. I looked up at the sky as if asking for divine intervention and let out a deep sigh. "Now, I have to pay for those."

"For Christ's sake, Tom. Stop being so uptight. There are extras in the box," he said as he picked up the gnarled string he just dropped. With an inaudible grunt, I went over to the box and began the task of deftly untangling the bulbs. The sound of laughter tickled my ear. I looked up from the bulbs toward its direction. My body tensed again just like it had moments ago. She never glanced back at me, but I had a nice view of her ass as she waved goodbye to Ellie and walked back toward The Inn.

"So, *that's* what has you so uptight. You're obsessed with your teacher."

I turned my head away from the most incredible sight, only to see one that wasn't as appealing. Paul had a smug look on his face, and he continued, "You actually cannot function when it comes to that girl. Your bedroom has been a revolving door for years, and some naked tub lady completely immobilizes you."

"Not true." I could deny it to Paul but not to myself. Whatever it was about her, I had to try to get a little taste.

"It *is* true," he argued, still battling the lights. "If you didn't have a plan in place already, you would have run after her just then, but your mind already has one. I bet it has something to do with seeing her reaction to your presence in her classroom." He shook his head and added, "I think you should have warned the poor girl. You might make her pass out."

"Well, then I'll have no problem giving her mouth to mouth resuscitation." I stared at him with serious intent. The bulbs hit the ground again as Paul shook in laughter. I couldn't help but join in his amusement.

AFTER FINISHING WITH the light debacle out at the festival

site, I showered and changed into jeans and a black button-down with the sleeves pushed up, determined to make myself look presentable. The class at the community college gathered in the left wing of the main building. The 6:30 history class started within moments. I got there a few minutes early, wanting my water goddess all to myself.

I strode up to the building, found the correct room, and peeked inside to see my beautifully breathtaking teacher sitting behind her desk, immersed in a book. The mere sight of her caused my chest to ache in an unfamiliar way, but I willingly gave in to this feeling. Her gorgeous brown locks lazily hung around her face as she hunched her shoulders slightly forward. She still hadn't noticed my presence, so I crossed my arms over my chest and leaned my shoulder against the door frame. My fingers twitched at the thought of running them through her long hair. I wondered if it felt as silky as it looked.

"Is this History 101?"

She looked up and her blue eyes grew almost twice their regular size. I panicked for a moment until the blush crept up her cheeks. My body was no longer in my own control. My feet shifted toward her as my shoulder pushed itself away from the door frame. My eyes never left hers as our chemistry pulled me closer. The drum of my heart solidified the start of something between us, a something I wasn't sure I would ever want to end.

"We haven't been properly introduced. Hi, I'm Tom McCloud."

When she didn't respond, I extended my hand to shake hers. She gracefully placed hers into mine and stammered,

"Hi… I… I'm Jordan Hawthorne. Your teacher."

With our hands still clasped and our eyes locked together, I knew there was something about this woman. I knew right then and there that I had to have her.

"Well, it's nice to finally meet you, Ms. Hawthorne. I think I'm going to enjoy this semester."

Our hands parted as my classmates started to enter. I turned away with a smile and took a seat close to the back. While the class filed in, I glanced up at her again and found her looking at me. The best part… she smiled back.

Chapter Nine

JORDAN & TOM

An unknowing grin eased up my cheeks as I tried to wrap my head around this new turn of events. The smirk on his face made my chest ache. His blue eyes drew me in. I had no idea how I could possibly teach this class with him watching my every move. The morning classes had started without any problem, but with his presence in this one, I didn't know if I would be able to function. I would love to have him in anything… *except* my class.

With the desks now filled up by students, I willed my eyes to move away from the cowboy who was sure to enter my dreams tonight. This was going to be a pleasant disaster. I grabbed the syllabi on my desk and handed them to the student sitting directly in front of me. While she took one and passed the stack onward, I greeted my students. "Good evening, class. My name is Jordan Hawthorne." Of their own accord, my eyes flickered back toward the hot cowboy, and I added, "But please, call me Jordan."

His eye cocked up with an amused smirk, and I turned away from the class momentarily in hopes of hiding any blushing embarrassment. I steeled myself in order to begin my lecture and stood behind the podium. While waiting for everyone to get a syllabus, I could feel his eyes on me. The glancing caress made my body tense. No matter where I looked, I ended up meeting his eyes with every pass. For the briefest moment, I let go of my willpower and allowed myself to give in to the temptation. A look of dire intent replaced the smirk that had once graced his face, and during that fleeting moment, something happened. I didn't know what, but something sparked between us. He wasn't looking at me like some girl he walked in on while taking a bath. He looked at me in a way I had never seen before. That look woke up something I had never felt before.

A student returned the remaining syllabi to the podium, and I blinked away from the eyes I had almost drowned in. With one more glance, he had blinked away and was now staring at his syllabus, his face etched in confusion. He didn't look like the confident cowboy who had leaned against the classroom door frame or the plumber who couldn't remove his eyes from my naked chest. What he had just showed me was the real him, a man as lost and confused as me.

As the silence remained thick throughout the room, I began my lesson. "Today we start at the very beginning of the United States with the discovery of the New World."

Like a moth to a flame, I peeked at him again, and having done so, I lost my train of thought. With a blink away and slight head shake, I glanced back down at my guide and followed along with my lecture. "Although the discovery of the Americas has been attributed to various other explorers, the modern study of US history started with the European voyages of Christopher Columbus."

Finally, his eyes focused on his desk as he diligently took notes. Maybe I could survive after all. I continued my lecture without a problem, and the hour and a half class flew by quickly. "Next week we'll discuss the colonization of Jamestown. Please read chapters one through three before our next meeting. Have a good evening, y'all."

The students left the class. I walked back to my desk to gather up my belongings. I felt a presence in front of me, and my breath shook as I inhaled. I tilted my head upward and focused on the man who distracted me both in and out of the classroom. He gave me a mix of nervous excitement and calm comfort. I didn't know how it was possible, but it was refreshing.

"So... Jordan, can I make it up to you and buy you a cup of coffee?" he asked with an anxious smile.

Any nervousness I had harbored evaporated when I noticed how he had changed from some random, hot cowboy into a southern gentleman. With the promise of something new and fresh in front of me, I grabbed hold of any chance I could get of finally leaving Ryan in the past. A little smile adorned my face, and I replied, "Well, Tom, I don't know if a cup of coffee will be enough to make it up to me, but it's a start."

Tom and I went our separate ways after leaving the classroom. He had parked in the student lot, but my car was located in the teacher's. We decided to meet up at The Inn and walk down to the café from there. I didn't allow myself to over analyze the situation. It was just a coffee… with a really hot cowboy. The *hot cowboy* part put me slightly on edge again. I tuned the radio to a country station and turned up the volume, hoping the music would calm my nerves. Blinding lights reflected off my review mirror. I blinked at the glare and repositioned my mirror until the light was no longer reflecting in my eyes.

As I continued driving down the highway, the loud roar of an engine came up behind me. I tried to reposition my mirror again, but I couldn't see against the blinding lights. With a wince, I tried looking out the side mirrors. Again, all I could see were bright lights.

"What the hell?" There was no one on this highway except this car behind me wanting to ride my bumper. "All right, fine. I'll slow my ass down. Bastard."

When I released the gas, he came uncomfortably close. I gripped the steering wheel tight and cringed. Just when I thought the car would slam into me, he slowed down and swooped into the passing lane. I continued to slow until he passed me, and when I thought the car was going to take off, I glanced toward it. I gasped when I saw Ryan. I blinked in terror and peered back, but the face blurred as he sped away. I reacted and swerved from the sudden shock. My tires drummed on the bumps in the emergency lane as I came to a stop.

"Shit!" I slammed on my breaks. I tried to check out the license plate, but the only thing I could see were the glowing taillights shrinking away. *It wasn't him. It wasn't him. He doesn't know where you are.*

I sat for a moment, taking a few deeps breaths. When I thought it was okay to drive, I pulled out onto the highway again and continued back into Olde Town. By the time I arrived, my nerves loosened somewhat, but I was still anxious for my date with the cowboy. As I parked my car in front of The Inn, a truck pulled alongside of me. I was welcomed by Tom's smiling face. The sight of him made any thoughts of Ryan and my near collision fade away.

I switched off the ignition and readied my handbag, which was nestled in the passenger seat. Before I could grab the handle, my car door opened for me. I was taken aback. Was it possible that cowboys and gentlemen still existed? Apparently, I needed to get out of the city more often.

My heels crunched against the gravel drive as I stood, nearly meeting his eye. I stepped away from the car, and he shut it behind me.

"Thank you. I didn't know guys still did that."

"Do what?" He met my step as we started walking down the street.

"Open doors for women. The only man I know who still does that is my father."

I continued down the street, but he stopped a few steps behind me. I turned around and looked at him with slight confusion. My shoulder's relaxed when he smiled the sexiest smile I had ever seen, and as he tipped an imaginary hat, he said, "Well, ma'am, in the country, we still respect beautiful women."

Wow.

A blush crept up my face and I turned away from him in

hopes that he wouldn't see. He met my stride, and in order to spark up conversation.

"So, Tom," I said, sparking the conversation. "You seem a little old to be a freshman in college."

My eyes stared forward as we walked, but I could hear his smile as he said, "Well, you seem a little young to be a college instructor. How old are you, anyway?"

"Twenty-three. You?"

"Twenty-four," he replied as he grabbed the handle of the café and pulled the door open.

"After you, ma'am," he crooned, making my insides tumble as his eyes bore into mine. I had to get an iced coffee, because it would be way too hot sitting across from this cowboy.

OKAY, TOM, PLAY it cool. Play it cool. Jordan was unbelievably gorgeous with a refined quality about her, proving that she was way out of my league. I couldn't treat her like any other farm girl, not that I treated any woman with disrespect. I had just handled previous situations with women differently, but my antics would soon be changing. The cafe was relatively quiet for a Wednesday. School had begun and students weren't yet flocking for the nearest form of caffeine. The smell of fresh-ground coffee beans warmed my senses as the soothing sounds of an old crooner filtered through the air. After finding two club chairs tucked away in the corner, I ushered her over to the dimly lit area, and we sat with our legs nearly touching. She crossed hers, and my eyes swept down their length, craving to have them wrapped around me. *Play*

it cool, Tom.

A young, blonde waitress came over to take our order. The man I was a week ago would have talked her up to no end, but with a woman like Jordan sitting next to me, I didn't believe my eyes would ever wander again. With complete ease, Jordan ordered, "Iced skinny cinnamon latte." Whatever the hell that was. Her lips became the focus of my attention when she spoke, just as they did during class. They weren't too plump or too thin. I wanted to know what they would feel like on me.

She turned to me. I had no clue why she was staring until I realized it was time for me to order. While I dared not look away from her, I responded, "Coffee, black."

The lips I now craved lifted into a smile as a blush darkened her cheeks. She bowed her head and stared at the floor with a bit of shyness.

I eased into a conversation and asked, "So, how do you like living at The Inn, Jordan?"

Her eyes blinked back up to mine. "It really is nice there. It's been a culture shock living out in the country, but it's starting to grow on me."

In my attempt to keep my eyes off her legs, I kept them fully locked with her eyes. Hoping to gain a genuine knowledge of her life, I asked, "What city are you from? Somewhere close by?"

"Charlotte. Not too far from here." She interlocked her fingers, resting them on her knee. Her head tilted down slightly, and she had a far off look about her.

"Do you miss home?"

Her eyes focused on me again as her brow creased in

worry. Something wasn't right about home, I gathered. She answered with a vague response, "Well, I miss my parents and my best friend, Katherine, but it was time to move on."

Unmistakable despair etched across her face. I knew there was more to the story, but I was going to leave that for another day. It probably had something to do with the douche bag from her picture. I wasn't going to push her into telling me all of her problems. I just wanted to be the one to fix them.

The waitress served our coffee, and after we both thanked her, Jordan continued with a brighter look, "Although, I don't know what I'm going to do on Sundays anymore. I used to go to all of the Panthers games with my dad, and it's going to be such a good year. I can feel it."

With the first sip of coffee just passing my lips, I almost spat it out from the shock. This chick liked football?

"You like football?" I asked, hoping that my pure excitement didn't make me look like a fool.

She laughed as she said, "Like is an understatement. I've never missed a home game in my life. Hotdogs, beer, and the Panthers… that's how I do my Sundays."

Yep, I had died and gone to heaven.

"Well, don't worry about missing the games because we always have a big group of people who watch them down at Dixie's on Sundays." I didn't want to imply that I was asking her out on a date. I still needed to work up to that.

"That sounds great. I'll keep that in mind," she said as she smiled, and my heart twinged. In my state of awe, I could not form a cohesive sentence. Thankfully, she graced me with a question. "So you know I'm a teacher, but what is it that you do, Tom?"

I sat my mug down on the adjoining end table and replied, "Well, I'd like to consider myself a cowboy because it sounds cooler, but I'm really just a farmer."

She placed her cup next to mine, and after returning her hands to her knee, she asked, "Do you have cows?"

My brow furrowed at the odd question. "Yes."

With a simple shrug of her shoulders, she concluded, "Well, then you're a cowboy."

She reached for her drink as I stared at her in amusement. She gave me a flirty smile, noting my amusement, and as she sipped her drink, we never broke eye contact. My cheeks rose into a grin as I also reached for my coffee, and I said, "I believe I like your logic, Ms. Hawthorne."

With her straw pinched between her finger and thumb, her smile remained flirty. In a sexy whisper, she added, "Well, a cowboy does sound sexier than a farmer."

Oh, shit. Settle down boy, settle down.

After we finished our coffee, we began the walk back to The Inn, and as we approached the front door, I asked, "Do you think you'll be heading down to Main Street for the End of Summer Fest on Friday night?"

Her face lit up. I smiled to see her trying to control her reaction as best she could. With a hint of hopefulness, she replied, "Yes. I made plans to meet Ellie there."

The need to be closer to her intensified; the lips I had been craving all night beckoned to be kissed. I stepped a little closer, but I knew that it wasn't yet the time. "Well, maybe you can save a dance for me, then."

It wasn't a question, because I wasn't going to give her

the option. I had to feel her arms around me, and my arms around her. She stepped a little closer and whispered, "I'd like that."

The breath caught in my throat as her lips drew so close to mine. She bit her bottom lip, and it nearly drove me insane. With the need growing to kiss her, I took a hold of her hand, and I said, "Well, until then…" I gave her hand the smallest peck while staring into her eyes and pulled her hand back down, "Have a good night, Ms. Hawthorne."

The eye contact remained locked as I stepped away. With the click of the door knob, she stepped inside and said in quiet voice, "Thank you. Good night."

She slipped inside and closed the door behind her. The drumming in my chest played an unfamiliar beat, a mix of excitement and hopefulness. One confident step into this new territory, and I believed I was lost forever.

Chapter Ten

JORDAN

After teaching my two morning classes, I decided to surprise my new friend at her boutique. As my feet crunched down the gravel drive of The Inn, it occurred to me that since it was afternoon, lunch sounded like a good way to get to know Ellie. Lunch would also give us a way to talk about her friend, someone I needed to find out more about, even though I knew this was way too soon. Across the street from Ellie's Boutique stood the café where Tom and I had coffee just the night before. I exhaled a calming breath and an unhelpful smirk rose up my face. I shook my head in disbelief over the rush I was having because of this man. I hurried my steps, strutting down the cobblestone street and stepping up onto the paved sidewalk.

When I reached the café, the welcoming aroma of coffee and vanilla soothed me, but the late summer heat had me yearning for something cool in hopes of keeping the sweat from dripping down my face. After glancing at the menu written on a big board with different colors of chalk, I ordered two chef salads with ranch dressing to go, paid the bill, and stepped aside so the next patron could order. I looked around the sleek, modern café in the daylight. It seemed almost out of place in the middle of the country, but it was comfortable for the lifestyle I had been accustomed to. The front and side walls were mostly filled by windows, with the afternoon sun hidden behind shades. The back wall housed the counter where customers placed takeout orders. Waitresses would serve anyone who sat at one of the wooden dining tables or overstuffed chairs in various deep colors of purple, wine, and chocolate. The far wall was the main focal point of the café. Bookshelves made of dark walnut lined it from floor to ceiling and from the front to the back of the café. The shelves were stacked with books upon books. I would have to make use of those bookshelves one day.

As I turned around, checking out the place in the daylight, the quiet corner I had shared with Tom came into view. There was no getting that cowboy out of my mind. I thought about him more than I ought to, especially considering the position I was in emotionally and professionally. It was unhealthy, I was sure, but the look he had in his eyes last night urged me to think about him even more and to not dwell on the consequences. A brown paper bag appeared in front of me, snapping me out of my continuously unhealthy thoughts about the cowboy and the consequences he would surely bring. I grabbed the handle of the bag and exited the café into the heat of summer.

As I crossed the quiet cobblestone street, I turned my head toward the sounds of hammering on Main Street. My heels clicked to a halt when my eyes feasted on at least twelve men assembling what appeared to be a wooden dance floor. Another man joined the group, adding even more to the jaw-dropping view. The tight fitted jeans and T-shirt hugged his physique, making my hands twitch with need. When those blue eyes shifted toward me, the power of his stare almost made me drop my lunch. The sound of a car horn snapped me back into reality and I scurried across the street.

Without a look back at the Cowboy Adonis and his minions, I swung open the door of the boutique to welcoming country music and crisp air conditioning. A quick look around the store. I didn't see Ellie anywhere in sight. I walked to the counter, and as I set the salads on top, the hum of a sewing machine rumbled from the back of the boutique. I followed the hum and found Ellie hunched over her work. Her hair was thrown up on the top of her head in a tousled knot, her eyes were baggy, and she looked as if she slept in her clothes from the day before. When she noticed me, her head twitched up from her zone and a tired smile brightened her face as she turned off the sewing machine.

"I brought you a salad, but from the looks of it, I should have brought you some coffee. Have you slept in the past forty-eight hours?"

Ellie rolled her eyes, and with added sarcasm, replied, "No, I was working." Her face lit up in a sleep-deprived smile as she continued, "You just gave me an idea about a new design angle, and my mind has been in overdrive. Come see what I've got, and then we can eat lunch."

As she grabbed my forearm, pulling me with her to a rack full of clothes, I could feel the caffeine pulsing through her jittery fingers. After dragging me through the organized chaos of random fabrics, she released my arm and rose up on her tip toes, reaching for a hanger. The excited smile colored her voice as she proclaimed, "I've got just the outfit for the fest tomorrow night."

She pulled out a rich orange one-shouldered dress that fit tight across the chest, flared out at the hips, and fell to just above the knee. It looked simple and casual, but elegant all at once.

"This line is a mix of the city and country flair. It just hit me while we were having lunch the other day talking about clothes. It's a perfect marriage between the two, the casualness of the country with the sleekness of the city."

"Ellie, this is really pretty. I love this color," I said as I glided my hand down the dress, feeling its texture.

While the dress was still in my grasp, she walked over to her work station and pulled out a pair of cowboy boots from underneath the table. She lifted them up and said, "Here you go. You have an outfit for the fest. You might even wrangle a cowboy." She gave me a wink that didn't even begin to be subtle.

I eyed her suspiciously and blurted, "Okay, Ellie. Spill it."

She twitched her mouth, trying to repress a smile, but then she admitted, "Err... I know about you and Mr. Coffee. This town isn't that big, you know." She finally released her smile and asked, "So, how did it go?"

Not willing to dish out all of the information just yet, I replied, "It was fine. Did you know he's my student, too?"

"I did find out about that yesterday…" She tucked her bottom lip in between her teeth as if she wanted to say more. Without being able to keep it in, she blurted out, "And I know about the tub incident!"

My eyes popped in disbelief. Shaking my head, I said, "Damn, how small is this town?!"

Ellie waved her hands erratically and said, "No, don't worry. Paul told me. The whole town doesn't know. At least I hope not." She shrugged her shoulders and added, "But Lance knows, too, so you never know."

"I don't even know Lance and Paul!" I perked up when I realized the connection. "Wait, if you know about the tub incident"—I cringed at the term—"from Paul, then Paul knows from Tom. Has he been talking about me?"

Ellie just grinned and nodded. My heart thumped in my chest. I bit my lip knowing that this wasn't good. It would only end badly. I had only been single for a few months, and I was still getting text messages from an ex, which I kept deleting for the obvious reasons. This situation seemed so easy to fall into, and I didn't trust myself around it. Ellie knew my reasons for fleeing the city, but she seemed to think that a person needed a new someone to help get over the old someone. I wasn't so sure my heart could take it.

"Look, Jordan, I know you had a bad breakup and all, but Tom is a really great guy. He doesn't normally date much, so there really wouldn't be any awkward situations with an ex. Well, except maybe Angela because she's not so bright," Ellie rambled.

My defense mechanism heightened, and I asked, "Who's Angela?"

Ellie's head fell back, and after a spurt of amused laughter, she said, "No one to be worried about. Let's just say Tom had one too many at a party a few years ago, and the girl thinks she still has a shot." Ellie shook her head as she continued, "Bless her heart. She really is clueless."

Ellie lead me back to the front of her store as the possibilities narrowed into reality. I slumped in my chair and propped up my elbow on my knee, resting my chin on my hand. "I just don't know how long I'll be staying here, Ellie. I might be leaving after this semester. I don't know if I should or could take on anything serious."

We prepared our salads, and as I dug in mine, I glanced up at Ellie. She smirked. I paused with a forkful of lettuce halfway to my mouth, and asked, "What?"

With a slight eye roll, she said, "Jordan, it's not like you're marrying the guy. I mean what's a roll or two in the hay!"

"Ellie, I—"

"Jordan, just live a little." She smiled and added, "Oh, and Tom loves that color orange."

The only comeback I had was to throw a crouton at her as we both sat back and cackled.

After a few hours of mindless chit chat with Ellie, I got ready to leave her sweatshop. I made her promise to get some sleep tonight—I didn't want my newfound friend getting sick or keeling over from exhaustion—before I made my way back to The Inn. Ellie was the polar opposite of Katherine, but she was also someone I could consider a long-term friend. It was nice to have a friend close by since everyone else I knew lived a few hours away. And, hopefully, a certain person would stay those few hours away.

As I was walking down the street and digging for the room key in my bag, the thought of Ryan being just a few hours away bubbled up from my subconscious and my shoulders tensed all over again. I felt sure someone was watching me. Continuing my walk to The Inn, I dug faster through my purse, but it was no use. I stopped to search more carefully, and while I battled the wind blowing my hair around, I cursed myself for not keeping the massive bag cleaner.

As I dug and dug, my senses alerted me of someone approaching. My eyes flickered up as I froze in place.

"Howdy, ma'am."

A gasp escaped me as the voice whispered in my ear, mixing with the howling wind. Fear and adrenaline surged through me. I was right—it had been Ryan on the road! I jerked around to find a Greek god of a cowboy only a few inches away from my face. I let out a sigh of relief, and while my hand brushed over his tight, muscular chest, I said, "Tom! You scared me!"

My eyes rose from his chest to his face. He wore the sweetest smile. I felt at peace with him. I don't know why I was so willing to let my guard down around him. Hadn't Ryan taught me enough about how men use women? But somehow, when I was with Tom, all those horrible memories faded away and there was nothing left but the two of us, here and now.

"Sorry, I just couldn't help myself. Are you headed back to The Inn?"

"Yes, but I think I left my key in my room. That's what I was looking for when you decided to scare the hell out of me." I couldn't help playfully swatting his chest again. He placed his hand on the small of my back, leading me back toward The Inn. My skin tingled from his touch and my heart fluttered from the anticipation that spread throughout my body.

"I can get you into your room. I have a master key. Remember, I'm the plumber."

When I glanced up at him, he winked. My cheeks turned a brighter shade of pink as I turned my head in hope that he wouldn't see.

"Well, what are you doing down here in town? Don't you have stuff to farm or something?"

He laughed a deep, husky chuckle. I couldn't help but watch his face light up.

"Stuff to farm? I like that. Never heard it put that way. Actually, I was finishing up with the festival setup for tomorrow night, taking extra special care of a certain area where I hope you'll be spending some time with me."

My face lifted into a knowing smirk, and I asked, "And what area would that be, Tom?"

"The dance floor, of course. Get your mind out of the gutter, Ms. Hawthorne." He grabbed the door handle for The Inn and opened it for me. Maybe one day I would be immune to his southern charm and would no longer blush at every little thing he said or did, but in all honesty, I doubted it.

As we entered the foyer, I didn't see Aunt Ethel by the counter, but Chef Al's singing filtered into the dining room from the kitchen. I walked through the foyer and up the stairs with Tom right behind me. When we reached my suite, I stood out of the way so he could unlock it. With a *click*, it unlocked, and he pushed the door open for me. I glided past him, and the part of my skin that touched him tingled as the electricity popped between us. I stood inside the doorway, turning around, and hesitated in deciding my next move.

"Thank you, Tom."

His charming smile lit up his face, making my knees almost turn to jelly. "It was my pleasure."

He backed away to head downstairs when an uncontrollable urge came over me. I no longer hesitated. I didn't want him to go. As soon as he took the first step down the stairs, I asked, "Would you like come in for a beer or something?"

He paused, his head turning back toward me. His cheeks twitched like he was trying to contain a smile, but with his face still gleaming, he answered, "Yes, I would like that a lot."

Tom brushed passed me as I held open the door for him, and I could smell a hint of sun and something else I couldn't describe. Maybe it was the scent of a cowboy. With the scent lingering and my body completely tingling, I walked to the mini fridge encased inside a wooden cabinet underneath the flat screen, and I grabbed two bottles of beer.

"Is light okay? That's all I have in my fridge."

As I turned around, my clutched fists landed against his ripped, rock hard abs. My eyes leveled just above his chest and I bit the inside of my lip. I dragged my gaze up to his piercing blue eyes, and I forgot to breathe.

"Jordan ..."

His hand caressed my cheek while his gaze flickered between my eyes and my lips. My heart fluttered as it drummed an anxiously hopeful beat. What was happening between us was inevitable, and there was no stopping the inevitable. Our breath intertwined just as his lips brushed against mine. My body almost lost all will to function as it hummed with need. His eyes found mine again as if seeking permission to continue. I wasn't about to stop him. He leaned into me once again. I responded with a passion, a hunger.

My arms wrapped around his neck, dropping the bottles of beer onto the rug-covered floor. He pulled me flush against his body, and my fingers instinctively laced through his brown hair. My tongue swept against his lower lip; his gently massaged mine. The arms that wrapped around me engulfed me in a heaven that I never wanted to leave. My inner desires pooled within as a moan rose up, but I didn't know if it came from him or me.

As much as I didn't want to, I broke the kiss, and as we both inhaled deeply, he rested his forehead against mine and whispered, "Did you feel that?"

My body strummed with desire as my heart thumped an erratic beat. I exhaled slowly as my eyes remained closed, and I whispered, "Yes."

His lips skimmed across mine again while his hands slid around to my hips. As we ended our kiss, my eyes flickered open to find his full and bright. His mouth fought against a smile, but his cheeks quirked, giving him away. As the smile finally eased up his cheeks, he asked in a whisper, "Will you have dinner with me?"

A nod was the only answer I could give. If I had anything left of a heart, I would be in love. I made sure I had my room key and we started down the stairs. As we walked, I asked, "Where are we going?"

We arrived in the foyer, and as he cracked that sexy smile of his, he said, "Not far." He led me into the dining room.

"Ciao, Bella," Chef Al greeted us in his best Italian North Carolina country accent.

"Hey, Uncle Al. What's your special this evening?" Tom asked as Chef Al led us to one of the tables in the corner. There weren't too many guests dining tonight, leaving us practically alone. This was perfectly okay with me. We sat next to each other while the chef poured us each a glass of wine and read off the evening's specials.

"Tonight we are serving Caesar salad to start, followed by Chicken Marsala, which is served with linguini in a light mushroom cream sauce."

"That sounds amazing. Thank you, Chef Al."

Breakfast at The Inn was a Southerner's dream with grits and country ham, biscuits and gravy, eggs any way you like them, but dinner seemed to be a whole different game with Chef Al.

Chef Al went back into the kitchen while we sipped on our wine. The sound of Italian music played subtly in the background. The perfection of this night seemed unbelievable. I looked down at my lap in hopes I could calm the giddiness jumping inside. As I twirled the stem of the wine glass, his fingers brushed gently across my knuckles; I bit my lip to keep from grinning too big.

"Well, Ms. Hawthorne, I'm afraid I have some bad news."

"What's wrong, Tom?" I asked while placing my hand unknowingly on his thigh. I flinched when I realized what I'd done, but when his sexy smile eased up his face, I didn't move my hand away. I really didn't care to. He leaned in closer and said, "I won't be able to call you Ms. Hawthorne any longer, because I have to drop out of your class."

"Oh," I said as I removed my hand and placed it back on the stem of my wine glass. My heart sunk a little; although, Tom's presence in my class had been a little distracting. "That's too bad. Have too much going on at the farm or something?"

His hand brushed mine before he pulled my hand away from the glass; I looked up into his eyes. He leaned in closer and whispered, "I just don't think it's very wise of me to be taking a class from a teacher that I have a major crush on."

While his fingers continued to brush against mine, he added, "I know I would fail when all I would be thinking about is how perfect your lips feel against mine, and how I so badly want to do that now."

He grabbed hold of my hand, pressing his lips to my palm just as Uncle Al brought us the salads. After his little kiss, we dug into our food. Searching desperately for a topic of conversation that didn't involve what each of us wanted to do with the other's body, I asked, "So, how is it that you run a huge farm by yourself?"

"Well," he said as he finished his bite, "I've lived there most of my life. My parents died when I was three, and I lived with my grandmother growing up."

"I'm sorry to hear that about your parents. That had to have been tough," I said, resting my hand on top of his.

"I really didn't know any different. My grandmother died when I was sixteen, which was pretty rough. I didn't want to lose the farm," he said as his eyes met my sad ones.

"You've kept up a farm since you were sixteen?" I couldn't understand how a sixteen-year-old could hold that much responsibility.

He shrugged his shoulders and said, "It was the only

thing that mattered to me. Aunt Et and Uncle Al took care of me until I graduated high school. Now you see why I'm just starting college."

I was in shock. I knew a very small number of men who had that great a sense of responsibility, much less a sixteen-year-old. I was utterly amazed.

The ease of conversation that flowed between Tom and me felt like we had known each other forever; however, I kept my reason for moving to the country out of the conversation. I did not need to discuss ex-boyfriends with hopeful, future boyfriends.

When it had appeared that Chef Al was long gone, and the bottle of wine he left for us was empty, I turned to Tom and said, "I believe we closed the place down."

He looked around and said, "Funny… I didn't notice a thing while I was talking to you."

"I didn't either." The blasted blush crept up my face again.

My nerves took over again, and I started biting my lip. He cupped my chin and leaned closer to me. I met him half way and kissed him. Not forcefully, but enough to let him know that I meant it. The touch of his lips made my heart flutter into over drive. He stood up and reached for my hand. "Let's get you to bed, Jordan."

My fingers intertwined with his and I followed him into the foyer. When we approached the stairs, he kissed me again with as much passion as he had in my room. He rested his forehead against mine, and with a low, husky voice, he whispered, "Jordan, I want to follow you upstairs, but I'm just going to say good night. I can't wait to have you in my arms tomorrow night on the dance floor."

He kissed me again and my heart melted.

"Sweet dreams, Jordan."

"Good night, Tom. See you tomorrow."

I slowly climbed the stairs, looking back before I lost sight of him. My eyes met his and he smiled, placing his hand over his heart. That one single motion told me that he wasn't playing with my heart. He was protecting his. When I got to my room, I shook my head and exhaled a long-withheld breath. I didn't know how it was possible after only four days, but my broken heart was slowly mending.

Chapter Eleven

JORDAN

Lush green grass softened under my feet. A vast field surrounded me, with gentle rolling hills merging into the distant mountains. The sun lightly kissed the tip of the mountain goodnight, slipping away behind its peak as the moon brightly dominated the sky. My fingers glided over the tall reeds of grass as my hair flowed behind me, dancing in the summer breeze and tickling my neck in loving caresses. Flickers of soft yellow lights swirled around me, touching my hands and landing upon my white sundress. I followed their alluring aerial dance as they led me to an old weathered barn.

As I approached the barn door, the fireflies danced one last dance before being whisked away with the breeze. I didn't recognize this barn or why I had been brought here, but I felt secure.

I stepped through the weathered red door, and called out,

"Hello?"

My bare feet cushioned against the hay-lined ground. Stalls lined the walls on either side of me, but there wasn't a horse to be seen. I knew I was here for a reason, but I wasn't sure what that reason was.

I stepped further into the barn and called out again, "Hello?"

"Good evening, ma'am."

I swiveled around, but I couldn't find the source of the voice. As I stood facing the side of the barn, a muscular man, wearing only jeans, boots, and a cowboy hat, jumped down from the rafters in front of me. My normal instinct would be to flee, but I was overcome with a sense of serenity. With one piercing look from those blue eyes, my insides clenched, and I whispered his name.

"Tom."

His breathing elevated for a moment, and before another word was spoken, he slid his arms around me, pulling me tight into an embrace. Even before I wrapped my arms around his brawny shoulders, his lips found mine, and my long-anticipated desire was finally fulfilled. Our mouths melded without hesitation. He lifted me up, and my legs encircled his waist. He broke our kiss, and his lips eased down my neck.

A hard, wooden beam pressed into my back as Tom anchored me against him. In a blink, we were completely naked. He pressed forward, relinquishing the need I harbored for so long. I screamed out in passion as he filled me completely. I used every muscle I could to urge him deeper. Our breath intertwined; our lips so close together. His mouth covered mine, our tongues dancing. I pulled away panting and screamed out *in ecstasy, nearing my peak as he whispered in my ear.*

"I've been dreaming about you, darlin'."

I gasped as my eyes popped open to the morning sunlight seeping through my bedroom window. I turned my head to the empty pillow beside me, and a sigh of longing escaped. I wanted to return to the dream. Covering my racing heart with my hand, I closed my eyes and regulated my breathing. That man had me craving things; things I wasn't sure I wanted to crave. I had to shake it off.

Stretching my arms and legs, I peered at the clock on the nightstand and read 8:52. After lifting off the light quilt, I pushed myself forward and sat on the edge of my bed, staring absently as my focus sank inward. Something felt different. Maybe I didn't have to shake it off. A small grin tickled my face, and for the first time in months, I felt hopeful. I had gotten used to the constant ache around my heart. It was still there, but this morning it felt slightly less painful. My fingertips glided over my lips, remembering Tom's effect on me. I didn't like to believe he was the reason I felt different, but it was hard to deny that he was. The way he looked at me, as if he could see the depths of my soul, made me feel almost human again, as impossible as that seemed. A light inside which had long been extinguished began to flicker again.

Since being with Ryan, I couldn't remember a time I had felt this good. I'd known Tom all of five days, and he had shown me more admiration than Ryan ever had in a whole year. I was such a fool to believe what Ryan and I shared was love. How could I have jilted myself for so long? I was no longer going to make plans for love. I was going to live one day at a time.

I had officially moved on.

As I headed into the bathroom to run a bubble bath, I grinned at the thought of the last one I had. It gave the term "Peeping Tom" a much different meaning to me now. I couldn't believe a man who looked like that could possibly give a damn about me. Just five days ago, I lay in this exact spot and cried my eyes out with hurt and anguish. I would have never believed in such a short amount of time I could feel whole again.

I heard a beep from my phone and I rolled my eyes. After finishing my bath, I reach over to where I'd left it near the sink, already prepared to delete another one of Ryan's messages. But I stared at the ID, puzzled; it was a local number. I clicked open the message.

Good morning, darling. Can't wait for our dance. – Tom

My heart sang with an indescribable giddiness. As I saved his number in my phone, I accidently opened a message from Ryan that I hadn't deleted.

I will find you. When I do, you'll regret ever leaving me.

Hate seethed through me. I threw the phone down; ruing the day I met him. It was time to move on.

After my bath, I headed down the street to the electronics store. I had today off and I intended to enjoy it. A new cell phone and new phone number were the way to go if wanted to ensure Ryan wouldn't ruin my day with endless texts. Once I had my new toy in hand, I texted Tom back.

Hey, cowboy! I decided to make a more permanent gesture and got a local number. Make sure you save it for future reference. ;)

Just as I opened the door to the café, yearning to have

a coffee concoction, my phone beeped. I sat down by the window and opened the message.

You know I'm going to text you like crazy. For future reference, of course.

I grinned like a little school girl.

Good. I hope you do. ;)

Since I didn't have Internet access at The Inn, I checked my email and saw I had received an official notice from the school that Tom had dropped out of my class. The more I thought about what he'd said, the more I realized he was right. A student-teacher relationship wasn't wise. I didn't want anything jeopardizing my career.

As I enjoyed licking the whipped cream off my straw, my new friend sat down in front of me. Ellie looked far more sunny than she had the last time I saw her.

"Well, I'm glad someone got some sleep."

"Hey, Jordie! Oh, that looks yummy!" She turned to the waitress approaching the table and asked to have the same as me. "So, I have a favor to ask of you."

"What's that?"

"Well, I have a booth at the fest, which most local business owners do. Would you mind hanging out for a little while, since you'll be wearing one of my designs?"

"Sure, I was planning on hanging out with you anyway." I tilted my head, studying her, as my brow wrinkled. We had already made plans on hanging together. Ellie had a little glint to her eyes. "Ellie, why do I have the feeling you're hiding something?"

"Because I don't hide things very well. And on that note, I'm taking this coffee to go." A guilty smile slid up her face as

I grabbed her arm.

"Ellie… have you been talking to Paul again?"

Ellie grinned and nodded. "Tom really likes you, Jordan. Paul and I were just discussing this morning how we've never seen him like this."

"So, why were you and Paul talking this morning?" I gave her a knowing smile. "Was this outside on the street, or was it somewhere else?"

Ellie stilled and smacked her forehead with her hand. Then she looked up at me and smiled. "Oh Jordan, I don't know what I'm going to do. I've been in love with him for so long, and I think he likes me, too. It's just that neither one of us wants to hurt Lance." She looked at her watch and said, "Okay, I really do have to get going. I'd like to set up my booth before I get ready for the evening. I'll see you in a bit."

Ellie darted outside toward the stands lined down Main Street. Most booths were draped in shades of dark greens and browns, but, of course, Ellie's stood out in a golden yellow. The street was bustling with the vendors. My nerves started to hum with anticipation. I looked at the time, and after realizing that I had been sitting in the café for a couple of hours, I hurriedly gathered my things and left as well.

After showering and curling my hair, I proceeded to style it in a low, messy bun, as directed by my favorite boutique owner. Once I finished my make-up, I opened up my closet and took the dress off the hanger. I stepped inside the dress, letting it graze up over my hips before placing the one strap over my shoulder, zipping up the side. I didn't need a bra because my smart designer friend had built a comfortable support into the dress. I pulled on brown lace panties, hoping

Tom would get a chance to see them later. I needed him more than I had ever needed anyone.

As I pulled on my cowboy boots and straightened my dress, I looked in the mirror, and had to admit Ellie was right. It was a perfect mix of country and city. A dab of perfume and I was ready. I opened the door to leave and noticed a bundle of daisies resting on the floor. My heart melted at the sight. I picked them up, smiling as I played with the petals. I went back into the room and set them on my nightstand. It was time for the fest.

While I was walking down to Main Street, the sun descended behind the mountains, painting the town with a glint of orange. Little flickers of light danced around the skyline. I stopped for a moment and watched them play. There weren't any fireflies in the city so I wasn't used to them. They were absolutely fascinating, hypnotizing as their glow blinked in the surrounding trees and continued into the foothills, leading to the mountains.

The fireflies hung overhead as I walked over to Ellie's booth. My presence went unnoticed. She and Paul couldn't tear their eyes away from each other. I cleared my throat to get their attention. Ellie looked over and gasped. Seeing me, she bounced up and down as she beamed, "It's beautiful! You're beautiful! I'm so awesome!"

A strong male hand touched my elbow, and I turned to see a handsome blond with smiling dimples. I could see why Ellie had been in love with him for so long. He was slightly taller than me, but only by a couple of inches. He extended his hand toward me and said, "Jordan, I'm Paul. It's really nice to finally meet you."

"Likewise." I smiled at him, and I eased my hand inside of his, glancing at Ellie. Her face radiated with happiness. I hoped this worked out for her.

"So, pretty ladies," he continued. "Is it a wine or beer night?"

Ellie and I both looked at each other. "Beer!"

Paul, Ellie, and I hung around the booth for a while, drinking beers and socializing with anyone who came by. I played the model a little bit while women from across the county came over to gush over Ellie's designs. Her country-meets-city style was a hit. I was having a good time until I noticed that it was nearly 7:00. Why hadn't I seen Tom yet? Where was he? When Ellie and Paul disappeared, I pulled out my cell to see if I had missed any texts from him. There was one, and luckily, it had only been sent three minutes ago.

When are you going to dance with me? ;-)

I put my phone back inside my purse and shoved it underneath the table where Ellie's belongings were. Feeling confident, I stood and walked over to the dancing area. It was packed with cowboy boots and cowboy hats. A wooden floor lay underneath a crisscross of twinkling lights, reminiscent of the fireflies twirling above. A perfect country night.

I weaved through the crowd of two-steppers, coming to a sudden halt in the middle of the dance floor. I stared at the most undoubtedly handsome cowboy in the world. He wore scuffed cowboy boots; dark, well-worn jeans; a plaid orange shirt, which happened to match my orange dress; and the typical cowboy belt buckle. My breath caught seeing his cowboy hat. It was just like the one from my dreams. The gaze in his eyes caught my attention. In that moment, no one else existed on the dance floor—no band, no dancers, not a soul. It was just Tom and me. The way it was meant to be.

His eyes bore into mine. My heart pounded against my chest. A slow exhale escaped his lips as he finally approached me without breaking his deep gaze. Mere inches away, his hand caressed my cheek, and he whispered, "You are the most beautiful being I have ever seen. Please dance with me."

I wrapped my arms around his neck, swaying with him to the music. While caressing the back of his head and playing with his hair, I buried my head in the crook of his neck. He bent down to my ear and whispered to me again, "You're making my heart do things it's never done before."

I pulled away from his neck.

He stared at me longingly and continued, "Jordan, I know something bad happened to your heart before you moved. I don't know what it is, and I'm not asking you to tell me. All I'm asking is for you to give me a chance to fix it."

His thumb rubbed across my lips, and I leaned in to kiss him. Allowing my heart to lead me, I said, "I trust you."

He didn't need to say a word. His eyes said it all. As the song began to change, he laced his fingers with mine, and we walked in between the dancers and behind the stage, away from the crowd. Our eyes locked and I melted into his gaze. I felt like I was the only one he had ever longed for. He coddled my face inside his hands as he inched closer. My heart raced with anticipation as he brushed his lips against mine. When he pulled back slightly, his beautiful lips twitched into a smile. I couldn't take it anymore. I looped my arms around his neck and kissed him with all the passion I felt for him. I grazed my tongue along his bottom lip, seeking admittance as he wrapped his arms tight around me, lifting me up.

The passionate kiss merged into a kiss beyond description. My back pressed hard against the wall of the stage as he hoisted my legs around his waist. I could feel him pulsing against me. My need for him grew more urgent. He broke away from my lips kissing slowly down my jaw, my neck, and over to my ear. I whimpered into the breeze. The kiss had ended too soon. His eyes brimmed with lust and he gave me another gentle kiss.

"Our first time will not be outside behind a stage," he said.

As I tried to even my breathing, I replied, "Well, cowboy, you seem to have some effect on me."

He lowered me to the ground but refused to let go of me. "Tell you what. Why don't you go over to Ellie's booth and give me a second to, umm… settle down. I'll grab you a beer."

"Sounds good. Don't make me wait too long."

Wanting to make sure he'd come back for more, I gave him a slow parting kiss before leaving him behind the stage.

Chapter Twelve

TOM

After letting Jordan go, I leaned against the wall behind the stage to compose myself. I ran my hand down my face in utter disbelief. I never expected that I could ever feel this way about a girl, and I hadn't even slept with her yet. As much as I wanted to, I wasn't going to rush this.

I decided to quit hiding and walked over to the beer booth. As I waited in line, an arm snaked around my waist, but this arm didn't belong to my girl.

"Angela, how are you this evening?" I asked, but dared not look at her.

She slithered her way in front of me, attempting to catch my attention. As she tried pulling me closer to her body, she said, "I saw you dancing with some girl. Are you trying to hurt my feelings?"

I reached around and grabbed her hands, which were clinging to me so tightly it felt like a death grip. Hoping to make my point clear, I narrowed my glare at her.

"Angela, you've got to stop. We've already discussed this."

"Tom, you told me you weren't ready for a girlfriend, and I'm fine with that, but you were dancing with another girl. You're obviously trying to make me jealous. Well, it worked. Why don't we leave here and go back to my place so you can make it up to me?"

"Hey, Tom, do you need help with those beers?"

I turned around to see Jordan standing about two feet from me. Her fingers were interlocked, hanging down in front of her, and a timid smile invaded her cheeks. My heart broke seeing her questioning eyes. A quiet tension filled the air. Jordan took a step forward and raised her hand out toward Angela.

"Hi, I'm Jordan."

Angela stared daggers at Jordan, ignoring her hand by putting hers on her hips. Angela's lip curled like a rabid beast. I shook my head and handed Jordan a beer.

"Here, darlin'."

"Darlin'? You call her darlin'?" Angela's voice rose a little bit higher than I would have preferred. I gazed at Jordan as she nervously bit her lip.

"Yes, she's my girl."

Jordan's eyes lit up as Angela rambled in the background.

"You've got to be kidding me." An added groan confirmed Angela's departure, and I moved to stand in front of Jordan.

"Am I your girl?" Jordan asked as her eyes searched mine.

"I would like you to be." I chuckled. I hadn't officially

been exclusive with someone since high school, and it wasn't like I really knew then what I was doing. "Is that what guys do? Do they ask?"

She laughed at my question and shrugged her shoulders. I took a step closer and caressed her face with my free hand. Her laughter stopped, but the smile never left her eyes. She tilted her face into my hand. I loved how she responded to my touch. She amazed me ever since I had literally walked into her life. It scared me that I wanted to be with her so much. Maybe the reason why I never put much into women before was because I knew they weren't right for me. Other girls didn't complete me the way Jordan had. I wanted that every day... for the rest of my life.

"I may sound like a sixteen-year-old when I ask this, but since I'm not sure of the right way of doing these things, I'm just going to put myself out there." I took a deep breath, wanting to remember this moment. "Jordan, will you be my girl?"

My breath stopped as I stared into her eyes, waiting for an answer. She bit her lip as her cheeks reddened. I couldn't help but smile at how absolutely gorgeous she was. She nodded and my heart filled with hope.

"Is that a yes?"

She laughed and grazed her hand down my chest.

"Yes, Tom. I would love to be your girl."

"Ms. Hawthorne, you're making me a very happy man right now."

"Am I?"

I took the beer from her hand and set our drinks on the counter of a nearby booth. Caressing both of her cheeks, I leaned closer, gazing into her eyes, then down at those soft, inviting lips.

"Yes, I'm a very happy man right now."

My lips found hers. In her kiss, I tasted the only form of heaven I'd ever want to know. Being with her, it felt as if the world had abandoned us, leaving her and I lost in our own intimate abyss.

I broke the kiss and smirked. "Well, girlfriend, I don't think I'm done dancing with you yet."

The dance floor was crowded with familiar faces, all the typical Friday night regulars from Dixie's were there, but they seemed a little rowdier tonight, the dancing a little more suggestive. My arms wrapped around Jordan, and her hips slowly started to grind against me. She glanced over at Ellie, who was dancing with Paul. With a wink, the girls pushed us away. They turned to each other and started to dance together. They weren't exactly holding back either. Paul grabbed my shoulder as our gazes fixed on the sexiest thing I'd ever seen. The girls noticed and laughed at our gawking. Ellie ran back to Paul. It looked like those two were progressing.

Jordan stood a few feet away from me and curled her finger, beckoning me to return to her. As I approached her, she turned around and started grinding that perfect ass against me. I placed my hands on her hips to hold her against me as I responded to the beat of the music. Thankfully, the crowd around us was dancing in a similar fashion. Her ass swayed against me, awakening a powerful craving. My hands gripped her hips tight as her ass bounced to the beat of the music. I sucked air through my teeth and my eyes almost crossed. The things this woman did to me. She bent at her hips, pressing harder against me, and scratched the tips of her fingers up my legs. I wrapped my arm across her chest, pulling her to me.

"If you keep doing that to me, I'm going to go back on what I said about our first time being outside," I whispered in her ear.

She turned in my arms to face me, nipped my ear, and whispered, "The sooner, the better."

Then she added a sexy wink.

I stared into her eyes and said, "Hey, Paul?"

"Yeah?"

Unable to break eye contact with Jordan, I spoke loudly in reply to Paul, "I think we're heading out."

Jordan's eyes began to smolder. Mine must have been doing the same because she grabbed my hand and led me off the dance floor.

"Don't do anything I wouldn't do!" Ellie laughingly called out to us.

With our arms around each other, Jordan grabbed her purse from Ellie's booth, and we slowly made the journey down the street. I couldn't keep my hands off her. I wrapped my arms from behind her and started kissing down her neck. Jordan stopped walking as her head tilted back, giving me greater access. My hands grazed across her stomach and cupped her breasts. As her breathing deepened, she twisted around in my arms, gripped the front of my shirt and pushed me up against the brick wall next to Ellie's shop. I held her tight as she kissed up my neck and nibbled my ear. I twitched against her, needing to be buried deep inside of her. She grabbed my jaw and slanted her mouth over mine. I grabbed her hips and turned us around, pressing her back against the wall. She let out a little yelp, but that didn't stop either of us. My hands glided up her sides as I possessed her. She pulled me close. I slid my hand down her leg, relishing in the silkiness of her skin. I wrapped one arm around her waist and hooked her leg around my hip. I pressed against her core, and she released a whimper of need. My jeans were now unbearably tight. My tongue danced with hers as the blood roared in my ears. I needed her, and I needed her now. I broke our kiss and we agreed to make an attempt to calm down; at least until we got back to The Inn.

"Come on, cowboy. Show me how you ride." Her seduction purred in my ear.

I wrapped my hand around hers, and we hurried back to The Inn with a pace that was more jogging than walking. The foyer was quiet when we entered. I followed her up the stairs. Not holding back any more, I cupped her ass and let my hand skim over her hips, around to her front, giving a gentle squeeze. She was wet and ready. She stopped climbing and let out a pleasing whimper as she almost fell backward. I wrapped my arms around her, holding her tight. I spun her around and saw the electricity sparking her eyes. I hoisted her legs around my waist and felt my throbbing against her. My mouth found hers as I kept my hands firmly on her ass.

My lips found her neck as I carried her up the last few steps and down the hall to her room. I released my hold of her and her body slid down against mine. Using the master key, I opened the door for her, keeping my arm wrapped around her hip. The door clicked shut behind us, and I spun her around. The wanton stare in her eyes almost brought me to my knees. Resting my hands on her hips, I leaned in close to her. She stared back at me, breathing unsteadily as her lips quivered with need. I pressed her against the wall and brushed my lips against her neck. Her breath changed from a trembling need to lustful pant as I started to thrust against the heat of her core. She moaned my name. My body quaked.

"Go sit on the bed," she whispered in my ear.

I didn't want to stop touching her, but the way she looked at me coaxed me into agreement. I unwillingly put her down. Still holding her hand, I walked backward to the bed.

As I sat down, she pulled away from me. I started to protest, reaching for her as her dress slipped out of my grasp, but she stuck her finger in the air and instructed me to wait. She pulled out a few pins from her hair and her beautiful locks flowed freely, cascading down around her shoulders. She reached around ever so slowly unzip her dress. The slowness with which she undressed was nothing short of torture. I wanted to rip that thing off her; and I could in two seconds flat.

The dress fell to the floor in one swoop, allowing my eyes to feast on her. My chest ached with an unfamiliar feeling, one that I wanted to feel again and again. She stood before me wearing nothing but brown lace panties and cowboy boots. I couldn't believe I was lucky enough to have this: every man's fantasy stood two feet away from me and coming closer.

I thought I had hyped up the memory of her body, but those memories didn't do her justice. Her hair lay over her chest, her nipples pebbling between the strands. Her waist tucked in before the curves of her hips, extending into smooth, long legs. My fingers twitched in yearning to touch her again. She was perfect in every way. I couldn't break my stare.

"My darlin', you are beautiful."

Something in her eyes said that she felt for me the way I did for her. My heart ached when I wasn't with her, and in this moment, it was so full of... *love*. I closed my eyes, absorbing what I just realized. How could I be? So soon? But every time I was near her, I got those weird feelings, and now I was beginning to understand them. I didn't care if it was too soon. *I'm in love with Jordan.* I opened my eyes to look back into hers and I couldn't help but smile. I was in love with this beautiful woman.

She swayed her hips while walking closer to me. I swelled painfully against my jeans. Her fingertips grazed the brim of my hat, yanking it off and tossing it to the ground. She bent over and placed her hands on my knees. I couldn't stop myself from staring at her breasts hanging before me. Her sultry eyes penetrated mine as she purred, "You've now seen me naked twice. It's my turn."

Jordan's hands roamed over my chest, gripping my shirt. She unbuttoned every button, followed with kisses on my chest. I couldn't stand it anymore. I gripped her hips and tossed her onto the bed. I pulled off my shirt and unbuttoned my jeans, but before losing the jeans I reached in my back pocket, dug out a condom, and tossed it at her. She started to laugh the most beautiful sound.

I stripped her of her boots and slowly proceeded to take the brown lace away, leaving me almost breathless as I gazed upon her beauty. I pushed down my jeans and my boxer briefs. She eyed me in near astonishment, looking up at me with questioning as I leaned over her.

"Tom, I don't think it's going to fit."

I lowered myself on top of her, nibbled her neck up to her ear and whispered, "I'll make sure it does."

Her blood pulsed as I slowly kissed down her neck, crawling over her body to have her perfect chest in front of me. Having craved these nipples since the first time I saw them, I savored the moment as I slowly wrapped my lips around one, sucking tenderly as I caressed the other. She released a cry loaded with need, pushing out her chest and making me hungrier than I was before. I left one nipple to devour the other. She squirmed, panting beneath my lips.

Another moan escaped her, and I decided to give her what she really needed – what I really needed. I left her luscious nipples and began kissing down her stomach until I reached the patch of hair pointing the way to glory. As I nuzzled so close to her core, she twitched and said my name breathlessly.

"Tom…"

The mere sound of my name leaving those precious lips drew out my animal instinct. I needed to feed. Hoisting her legs in the air, I slowly flicked my tongue against her, and she shuddered in pleasure. I wrapped my lips around her nub, sucking gently with a need to feel every throb coursing through her. Jordan's fingers combed my hair, begging me to continue, and I slowly slid one finger inside her. Her breath caught.

"More."

I slid another finger inside, spreading her deep while flicking her. Her back arched off the bed as I gripped her hips, holding her down. Her breathing hitched with a gasp. She came undone before me, allowing me to taste what I had been thirsty for ever since I saw her in that bathtub. As I crawled back up her body, she grabbed my head and kissed me hard, tasting herself on my tongue. I gazed back into her eyes, but I didn't see what I expected. She seemed almost worried.

"Jordan, I want you to know I'll never ever hurt you. You mean so much to me already. I couldn't stand ever hurting you, but, baby… if we start this, I'll never want to stop."

A calming breath passed her lips, and as I rolled on a condom, she bit her lip. *God, she's sexy as hell.* Hovering over her, I slid my tongue between her lips, slowly massaging hers as I nudged inside of her. She pulled out of our kiss with a gasp. I locked my eyes with hers as I slowly eased in deeper. When I reached that one spot, her breath caught, and I rocked into her with a gentle beat. Her eyes fluttered closed, and she exhaled her tension. Finding our rhythm, she wrapped her arms around me, scratching her nails down my back.

"My God, woman, you're beautiful."

As I raised her hips higher, she cried out, meeting me thrust for thrust. Her breathing became more rapid, her walls clenching against me. Wanting to fulfill her desire, I reached my hand down in between us and started flicking at her mound. I bent over and took one of her nipples in my mouth, swirling my tongue around it. She called out my name over and over. I started going faster. She screamed out, erupting in climax.

As she came down from her high, I continued to thrust slowly inside her. I licked her lips and tasted the beautiful life before me. With her eyes still filled with lust, she flipped me over onto my back. Straddling me, she bent down to my ear and sexily whispered, "I'm not done with you yet, cowboy."

Her eyes remained hooded with lust as she slid me inside of her again. I gazed up at this goddess, claiming her as mine. As she took me in, I roamed my hands over her body, molding them over her every curve. Needing my own release, I sat up and wrapped my arms around her as I pumped her from underneath.

Her head fell back, and I knew she was close to coming again. I flipped her over onto her back and pumped into her hard. As my own climax came over, I begged her, "Come for me, baby. Come for me, Jordan."

The rush flowed as we both came together. Her moans turned into screaming pants. It felt like we were in our own world of ecstasy.

As I rested on top of her, pecking her lips, I gazed at her sleepy smile. I scooted off her to dispose of the condom and then quickly pulled her against me. She rested her head on my chest as our legs intertwined. I fingered her long hair, bringing us both into a relaxing state, and when her breathing returned to normal, I knew she had fallen asleep.

"I love you, darlin."

I kissed the top of her head and drifted off with a breath of satisfaction.

Chapter Thirteen

JORDAN

*S*trong arms held me tight against a muscular chest as the dawn's light glowed through the lace curtains and the smell of freshly brewed coffee awoke my senses. My hands slid over a man's embrace as my legs ached with pleasure. I twisted around in his arms and found the most beautiful face smiling at me.

"Good morning, darlin." Tom pressed his lips to mine.

"It is a pretty good morning." I nuzzled into his chest, consumed by his manly scent of sunshine and leather. As I breathed deeply, the hint of something rich and bold perked me up. I lifted my head off his chest, eyeing him.

"Why do I smell coffee?"

A soft smile eased across his cheeks. I sat up, becoming aware of the table in the corner completely dressed with linens and table settings. Silver domes covered what I assumed was breakfast. The daisies he had given me last night were in a vase in the middle of the table.

"I can't believe you did this." My hand rested on my sheet-covered chest as my heart fluttered in total awe.

He wrapped his arms around me, and after pecking my shoulder, he whispered, "I'd do anything for you, Jordan."

He got out of bed and walked over to the bathroom to grab my robe. I noticed he'd already put on his jeans. *Pity.* He came around to my side of the bed, holding the robe open for me. "Would you like to join me for breakfast, Ms. Hawthorne?"

I let the sheet fall off me as I stood up, completely naked and open to the bright morning light. His eyes roamed up and down my body, a look painted with temptation. I turned slightly to ease my arms into the sleeves, and with a glance over my shoulder, I said, "Give me one minute."

His eyes lingered on me as I strutted into the bathroom with every ounce of sexiness I could fake. The door shut behind me and my knees almost buckled; I gripped the edge of the bathroom counter to steady myself as I stared into the mirror, lost in a dreamy daze.

Did last night just happen... with a cowboy?

The reality of last night hit me with full force—his thoughtfulness, his caresses, his skilled kisses, his body, his words of love.

His words of love?

Sleep overcame me while he played with my hair, soothing my racing heart. I laid my head upon his chest, his heart drumming a contented beat. My body slowed to a diminutive hum as words echoed into my dreams.

"I love you, darlin'."

A silent gasp escaped as I stared at my shocked expression in the mirror. He couldn't have meant that already. Obviously, it had to be some well-mannered custom of the country boy way.

I turned on the faucet. As the water warmed, I stared at the bathtub; the thing that brought us together. My fingers eased under the stream, and when it was warm enough, I scooped up a handful and splashed it on my face.

It was too soon. It had just come out, I told myself, like a post-orgasmic spasm. He couldn't possibly be in love with me. If it were any other man, I would have kicked him out.

So why was he still here?

My face softened. *I won't let this one get away.*

As I came out of the bathroom, he was fully clothed and standing behind one of the chairs at the table, waiting for me. I walked over to him and wrapped my arms around his neck, slowly kissing him good morning again.

Breaking away, I said, "I can easily get used to this treatment."

He smiled. "Good, because I like treating you this way."

My heart melted again.

"Sit, sit. The biscuits and gravy taste better warm."

As I sat, he scooted in my chair, and then he dropped into the one across from me. He lifted off the domes from the plates and set them on a serving tray standing behind the table. I knew all this delicious country food was bound to make me fat, but it was too good to pass up, and I needed to replenish from last night's caloric burn. I imagined Tom wouldn't mind helping me burn some of these calories off later.

"Your uncle really knows what he's doing," I said in between bites.

"Well, he did teach me a thing or two. Would you like to have dinner with me tonight? I'd love to be able to spend the day with you, but I have stuff to farm – as you like to put it."

"I would love to have dinner with you, Tom."

He smiled again. I liked when he smiled and the way it brightened his face. I feared the early onset of the feelings I had for him, but I knew there was no way I could stop it. He would be the one to break down my walls, and by God, I was going to let him.

After we finished eating, he came over to my chair and knelt down in front of me. He brushed his fingertips across my cheek, tucking a strand of hair behind my ear and leaving his hand to linger against my cheek.

"Jordan, I don't want to scare you off by seeming too forward, but what happened between us last night was incredible. I don't think I've ever felt anything like that." He smiled nervously at me and continued, "I just want you to remember that I'll never hurt you, and if you ever want to talk to me about anything, I will always listen."

He knew I had built a wall around my heart. Looking back into his eyes, I only nodded in return. Tears pricked the back of my eyes and I was afraid I would start to cry if I spoke. My heart tore, pulled between the pain and the hope. I could still feel the ache left by Ryan, but this cowboy gave me so much hope. Tom leaned forward, pulling me into an embrace. My chest relaxed, the tension easing within his arms. Hope was winning.

Kisses brushed against my cheek and my lips. I ran my fingers against his chest, returning his kiss. Our kissing progressed in the natural way it always seemed to do. I licked his bottom lip, and he allowed me access inside. An exhale escaped as he eased his hands inside my robe, pulling me to him. I instantly molded against his body as if we fit so perfectly together.

"I don't want to go, but I have to." He leaned his forehead against mine as we brought our heavy breathing back to normalcy.

"You have stuff to farm; I understand." I grinned, lost in his eyes. He kissed me again. Despite how much we'd kissed in the past twelve hours, my heart still fluttered like it was the first time.

"Go take a nice bubble bath, and I'll clean up breakfast. But your next bubble bath will not be alone." His sexy smirk made my skin warm and it was hard to keep him at a safe distance.

"Are you sure you don't want to join me?" Seeing the torn look on his face, I conceded. "Okay, I promise my next one won't be alone."

His lips pressed against mine with a tenderness I was growing used to. My heart released a happy sigh.

"Pick you up at 6:00," he said with that perfect smile. "If that's okay with you."

"Perfect." Everything seemed perfect with Tom.

As I began preparing my bubble bath, the door to my room clicked shut. He had gone. The silliest grin brightened my face while I stepped into the warm, relaxing bubbles. I eased down with a pleasuring wince from the dull ache in between my legs. I had never felt this sated before, and yet I couldn't wait for more.

I couldn't remember ever feeling this way with Ryan. I knew I shouldn't be so bitter and I should let things go, but a year was a lot of time to waste on someone who didn't truly love you. I was angry with myself for not noticing the signs. Was I that gullible?

What if I was doing it to myself? What if I wasn't capable of having a happy relationship? What if I fooled myself into thinking things were perfect just to have them come crashing down again?

Could I allow myself to be happy?

Frustrated by personal sabotage, I finished my bath and pulled on my robe again, planning for a lazy day. As I came out of the bathroom and walked over to my bed, I noticed a note on the nightstand underneath one of the daisies he'd left by my door last night. I picked it up to read what he said.

> *I hope you enjoyed your bath, beautiful.*
> *I miss you already.*
> *Wear something comfortable tonight.*
> *Tom*

Putting an end to my mental debate, I decided to allow myself happiness, at least for tonight.

The clock read quarter to six. My closet was empty. The entire contents lay in a pile on my bed. What was comfortable *and* sexy? Okay, skinny jeans were on. We would go with that. Boots! Okay, brown, flat, side zip boots. Okay! Now I needed a top. Top, top, top, top… *Damn, I need Ellie!* Taking inspiration from my matching navy blue lace underwear, I donned a navy tank and a white sweater. He said comfortable and sexy, but he didn't specify whether I could wear one over the other.

A knock on the door startled me from my stance. I jumped around to look at the clock. It was exactly 6:00. In a mad dash, I grabbed all of the clothes and tossed them back into the closet, shoving them into a pile on the floor with my foot. I slammed the closet doors shut and grabbed my chest, trying to ease my rapid heartbeat. Now was not the time for tidiness! Why was I so damn nervous?

As I took a deep breath, I grabbed the doorknob, and with one final exhale, I opened it to my favorite cowboy and his mesmerizing blue eyes. The tingles immediately started to erupt throughout me as the recent memory of the things he did to my body swam into my thoughts. He wore his trusty cowboy boots, faded jeans, a tight black T-shirt, and a brown leather jacket. How could one man be so damn sexy?

"Hey, darlin'," he whispered, stepping closer to me and caressing my cheek.

"Hey, cowboy." He bent down to give me a lingering peck and a tingling need touched every nerve.

"Are you ready to go?"

I nodded as I grabbed my purse. Sometimes I was utterly speechless around him.

Tom weaved his fingers through mine and we made our way downstairs. We passed Mrs. Ethel standing at the counter. She didn't say anything but grinned from ear to ear. I smiled back at her. His hand resting on the small of my back, he guided me to the passenger side of the truck. He opened the door for me in a gentlemanly fashion, but he also copped a feel as he boosted me into the seat. A smirk adorned his sexy face as he slammed the door behind me. As I buckled my seat belt, he climbed into the driver's seat. My body reacted to his closeness, instantly humming with need.

"That was pretty smooth, Tom," I said as he started the motor.

"I didn't think you'd mind." He shifted gears with a wink in my direction.

The giddy schoolgirl grin plastered itself on my face. I worried that these feelings were consuming me too soon. When I glanced up at him, his eyes sparkled with happiness, and his cheeks twitched, holding in a smile. He turned the radio onto a country station and interlaced our fingers again. I felt completely comfortable around him, even when we weren't talking. My nervousness was disappearing. He started to chuckle.

I looked over at him. "What?"

Continuing to chuckle, he shook his head and replied, "You're going to think this is probably really stupid, but I was so freaking nervous about our date."

I started laughing. "Me too! I had no idea what to wear! My whole closet is torn apart!"

"Well, you could wear anything and you would still look beautiful," he whispered, squeezing my hand. "Or you could wear nothing."

We pulled up to a stop sign. He turned to look at me, bringing our interlaced hands up to his lips and giving the back of my hand the sweetest peck. My head rested against the seat as I stared at his magnificent beauty, so bright it melted away the ice around my heart; pounding in my chest like a wall being torn down brick by brick. It beat warmth through my body, instead of the cold I had known for so long.

He turned the truck onto a long stretch of dirt road. The setting sun hid behind the tall trees that lined either side of the drive. A clearing approached, the most adorable country farm house coming into view. Sage green siding adorned a traditional, two-story farm house with white trim around the doors and windows. A large wrap-around porch harbored a pair of rocking chairs that swayed in the light breeze. A colorful flower bed flanked each side of the steps that climbed up to the porch.

"You keep this up all on your own?"

He nodded.

The view of the Blue Ridge Mountains was unlike anything I had ever seen. From the inside of the truck, I could see just a bit of a lake set off in the area behind the house, where the actual farm stretched over acres and acres with a wooden barn standing at the farm's edge. Rows upon rows were filled with vegetation, and on the other side of the farm, an open pasture with roaming cattle. My jaw dropped. I was on a real farm.

"I can't let the one place that had brought me so much happiness just fall apart," he said, his voice soft.

I could feel his eyes on me, tickling my skin. I tore my gaze away from the landscape to his beautifully rugged face. My breath caught as his eyes gave him away. Maybe it was possible that this cowboy loved me. How did I wrangle a cowboy?

I blinked away from his stare. If I hadn't, I might have

just straddled him right there in his truck. I had never had a craving for a man so intense before. After looking back at the house, I glanced to him and asked, "Had? Does it not bring you happiness anymore?"

"No, it does. It's just that something else makes me even happier now." His smile warmed my heart.

As he got out of the truck and sauntered over to my side, I fought against the hope rising within me. I mustn't let my guard down, although it would be easy to do with Tom. A little too easy.

Tom offered his hand to me as I hopped down from his truck. He placed his other hand in mine and looped my arm through his while we walked up the pathway to the stairs of his porch. He opened up the front door. Inside, a chocolate Labrador retriever sat in the foyer as if he had been waiting for Tom the whole time.

"Jordan, I'd like you to meet Hampton."

We walked over to the dog, Tom held out my hand to him, and Hampton instantly placed his paw inside. I giggled and looked at Tom.

"He's shaking your hand hello," Tom told me.

"Well, it's nice to meet you, too, Hampton." I shook and then released his paw. I scratched his head.

Tom let out an exaggerated breath. "Good, I was afraid he wouldn't like you."

I laughed. He turned to me with a look of confusion. I stopped laughing for a second, afraid he was being serious. Then he laughed, pulling me to him and wrapping his arms tight around me. I giggled into his chest at his silly antics. He pressed his lips to the side of my head as I melted into his embrace. I closed my eyes, breathing in his calming scent. I shouldn't allow myself to become this comfortable with him, but feeling his arms around me as he kissed me with genuine affection . . . I couldn't help but to smile.

"Let's go have some dinner." He guided me through a comfortable living room with a stone fireplace centered in the middle wall. Built-in wooden shelves lined either side of the fireplace from floor to ceiling; shelves filled with books and a few photographs, and, of course, one shelf held a huge flat screen TV. Dark paneled wainscoting wrapped around the room, the same dark trim framing two large windows. The walls were painted a neutral khaki in contrast to the wooden elements. The hardwood floors were bare except for a plush rug lying in between an oversized leather sofa and the fireplace. A recliner sat opposite the window, in direct view of the television. As we walked into the kitchen, the warm, familiar aroma of beef grabbed my stomach.

"It smells so good. Whatcha cookin', good lookin'?" I said in my best country accent.

"Pot roast." He pulled out a covered pot from the oven. I stood in awe as he lowered it onto a trivet. He glanced up at me with a sense of pride, but I just stared back at him unable to form a cohesive sentence. He couldn't have possibly known that pot roast was my absolute favorite meal!

His smile fell with his shoulders as a wrinkle of concern formed on his brow.

"Oh God, I realized I don't know if you like beef… I can make chicken… or we have salad…" He frantically looked through his fridge.

I walked up behind him and tugged at his shoulder,

pulling his attention from fridge. He stood there in confusion with a head of lettuce in his hand. I grabbed his face and drew his lips toward mine. He pulled me to him, with lettuce pressing against my back.

"Really, if you don't like it, I can make chicken. It won't take ver—"

I interrupted him by putting my finger up to his lips.

"Tom… I love pot roast. I was trying to think if I told you that before. That's why I was so shocked because I know I never did," I said with a reassuring smile.

"It's the best thing I can cook, and I wanted to impress my girl," he said with a proud smile. I looped my arms around his neck, guiding him back to my lips as I kissed my way toward happiness. He ended the kiss with a peck and tossed the lettuce back into the open fridge, shutting the door after it.

"Stay here for just a minute. I need to go fix the table," he said as he grabbed the pot. He leaned over and kissed me again before his face grew stern. "Don't move."

I nodded with a smile as he departed out the back door. I glanced around the kitchen, admiring the mix between old and new. A rich granite slab, anchored to rustic cabinets, covered half of the kitchen. An island sat in the middle as a cooking workstation. Glass tiles in various shades of red and brown served as a backsplash to the stainless steel appliances, all of which were of high-end quality. He knew how to cook, which put me at ease. I couldn't find my way around this kitchen, or any kitchen for that matter. If it didn't involve a microwave, I was hopeless.

As he came back inside, he wrapped his arms around me, kissing my cheek. It was all too good to be true. I had no clue how all of this happened so fast, but I knew one thing: I was tired of questioning it. I was going to accept it for as long as I could hold on.

"Do you trust me?"

I gazed into his eyes, and the only thing I saw was the love beating in his heart. "Of course."

His smiled widened. "Okay, close your eyes."

I closed my eyes like a good girl. His arms wrapped around my waist and he guided me through kitchen and onward until the autumn breeze hit my face.

"Keep them closed, okay?" I smiled as he picked me up and carried me down a few steps. When he set me on my feet again, he shifted behind me, wrapping his arms around my waist once more.

He kissed my cheek and whispered, "Open your eyes, darlin.'"

When I opened them, the breath caught in my chest and I couldn't wipe the grin from my face.

Chapter Fourteen

JORDAN & TOM

Thousands of twinkling lights fluttered over the expansive farm. The lights dazzled in the night, performing their fire dance and flirting about while attracting their mates.

Fireflies.

"This is unreal," I murmured, unable to take my eyes off the night sky. Millions of stars adorned the heavens with the fireflies mimicking their sparkle.

"This is beautiful." I tore my gaze off the sky and into the eyes of my heart's captor.

"Yes, it is," he whispered, never shifting his eyes away from my face to gaze on the night's wonderment. He watched my expressions evolve from utter disbelief to utter astonishment.

It would be so easy to let myself fall.

Caressing his face in my hands, I leaned up to kiss him.

He met me halfway. I roamed my hands down from his face to his chest and around to his strong back, pulling him closer to me. One of his hands wrapped around to my lower back as he held me tighter. His other clutched the back of my head, entangling his fingers in my hair. He had me in such a hold that I couldn't even move if I wanted to, but I didn't want to. I wanted to stay in this moment until the sun came up.

Our tongues continued to dance with each other, and I moved into him, forcing him to walk backward. My body throbbed with need, and the only man I wanted for the rest of my life was this man in front of me. I pushed him down on the bench behind him, and as our kiss broke, we panted for breath, feeling the desire pulsing between us. He reached out for me, but I took a step back. His brow creased in confusion. To ease his worries, I graced him with a sexy look and took off my sweater, letting it fall slowly to the wooden deck. His eyes popped up to mine, filled with lust as he stood up again, trying to pull me close. I stopped him, pushing my hand against his rock hard chest.

"Not yet. It's my turn."

After pushing him back down to the bench, I placed my foot in between his legs. He reached up to the zipper of my boot. His fingers slowly unzipped one boot and tugged it off, repeating with the other boot. His gaze remained locked on mine. Standing barefoot on his deck overlooking his farm, I peeled my tank over my head, allowing him to see my bra-covered chest. As his eyes were immediately drawn to it, I slid my hands up the sides of my body and grasped my breasts. His eyes pained with lust and need. I knew he wouldn't last much longer. Soon he would pounce.

Sliding my hands down to the waistband of my jeans, I unfastened the snap and skimmed down the zipper. I pushed down my jeans and stood in front of him. He breathed in sharply as his hands reached out toward me, brushing his fingertips down my sides and resting his hands on my hips. After pulling off his jacket, I gripped the hem of his shirt, drawing it over his head. The only time his hands left my body was to let his arms come out of his clothes. As I bent down to unbutton his jeans and lower his zipper, his lips crashed into mine and he stood up to shove his own jeans down. I pushed him back down on the bench and straddled him.

He throbbed between my legs as he thrust against me. His hands gripped my hair as he kissed down from my lips and buried his head in the crook of my neck. I steadied my hands on his broad shoulders, holding on for the oncoming ride. When his lips reached my ear, he whispered with heated breaths, "Darlin', I don't know what you're doing to me."

As I released my hold of his shoulders, I reached around to unsnap my bra, allowing myself to pour out before him. His eyes penetrated mine as he cupped my breasts, sending throbbing pulses throughout my body with his touch. He caressed my right nipple, pinching it lightly with his thumb and finger while licking and sucking my left. My head fell back as I released a low, passionate moan. His lips left one nipple for the other, and his tongue drew circles around my hardened tip. My hips bucked against him, needing him to fill me completely.

While he was immersed in my chest, I asked, "Condom?"

He pulled his face away from my chest as he shoved his hand inside of his jeans that were wrapped around his ankles and pulled out the foil wrapper. I tore off the side with my teeth and slowly sheathed him as he moaned with my touch. I pushed my panties aside to allow full access and brought myself down on him. He grunted with a deep thrust into me, stealing my breath away. His tip touched places inside of me that had never been touched before. My body jerked with every plunge, and I gasped for breath as I tore into his back, scratching for more. As I finally adjusted to his size, my tongue darted inside of his mouth. I held his head with security as we kissed and panted, our breath intertwined.

The walls of my core throbbed, clenching with an aching need. An inner explosion began to erupt from the pit of my stomach, pulsing down. My head rolled back.

"Tom..."

He squeezed my hips tight, thrusting deep and once again hitting that spot that no man had ever reached before.

"Come, darlin.'"

One final hard thrust and I hit my peak, flying into ecstasy. I rode through my screams of pleasure as Tom shook.

"I love you, Jordan. Oh God, I love you."

He pulsed into me and I clenched around him, milking every last throb. I slumped over him as he buried his head in the crook of my neck. As we both waited for our erratic breathing to settle, I sat back and looked into his eyes. His words echoed in my head. He'd said he loved me. I tensed within his arms.

"Tom..."

"Jordan, don't say anything. I'm not going to say that I didn't mean it, but I don't want you saying anything either way. Just let us be in this moment right now."

He showed more love in his eyes than I had ever seen from anyone before. I believed him and his words of love. I just didn't know if I was deserving of it. I reciprocated with tender kisses across his jaw while still remaining connected. Regardless of the unexpected announcement, this was undoubtedly the most perfect night of my life.

TOM, YOU DUMB *fuck. Why did you tell her you loved her?* It was the truth, but a truth that might scare her away. I hadn't meant to say it so soon, but like hell if I was going to take it back. I didn't want to scare her, though. I needed her like I needed air to breathe. How was this possible? It had only been a week. This was not some blind infatuation. I knew my heart. Even if she never loved me back, I would never regret telling her, and I would never regret being with her.

But the way she withdrew from me… I needed to figure out what had happened. I needed to figure out what he did to her, but now wasn't the time, not while I was still buried inside of her. I kissed her neck and across her jaw.

"Are you hungry yet? For food… I mean." I cocked my eyebrow and added a smirk, trying to move past any awkwardness from my premature declaration. *Good job, Tom. Awesome.*

"I'm starving." She grinned with a heavily sated gleam in her eye. God, she was gorgeous.

Reluctantly, we both got up and put our clothes back on. I enjoyed looking at my water goddess in her natural form. She remained barefoot, though, which was still hot as hell. I led her over to the table I'd prepared with the intent of dining outside. I pulled out her chair so she could sit down. The food was still warm, and I made us both a plate of pot roast, potatoes, and carrots. To complete the feast, I poured each of us a glass of red wine, a nice buzz to top off our evening under the night sky. We easily rolled through conversation as we enjoyed our meal. Once we were finished, I refilled our wine glasses and led her over to other side of the deck to sit in front of the fire pit. She snuggled up under my arm, and I kissed the top of her head, memorizing her scent of lavender. I just needed her to talk to me.

"Jordan?"

"Yes, cowboy?" she whispered so sweetly. I steeled myself for any impending backlash for prying, but if I was in the process of giving her my whole heart, I had to know.

"Will you tell me what he did to you?"

As soon as I asked the question, she tensed up, freezing in place. I shifted my arm from around her so I could look into her eyes.

"Baby, I know something happened, and I hope someday you'll allow me in here," I said as I placed my hand over her heart. "You already know how I feel about you. I'm not asking you to return the words, but I want to be able to call you mine." I sighed, looking straight into the fire. "And I need to know what that bastard did to you."

Thankfully, I had already set my glass down, because with the way I was clenching my fist, I would have broken it. I glanced up into her eyes, begging her to talk to me. She nodded as she set her wine down and scooted around out of my arms in order to face me straight on.

"I was engaged to Ryan. I had dated him for exactly a year." She paused for a breath. "We… ended three months ago."

"Why did you end things, Jordan?" I asked with concern.

She took another deep breath. I grabbed her hands, holding them tightly.

"Three months before our wedding I came home early to surprise him, and he was… with someone else."

I looked away. I hurt for her. I was glad that bastard was out of her life, but I hated to think of what her heart went through.

Wait…

"Baby, doing the math… when was your wedding day supposed to be?"

She stilled in my hands and looked at me.

"I didn't even realize…"

I thought she would be crushed, but she actually smiled and wrapped her arms around me.

"You made me forget. It was today and you made me forget."

I hugged her back and smiled to myself. She had allowed me to help her forget, and that meant more than anything.

"There's more, though, and this is something I need to tell you because you're in my life now," she said with a serious look.

I nodded and said, "Go on. I want you to tell me everything."

She took another deep breath. "He was calling and

texting… threatening me. Before I decided to move here, he… he almost forced himself on me, and he would've had if my best friend hadn't prevented it."

My blood boiled and my teeth clenched. "Is he still in contact with you?"

She shook her head. "That's why I got a new phone number. Only you, Katherine, my parents, and Ellie know my number, besides the college, of course."

"You make sure you stay up front with me if he tries to contact you again. Okay? I'll never let anything happen to you." I wrapped her in my arms and kissed her. My heart clenched, knowing how bad it must have been for her. In time, I would let her explain more, but for now, I had heard enough.

"It's getting kind of cool. Do you want to go back inside?" I started getting to my feet.

"Before we go, I want to be honest with you." She held my hand, keeping me in my seat.

My heart pounded as my nerves buzzed. I knew I scared her. I threaded my fingers through hers and whispered, "You can talk to me about anything, Jordan."

She scooted closer to me and caressed the side of my face. I closed my eyes, dipping my head into her hand. When I opened them, her face was closer to mine. She had a look in her eyes, but I couldn't tell what kind it was.

"I was only intending to stay here for one semester, but with everything between us…" She exhaled, looking down, and then found my eyes again. "I'm almost there. Just don't give up on me, okay?"

I gazed on her with hope, nodding my comprehension because I had no words. That was almost as good as her saying she loved me. I leaned in, stealing her lips. They would be mine forever.

Chapter Fifteen

JORDAN

The chill of the early fall air brought us back inside following our shared dinner and my feast of a cowboy. Hampton rose from his blanket and stretched before following the smell of the leftover pot roast that Tom carried inside. He fed Hampton while I put the dishes and the wine glasses in the sink. For good measure, I washed them while he put the leftover pot roast in the fridge. As I soaped up the plates and the glasses, my mind reeled. In such a short amount of time, it was almost as if my soul knew what my brain kept shutting down. He wanted to be with me. He wanted an "us." I just didn't know if I could trust my heart again. It had really screwed me over the last time, but I desperately wanted to trust it again. I wanted to trust Tom.

I dried my hands with a kitchen towel and placed it next to the sink. Calming warmth spread through me. Doing a simple task like washing our dishes made me feel like I belonged. With my hip resting against the countertop, I admired the view as he bent over to make room in the fridge. I didn't think I would ever get tired of the way his ass looked in jeans. The longer I watched him, the more I felt the wall around my heart breaking bit by bit. It was so easy to fall.

When he closed the door to the fridge and turned around, he caught me staring. His eyebrow lifted in amusement as a smirk eased up his cheek. I bit my lip, but not from shyness. It was hunger. He pushed away from the door, closing the distance between us. He lifted his hand up and brushed the back of it down my face. I closed my eyes, absorbing his touch. His thumb grazed across my lip, releasing it from its bite. My eyes flickered open, the love exuding from his blue depths. I told my head to trust my heart. It was okay to fall.

He slowly pressed his lips to mine, kissing me tenderly, and gently sucking my bottom lip. He coddled my face inside of his hands as his heart beckoned to mine.

It's too soon.

Without breaking our kiss, he leaned down, scooped me into his arms and carried me out of the kitchen, through the living room and to the base of the stairs. He continued to kiss me deeply as he carefully carried me up each step.

As we entered a room, he pecked me one more time and set me on my feet. Looking up at him, our fingers interlocked.

"I have one more little surprise for you," he whispered.

"Do I have to close my eyes for this one?" I cocked my head to the side with a hint of humor. His eyes lit up with his smile.

"No, but stay in here for just a minute." He pressed his

hand against the back of my head and kissed me lightly on the forehead. With a smile, he slipped away into the bathroom.

The room around me held the same richness as the living room. The walls were painted the same natural khaki and dark wooden wainscoting layered over the bottom half of the wall. An overstuffed leather chair sat nestled in the corner with a reading lamp and a table beside it. Curiosity took over as I walked over to the table to peek at the book resting on top. The front of it faced the table. I lifted it up, smiling when I saw he was in the middle of reading *Lonesome Dove*. I lay it back on the table.

He had a king size bed with a headboard covered in the same brown leather as the chair in the corner, with a neutral coverlet on the bed. A pair of dark walnut nightstands flanked the bed, each holding a lamp. On the far nightstand, a picture rested underneath the light. I crossed around to the other side of the bed, and, after studying the dated picture for a moment, I picked up the photo. A cute couple and their young boy. Tom came back into the room, but I didn't try to hide my snooping. If he was in love with me then he wouldn't mind. My heart needed to get to know him if I was ever going to let him in.

"What were their names?" I glanced up at him.

A small smile eased up his face. "Thomas and Susanna."

I set the picture down and walked back around the bed, wrapping my arms around his waist.

"Are you a junior, then?"

He shook his head, pulling me into a warm embrace.

"Our middle names are different. His is Douglas, and mine is Everett after my grandfather."

"Oh, that's what the 'E' stands for." As he looked at me in puzzlement, I smiled and continued, "Your initials are on your tool bag. Remember? The one you dropped when you were perving on me?"

He laughed. "Yeah, I was perving on you, wasn't I?"

"Just a tad."

For a moment, we gazed into each other's eyes. I didn't understand how it had happened, but I was determined not to ruin what was going on between us. He nuzzled his face into the crook of my neck, kissing down to my collarbone before peeling away my sweater.

"Well, I'm still waiting to see my water goddess." He kissed a little more, pulling me along with him toward the door. "And I said your next bubble bath wouldn't be alone." He pulled the shirt over my head. "So, will you join me?"

The twinkling effect carried over from our outdoor dinner. With the lights turned off, the bathroom glowed with what looked like hundreds of votive candles surrounding a huge jetted bathtub filled with bubbles, of course. My mouth dropped open in awe as moisture dripped down my cheeks. His thumbs swept over them, wiping my tears away.

"Darlin'," he whispered, "don't cry."

"You don't have to work so hard. I *want* to be with you." I shook my head and wrapped my arms around his waist, resting my head against his chest.

"I want to do this for you. It's because I care for you, Jordan. I want to treat you the way you should be treated. You are an amazing woman, and I'm in love with you." He looked into my glazed eyes. "This is nothing compared to the things I'm willing to do for you. I want to make you happy,

Jordan. I want to love you with everything I have. And I plan to." He leaned in close, giving me one more peck, and a silly grin rose up his cheeks. "Let's go, lady. Strip. We have bubbles waiting for us."

I laughed and obeyed his command. He stepped in first and held his hands out for me to hold onto. I eased down into the soothing bubbles and leaned my back against his chest. His arms wrapped around me, holding me close. For the first time since I had left Charlotte, I felt complete. I felt protected. I just hoped nothing would happen to ruin this feeling. Our fingers intertwined, my arms wrapping with his. In my state of contentment, I broke the silence that hung in the air.

"Where do you want to be in five years?"

He kissed my cheek and my neck.

"Doing exactly what I'm doing now... sitting in a bubble bath with my arms and legs wrapped around my girl." His gruff voice aroused me as his breath tickled my neck. He resumed kissing my cheek and down the side of my neck as I let out a moan. How could one man's kiss have this effect on me? I turned my head toward his chest and closed my eyes. The drumming of his heart soothed the unsure clatter of mine. My heart wanted to put itself out there for his to take.

Soon.

Before I knew it, he lifted me out of the tub. He dried me off with a warm, oversized towel, and then picked me up again and carried me out of the bathroom into the bedroom. He laid me down on his bed and scooted in behind me, planting kisses on my shoulder.

"I'm sorry I fell asleep," I whispered into the darkness of the night. He leaned up behind me and I turned my face, meeting his. The moonlight from the window sparkled in his eyes.

"The only thing better than you falling asleep in my arms is you waking up in my arms."

As my eyes fluttered closed, a weight lifted off my chest. I knew in that moment that I was falling in love with Tom.

I AWOKE THE next morning feeling completely and utterly loved and in love. My cowboy's arms wrapped tight around me as he snored softly, still out cold. Something was wide awake, though, and standing at attention and poking the back of my thigh. I nudged Tom over onto his back and decided that he needed to be properly woken up.

I slowly and quietly scooted my way down the bed until I found him pulsing at attention. After lightly licking the pearl essence from the tip, I proceeded to lightly suck and lick all over his engorged head. He hummed in anticipating appreciation and I smiled as I started taking him ever so slowly into my mouth as far down as I could, and then making my way back up. He whispered my name in his sleep and I continued my assault on him. I heard him gasp right before he threw back the covers.

"Oh my God, baby, what are you doing?"

I gazed upon him with a sexy smile.

"Telling you good morning." I didn't hold back any longer; he began to buck under me.

"Jordan, baby, you don't have to do this," he panted.

I gazed up at him, slowly keeping the rhythm with my

hand.

"Oh, but I want to."

Keeping my eyes locked on his, I started to lick up his length, holding him in my hand. He finally moaned and wove his fingers through my hair. I resumed the dive, massaging him the whole time.

"Oh God, baby… holy shit …"

I continued using my hand to guide further down while my lips sucked him at the tip. He tried to tug me back.

"Baby, stop, I'm going to come."

I ignored him and laid my hand on his chest as I continued working him in my mouth. He grunted again and thrust back into my mouth. I started working faster as his breathing grew more rapid.

"Oh, shit, baby." He hardened and throbbed as he grunted. His body tensed as he came, hot liquid filling up my mouth and down my throat. I licked off the remnants and swallowed. I crawled back up his body, and he grabbed my elbows and guided me up to his face, kissing me passionately.

While straddling him, I kissed him the way any woman would kiss the man they loved. I needed to tell him. I didn't care that it had only been a week. I needed to tell him even though it scared the hell out of me. Pulling out of the kiss, I gazed into his eyes, getting his undivided attention. I took a calming breath and willed my voice to be steady.

"I love you."

His face blanked in shock, his eyes popped open. He exhaled a breath as his face relaxed and all of the tension melted from his body.

"Are you sure, Jordan?"

A smile eased up my face. I bit my lip and nodded my answer.

As he coddled my face, he brought my lips down to his and he kissed me with more love and affection than I'd ever felt before. Pulling away slightly to look into my eyes, he whispered, "I promise to make you happy and never let you down, Jordan. I love you so much."

I kissed him back, knowing he was right.

Chapter Sixteen

TOM

The early weeks of autumn amazed me. I never expected I would be head over heels in love with a woman, much less one as incredible as Jordan. Except for the times we had to spend working, we were inseparable. Women usually tended to annoy me with their constant harping about settling down; I was only twenty-four, so I believed it wasn't necessary yet. The task of carving out my life and my future was important, but women and marriage hadn't come into play.

Jordan changed me.

Every thought of the future had Jordan in it. I dreamed of our future. I knew for a fact the only reason so many other girls annoyed me was because I was waiting for Jordan all along.

I continued to wait for her on a stool at Dixie's Tavern.

Paul and Lance sat on either side of me, sporting our Carolina Panthers attire and waiting for one of the first big football games of the regular season. With a bottomless mug of beer in his hand, Lance began his normal prowl.

Paul seemed slightly on edge.

"You okay?" I asked, looking at his reflection in the mirrored wall behind the bar. His eyes met mine in the glass. He shook his head and shrugged his shoulders. I took the hint that there was possibly some issue with Ellie, but I couldn't be sure. His feelings for her must have finally been taking their toll. I nodded at his shrug, letting him hold his pain inside as he usually did.

After ordering yet another beer, I looked at my watch and realized that kickoff was in less than ten minutes, and Jordan still wasn't here. Worry started to grow in my chest until a breeze hit my back from the opening of the door, and her laughter tickled my ear. Paul and I turned around at the same time. Our breath caught, along with the breath of probably every other man in the tavern. Ellie and Jordan strutted through the door, both wearing cowboy boots, short jean skirts, and oh-so-wonderfully-tight Panther jerseys.

"Holy shit..." came a whisper from Paul's mouth. My only response was a disbelieving shake of the head. Jordan's stare caught mine, and as it usually did, the room around me vanished. She came to me like a moth to the flame, and I relished every second of it.

"Hey," she whispered in two strides, sealing my lips with hers. Her tongue playfully licked my bottom lip as I licked her top. I pulled her close and held her against the bulge developing in my jeans, proving to her that I would never tire of her. She released my lips and kissed her way around to my ear.

"Settle down, cowboy, or you'll have me on my knees before kickoff."

My eyes popped for a moment until I recognized a faint taste on my tongue.

"Had some whiskey, darlin'?" I winked at her sexiness.

"Just a smidge." She beamed at me, changing from a sex goddess to the girl next door in a snap.

As I pulled her close again, I whispered, "I think I like you drunk on whiskey."

"Oh, I bet you do." The sex goddess came back with a secretive grope against my jeans.

Hiding under the cover of her hair, I nipped her ear and whispered, "You might get a spanking for that."

"It's about damn time, cowboy. I've been a very naughty girl."

I pulled my head out of my protective cover and gave her a stern yet playful glare.

"Evil. You are pure evil!"

Her head tilted back in laughter, and she gave in to me with a hug. The crowd started to get rowdy as everyone surrounded the televisions. I pulled my girl up on my lap, making sure my hand was firmly on her thigh the whole time.

Ellie stood next to us, dragging her finger around the rim of a beer mug. I looked through the mirrored reflection at Paul. His eyes were cocked to the side, watching Ellie's finger. There had to be something going on. More than likely, Jordan would fill me in later.

"Ho–ly shit."

We all turned past Ellie as Lance roamed his eyes up and down his former girlfriend.

"Hey, Lance."

He whistled his appreciation, but I could see in his eyes that he was already tipsy.

"Did–didn't I used to date you?"

Ellie cocked her hip out, resting her hand on it, as she said, "Yes, Lance, for about four years."

Without a blink, he pulled her against him, bending down to her height, and in an elevated whisper, he said, "Can't seem to figure out why we broke up."

I glanced back in the mirror and saw Paul seething, looking in the opposite direction.

"Lance, stop," Ellie said.

Paul's eyes darted back, and I quickly looked away. Before I could help Ellie, Paul was off his stool and had a firm grip on Lance's arm.

"Come on, buddy. Don't do this now."

Lance laughed in his playful manner and said, "Don't I have some sort of claim over her?"

Paul responded with a push—I could see he was controlling himself—and said, "No, you lost that right a long time ago."

Lance surrendered his hold of Ellie, and Paul offered his hand out to her. She looked up at him with eyes full of hope, accepting his hand and joining him on the other side of me.

"And who might you be?" Lance asked, resting his elbow against the bar. Jordan twisted on my lap, facing the best friend who seemed to have no sense of right and wrong.

"Lance, this is my girlfriend, Jordan."

Jordan stuck her hand out, and Lance eased his hand inside her grasp. I knew Lance. He was a player, but he would never go after my girl. I knew that. He leaned off the bar and looked at me.

"You lucky bastard, you. Is this the tub chick?"

Jordan nudged me in the ribs.

"Did you tell everyone about that?" she asked, tossing her head and pretending to be offended.

"They wanted to know how we met. I'm not that good of a liar." I shrugged in amusement and took a sip of beer, trying to hide a smirk, one she definitely saw me attempting to cover.

"Well, it's so good to fi—" Lance stopped mid-sentence as Angela, the leech, walked by, tossing her hair back, trying to get his attention.

Lance slapped my back and said, "Well, Tom. Looks like I'm gonna go have at your leftovers."

"By all means, have at it," I said as he walked off, chugging his beer and trying to find someone to fill his time, maybe to take home. One day, he would change, but not today.

I kissed Jordan's cheek and whispered in her ear, "Do you know what's going on with Paul and Ellie?"

She nodded, turning her head toward me, and said, "I just don't think she can fight it anymore."

"Bartender, two shots of Jack, please," Paul hollered, and then looked down at Ellie with the kind of smile he only wore for her.

I turned away from their craziness and snuggled in close to Jordan as the Panthers took the field against the Atlanta Falcons. Jordan took a tight hold of my arm. I looked up at the girl perched on my lap, but her eyes were glued to the television and she was grinning from ear to ear. The only thing I could do was to hug her and thank the dear Lord for giving me a girl who loved football.

IT WAS THE bottom of the fourth quarter, and the Panthers led by three. The Falcons lined up on our five-yard line on their final down.

"Oh, my God, I can't look," Jordan said, burying her head in my shoulder. She lifted her eyes to look again, but just as quickly put her face back down against me. She was adorable enough to distract me from football. The whistle blew through the speaker, and Jordan lifted her head up from my shoulder again to watch the game. Her teeth gripped her bottom lip as her brow creased. She mumbled a chant over and over.

"Defense, defense, defense…" Her chant became louder, and I was entranced.

She jumped off my lap and started screaming and jumping up and down. I looked at the television and realized something had happened that had never happened before. A woman had totally distracted me from a goal line stand, and I didn't care one damn bit. I wrapped my arms around her while she cheered, screamed, and kept on wiggling excitedly in my lap.

Through the eruption of the fans in Dixie's Tavern, Lance's voice rose above all the others.

"Hey! What the hell?"

Jordan and I looked in his direction as he stormed passed us. My eyes bugged in shock as I saw that Paul and Ellie were lip locked to no end. Lance gripped Paul's arm, pulling him away from Ellie, and then screamed in his face.

"What the hell man?! That's my ex!"

"Lance, stop," Ellie said, but Paul's voice rose over hers.

"You let her go." He pulled his arm out of Lance's grasp and continued in a slurred voice. "You gave her up years ago. Am I not supposed to go after the woman I've wanted all my life just because you got to her first over ten years ago?"

I scooted Jordan off my lap and stood in between my two best friends.

"Y'all, come on. Not here."

"No, dammit, we're gonna do this here," Lance said, pushing me out of the way. He got in Paul's face and continued, "Whatever happened about not going after each other's girls?"

"Well, you slept with damn near half the town, so the pickings are slim, Lance."

Lance unleashed on Paul, throwing a punch square in his face. Paul stumbled back a few steps, but didn't hit the ground. I moved out of the way and stood protectively in front of Jordan.

"Is this a normal occurrence?" Jordan asked.

I shook my head. "No. I just think Paul couldn't take it anymore."

Ellie helped Paul steady himself. After making sure he was okay, she turned toward a seething drunk Lance, stepping up to him and getting as close to his face as she could.

"You gave me up to whore around," she scolded, "and

now you're mad because, years later, someone shows me attention? You've got to be kidding. There are a lot of legs to spread; go find someone else's."

She turned back, grabbed Paul's hand, and they marched out of Dixie's together. Lance fumed as he turned around to face us. Now that the floorshow was over, the folks at Dixie's resumed the celebration of the win.

"Did y'all know about this?"

"Lance, everyone knew about this. Paul has been in love with Ellie since we were kids."

He exhaled. "Really?"

I nodded at his stupid question.

"Shit," he said under his breath, running a hand through his hair. He realized the scene he'd made. Throwing his hands up in the air, he drudged across the floor and out the door.

Jordan wrapped her arms around me. I rested my hands on her hips.

"That was explosive."

I nodded my head in agreement. "So, back to the whole spanking thing…"

She laughed at my comment and said, "Whenever you're ready, cowboy."

I grabbed her jaw gently, pressing my lips to hers. Our tongues danced together. Reluctantly, I pulled away and said, "Let's go."

She walked in front of me, but I opened the door and held it for her like a gentleman as she exited. As she passed me, I playfully slapped her ass and she squealed with a little hop.

"You said you needed one." I gave her a little wink and we

laughed about it all the way back to The Inn.

There would never be any further question. I was wholeheartedly in love with this woman.

Chapter Seventeen

TOM

"Baby, go wait at Dixie's. We're going to be so late," she purred as my hand glided up underneath her work skirt. Skin of silk possessed me to glide higher, caressing her curves and never wanting to stop. The evening sun lit up her suite at The Inn as I buried my face in the crook of her neck. I couldn't get enough of her. I knew I loved her. I loved her more than anything in this world, but what I felt was something words couldn't describe. I craved her. I needed to be constantly touching her. If we could spend the rest of our days like this, I would be the luckiest damn bastard alive.

When my lips traveled to her ear, her body gave up its fight. Her fingers threaded through my hair, pulling me into a mind-blowing kiss. I lifted her knee up and wrapped her leg around my hip. Her head tilted, deepening our kiss, and my fingers nestled between the lace of her panties and her shaven skin. Her slick heat spread across my fingers, and when I pushed inside, she moaned through our kiss. My thumb flicked in time with my finger as I pressed my lips to her neck, inhaling her scent full of sex.

The craving I harbored turned into an undying hunger. I unzipped her skirt and let it crumble to the floor. My hands slid over her silk blouse, cupping her breasts and flicking her hardened nipples.

"You don't like this shirt, right?

"Well, I actu—"

I tore the shirt, splitting it down the middle as buttons popped to the floor.

"I'll buy you a new one."

I swept her into my arms and lowered her down onto the bed. I held myself over her, peppering kisses down her collarbone and onto her chest, whispering, "You're so beautiful."

Her fingers threaded through my hair as I pulled down the cup of her bra, her nipple budding in the cool of the fall. I swiped my tongue gently across the tip. Her faint breath begged me to let my greed have its way. I lapped at her peak, sucking just enough to make her whisper my name. I pulled down the lace covering her other breast as my fingers slid across the smoothness of her skin. Her back arched into me and I sucked harder. My fingers trailed down her flat stomach, reaching into her panties again and resuming their previous task. I lightly pulsed inside of her, keeping my mouth on her breast. When her hands gripped my hair, I wasted no time ripping away the lace, exposing all of her to me.

"I'll buy you a new pair of those, too." I gazed up at her

as I inched down her body. She nodded her reply, and with one swipe of my tongue, her head fell back as she writhed underneath me. The easy thrust of her hips told me to go faster. I knew this woman's body. I had memorized every sound and every shiver from every place my hands touched. When she fed into me, I gave her more. I slipped one finger inside. My tongue flicked at a faster pace, and I eased another finger inside. She screamed out as she lost control of her body. I repositioned quickly and held her legs down. The buildup within her was growing rapidly; I knew that when she finally came, she would come hard.

I twisted my fingers as I pressed into her, sucking harder. The walls of her core clenched to a quicker beat, her legs quaking under my grasp. Her hips thrust faster as a moaning whisper escaped her lips.

"Tom… please don't stop…"

I shook my head, not that she could see. I wanted this more than she did. She cried out louder,

"Don't stop." She heaved a breath, "Please."

Her begging drew out a deeper hunger. I adjusted slightly to lift her hips higher. She cried out once, but when I hit that one spot, she screamed out my name as she came harder than she ever had before. Her sensitivity made her push away slightly, but I held on tight, drinking everything she gave. I kissed her inner thigh and slowly up her body until her fists clutched my shirt, pulling me to her lips. Her tongue swirled with mine as she sucked my bottom lip between hers. When our kiss slowed, her gaze melted into mine. She glided her fingers down to my belt, unbuckling it with pure intent in her eyes. I shook my head and she froze underneath me.

"This was just for you."

She grasped the button anyway and unfastened it.

"No, this is for you," she whispered, but I stopped her hands and shook my head again. She looked confused. "I don't understand."

"Darlin', you gave me everything I needed."

"Are you sure? Aren't I supposed to return the favor?" She pulled back like I had scorned her.

"Yes, Jordan." I pressed my body against hers, lifting her hands and holding them above her head. "Loving you is the only favor I ever want. This could not be more perfect."

I felt the touch of her lips against mine again, but I seriously needed to calm down. I pulled out of our kiss and pushed off her, but with the sight of her lying in the bed with shredded lace panties and a bra exposing her curves, I didn't think I would be able to contain myself again. I still craved her.

"God, you're so beautiful." She leaned up on her elbows with her legs still spread apart. Maybe I would let her return the favor later. "We're going to be late. You better find some clothes to wear."

She peeked over the bed, eyeing her shirt and panties, and she shook her head as she giggled. "Good thing I wasn't planning on wearing those tonight."

"I'll buy you some new ones." I reminded her as I leaned over her and pressed my lips to hers briefly. I grabbed my hat and headed to the door. "Meet you at Dixie's."

When the door closed behind me, I slid my hand down my face, still smelling her on my fingers. I didn't understand this carnal need for her. This was a feeling I would never understand, but I didn't need to understand it, I only needed it to last.

I pushed away from her door and headed down the stairs. My uncle's voice echoed a tune from the kitchen. Aunt Ethel was nowhere in sight. I headed out into the evening, the chill beginning to creep into the air. I pulled the brim of my hat down on my head to shade my eyes from the setting sun. Paul and Ellie were to meet us at Dixie's. From there, we had a plan to head down the highway to the Silver Bullet for our first official double date.

The walk down the block to Dixie's Tavern felt lonely. I turned to look back at The Inn and hoped my girl would hurry up. I glanced inside of Ellie's Boutique as I passed by, and saw that she was standing behind the counter talking to a guy. Probably some dude buying clothes for his girl. A smile slipped across my face, reminded of my promise to buy Jordan new clothes to replace the ones I'd ruined in the heat of the moment. I checked the time on my watch and noticed that the boutique should have closed ten minutes ago. I guess we weren't that late after all.

When I reached the corner door of Dixie's, I yanked it open and heard soft country in the air. Being just past 6:00 on a Thursday, the bar was relatively quiet; just some of the locals having an evening beer before heading home for dinner. As I sidled up to the bar, Mrs. Betty handed me a draft right away.

"I love how you know my order." I smiled as if I was the happiest guy in the world, because I was.

"Lance is rubbing off on you a bit, Tom."

I laughed as she headed off to the other side of the bar.

The smile didn't leave my face with her departure. I sipped

my beer as I watched a sports news show on the TV. Images from moments ago flashed through my mind. I couldn't believe I could call such an amazing woman my own. Her shocked expression when I had said she didn't need to return the favor raised a question. I chalked it up to how she was treated before. The smile fell from my cheeks when I thought of her life before we met. I just prayed I would always be in it from now on. I would fall asleep with her tonight and wake up with her in the morning, but it still didn't feel complete. Something was missing.

Is it too soon to ask her to move in with me?

A smile crept up my face again. I rarely dated girls longer than a month, and after a few months with Jordan, I was ready for a commitment of vast proportions. It just seemed right. Maybe I would give it a week or two, but I felt confident in my decision.

"Ma'am, could I have a draft?"

I turned my head to the side as someone sat down a barstool away from me. He turned his eyes toward me and I could swear he looked familiar, but I just couldn't place him. I nodded in his direction.

"Hey. How's it going?" he said in reply.

"It's going well, and yourself?" I didn't want to talk, but Aunt Et taught me better than to just brush someone off.

Mrs. Betty placed a beer down in front of this new guy and he took a sip before he answered. "It could be better, I suppose."

His accent wasn't quite country, but he was definitely from the south.

"Woman troubles?" I asked to pass the time and glanced

back at the TV.

"You can say that."

I felt his stare on me and right away I disliked him. I took a sip of beer in an attempt to ignore it. I glanced back at him. Instead of looking away, he lifted up his beer in a mock cheer and took a sip. I wanted to move away, but didn't want to seem rude. I'd just rather not talk to every Joe who passed through our town.

"Did she ditch you for another guy?" I sounded smug, but I wasn't sure why. Something about his attitude rubbed me the wrong way. Why did I care? I didn't know this guy

"You can say that." He repeated his answer from a moment ago, but it wasn't as nonchalant this time. I cocked my eyes at him and saw the way he clenched his jaw. He cleared his throat as his voice changed back to casual. "Know of any good restaurants around here?"

I wasn't about to tell him to go to The Inn for dinner. I didn't want a guy like that in my town, I didn't care who he was. "Not so much around here. Might have to drive up north to Lenoir. It's a bigger town."

"Good to know."

I glanced back at the TV, hoping he would get the hint, but he continued like any annoying guy would at a bar. "So, you from around here?"

"Close by." I sipped my beer, pretending to be really engrossed in the commentary before the Thursday night NFL game. The Chiefs and the Broncos didn't affect the Panthers' standings, so it really didn't matter too much to me.

"Excited for the game tonight?"

What is with this guy?

"It's football. It's no Panthers, but it'll do."

"My girl was really into football."

I took a sip of beer to disguise my annoyance and kept my eyes on the TV. He even had the nerve to side-lean closer to me.

"Yeah, it's the south. Chicks dig football down here."

He laughed as I sipped my beer again. He shifted from his seat and tossed down a ten dollar bill.

"Thanks for the chat. Lenoir, you said?"

I nodded, not wanting to engage in the conversation anymore.

"Yep. Up north on the highway." Anywhere but here would be good. He slapped my back.

"See you around, buddy."

Jesus, I hope not.

I nodded goodbye as my phone beeped. I flipped it open to find a text from Paul.

We'll meet y'all at the Silver Bullet. Ellie is running late.

I turned around and watched the weird guy exit the bar. I quickly typed Jordan a message.

I'll come get you. Stay put.

Something about him gave me a weird feeling I didn't much care for. I didn't want Jordan wandering down the street with people like him slinking around.

Chapter Eighteen

TOM

The walk back to The Inn was faster than the walk to Dixie's. The way that guy's eyes had devoured every girl passing him on the way out of the bar made me uneasy. I had a bad feeling about him. I slowed my walk as I dug out my phone. I flipped it open and dialed Caleb's number. After a few rings, he answered.

"Caleb Harris."

"Caleb. It's Tom McCloud." I came to a stop in front of the door to The Inn.

"Hey, Tom. What's up?"

I exhaled to rid some of the concern in my voice. "Can you run a check on Ryan Gordon?"

"Can I ask why you want to know?"

"There was some douche at the bar earlier and it threw up a red flag. I can't remember exactly what Ryan looked like, so I figured I'd ask you to check on it."

He paused for a moment as I heard what sounded like papers shuffling in the background, and he asked, "Is this Jordan's ex?"

"Yeah, she had some issues with him when she first moved here, but he seemed to have been quite for a while. It's just this new guy I met at Dixie's really threw me off."

"I'll look into it right away."

"Thanks, man."

I closed my phone and opened the front door to The Inn. The fact that this entrance remained unlocked at all times made me a little anxious, but at least there was a deadbolt on all of the rooms and my aunt and uncle's apartment. I exhaled, realizing that a deadbolt wouldn't save anyone. I shook my head. This was a night for my girl, and I wanted to show her a good time without the stress that she had just managed to get rid of.

I took two steps at a time up to the third floor and knocked on her door, but she didn't answer. I tensed up, listening for any sounds of distress coming from inside her room. It was quiet. I looked up and down the hall to make sure no one was lingering around, and I knocked again a little louder. Thankfully, the door flew open then.

"Calm down, cowboy. I was in the bathroom."

I wrapped my arms around her, pulling her as close to me as I could. She hugged me back and felt the tension in me, "What's wrong, Tom?"

"I just missed you. I don't like leaving you." I faked a smile in hopes of disguising the concern in my voice. I didn't want to worry her if there was nothing to be concerned about. She had been through so much already.

"So, why am I not meeting y'all at Dixie's?" She pulled out of our hug a little and I couldn't help melting under her stare. It was no question why Ryan still wanted her. He was just *never* going to get her.

"Ellie was running late, which more than likely means another hour. We're going to meet up with them at Silver Bullet later." I pulled her close to me again and whispered, "So, I figured you and I could have our own date before we join them."

"You're only allowed to rip one clothing item a day, and two are now in the trash."

I cackled at her statement. I loved this woman so damn much.

"Food, Ms. Hawthorne. I'm taking you to dinner. Get your mind out of the gutter."

WE DROVE DOWN the highway as I tried my best to not worry about the events that had happened earlier this evening. Jordan told me about some teacher drama at the community college, but thankfully, said she wasn't involved. After pulling into a parking spot, I hopped out to help her down from the truck, but before I could get to the door, her cowboy boots smashed against the gravel.

"You can help me the next time I wear a skirt. Sound good?"

I threaded my fingers with hers as I walked just a half of step behind her. Jeans sculpted her ass in such a way it was hard not to stare. I heard the slam of a car door as we passed, followed by the whistle of its owner. I made sure to walk directly behind her after that.

This barbeque joint was a little hole in the wall, but the pulled pork brought people in truckloads. We sat near the back as a waitress took our orders of sweet tea and pulled pork sandwiches. I stared at Jordan as she looked out of the window into the night.

"What are your plans after the semester, darlin'?" My heart was already so far gone. I needed to know if she still planned on just the one semester.

She moved her hands to her lap as she looked down at the table and then back up to me.

"I think I'd like to stay here. I feel like I'm putting a lot of faith in our short relationship. I have a track record of moving too fast in these situations, but I trust my heart, and I want to stay here with you."

A weight lifted off my shoulders. I reached out my hand for hers, and she lifted it from her lap to place it inside of mine.

"Are you happy here?" I squeezed her hand gently.

"I'm happy being with you. I want to be where you are."

"I love you, Jordan." And as if on cue, two pulled pork sandwiches appeared in front of us. "And I love me some pulled pork."

She laughed as she smothered her sandwich with barbeque sauce. I was going to enjoy watching her lick the sauce off her fingers when she was done.

THE CROWD AT Dixie's on a typical Thursday was impressive, but the massive crowd at Silver Bullet was pure insanity. It was like a busy Saturday at Dixie's and the fourth of July rolled into one. Jordan and I walked into the bar and immediately adjusted to the noise and the crowd, but then I heard her gasp beside me as she tugged frantically at my sleeve.

"What? What?" I started to freak out. For some reason, my brain instantly thought of Ryan and the need to protect my girl.

"They have a mechanical bull!" she declared, smiling.

I started to laugh to cover up my relief.

"Can I ride it?" she asked, her eyes big like a kid in a candy store.

"Why are you asking me?"

"Well, I don't know," she said as I pulled her hips to me until her lips were so close to mine.

"You feel like ridin'?" I asked as she mimicked my smirk.

"Not so much a bull, but maybe a cowboy."

Sexy as hell.

"God, I love you." I pressed my lips to hers, and on breaking our kiss, I patted her ass. "Go get up there!"

Jordan grinned and wove her way through the people surrounding the ring, with me following close behind. The attendant ran through a list of rules as I got closer to the railings. Jordan agreed to them with a nod as she signed a release form and hopped up onto the mat surrounding the mechanical beast. She held onto a rope, and with one jump, hoisted herself up onto what was called a bull; no legs or head, just a sturdy body made of rubber. She adjusted her legs and got a firm grip on the rope.

"You ready?" the attendant yelled out to her. She smiled and nodded as she kept her eyes focused on her grip. The beast began to move. Just watching her hips flex to such a slow rhythm, my jeans instantly became tight. The machine shook and twitched, Jordan's breasts bounced to the beat. I glanced around the ring, and, of course, every guy was staring. Some took pictures, which made me very uncomfortable. Jordan was my girl. I didn't want pictures of her on the internet, but I did nothing more than glare at a few and enjoyed the show with the rest of them. The good thing about it, she was coming home with me.

"Oh my God. Is that Jordan?" Ellie piped up from behind me and wiggled her way next to me.

"I can't watch this! I'm going to get a pitcher and a table." Paul was the only man in this place not watching my girlfriend ride the bull, and I was thankful. If it was Lance, he would be watching like everyone else.

The bull stopped kidding around and began bucking at a breakneck pace. Jordan held on to the rope with both hands, her knees gripping the sides of the beast. I winced when it threw her around harder. I was sure she would get bruised up. Maybe we would soak in the tub later. The mechanical bull gave a solid jerk, I was positive that we'd soak in the tub later, but would probably have to forfeit on collecting any earlier favors.

The beast stopped in mid-air, throwing Jordan off its

back and into the padded railing. She jumped up quick and threw her hands in the air. The hoots and hollers from the crowd lasted until she moved out of the ring. I ran over to the exit and scooped her up into my arms, kissing her hard for everyone to see.

"That was incredible! I didn't know you could ride like that."

Her cheeks darkened as she pulled at my shirt. "Sure you do. I ride you all the time."

She returned the kiss, and from the way she ignored the crowd around us, I figured I had a small chance on collecting that favor after all.

"Paul found a table," Ellie said as she met us by the exit of the bull riding ring. Jordan released her hold of me and linked arms with Ellie. I followed behind, making sure no one stared at my girl's ass. Paul sat at a four top, alone with a pitcher and four chilled pint glasses. When we got there, he stood and pulled a chair next to him for Ellie to sit. I did the same for Jordan, and as soon as I sat down, I pulled Jordan and her chair closer to me, resting my hand on her crossed knees. Paul poured us each a glass of beer.

"I'll get the next round," I offered. We would probably go back and forth like this all night. He nodded as he took a sip. People were already dancing, but this wasn't our normal crowd. We needed to ease into it slowly.

"Why were y'all running late?" As Jordan asked the question, my phone vibrated in my pocket with a text. I adjusted my hold on her knee and dug out my phone.

"This weird dude came into the boutique asking all these questions," Ellie explained, "and I was just like, are you going to buy something or just keep talking?"

I flipped open my phone and saw a text from Caleb.

Pulled in a few favors. That Ryan guy you asked about hasn't been to work in over a week.

My stomach bottomed out.

"He kept asking about what schools were in the area and if I knew any of the teachers," Ellie said with a look of disgust.

I rubbed Jordan's leg, hoping that she wouldn't get too anxious from Ellie's story. I had only just gotten her to the point that she didn't constantly worry he would show up.

"I had to pretty much throw the guy out. What a douche!" Paul said as he shook his head and chugged the rest of his beer.

"I need a ladies room. Ellie, come with?" Jordan asked, and they both stood from the table.

I squeezed her hand before she left, and asked, "Can I use your phone? This flip phone shit doesn't have the internet."

She pulled it out of her purse and handed it to me.

"Whatcha need it for?" she asked.

"I was just going to check what time the band comes on."

She smiled that beautiful smile of hers and my heart sank. Ellie's customer. The guy at the bar. It had to be him. After Jordan and Ellie left for the bathroom, I swiped the screen to unlock the phone.

"Dude," Paul said, "there is no band on Thursday nights here."

I tapped open her social media app.

"I know." I waited impatiently for the internet to work.

"Then what are you doing?" Paul asked, not waiting one damn minute.

"Just hang on." My knee bounced as the anxiety kicked in harder. I tapped on the settings, and then the blocked list. Only one name showed up. Ryan Gordon. I tapped on his name as the internet spun. *Fuck. Come on.*

Only a picture showed up. All of the blood drained from my face. My hands started to shake as I slid the phone across the table to Paul.

"Is that who you kicked out of the boutique?" I leaned my elbows on the table as I swiped my hand down my face.

"Motherfucker, is that …" He picked up the phone and examined it closer. "He was right there!"

"I know. I had a beer with him at Dixie's."

"Do what?" Paul looked at me with a blank stare.

I nodded, confirming what I'd said.

"Son of a bitch."

"He knew me. He knew who I was. He knew where Jordan was." I banged my fist on the table. "He was fucking right next to me!"

"Just be cool, Tom. The girls are coming back."

"Don't say anything. I can't have her freaking out. Text your brother for me and tell him Ryan is, or was, in town today, and tell him he's stalking Jordan."

Paul nodded and pulled out his phone.

I hated that this decision came from all the wrong reasons, but this settled it. I was asking Jordan to move in with me. I refused to lose her the way I had lost so many people I loved. I was never letting her out of my sight again.

Chapter Nineteen

JORDAN

The dawning sun flickered light through the lace curtains, the shadows of the trees danced across my suite in the fall breeze. Warmth embraced me; a tender beat drummed in my ear. I drew my finger down the bare chest of my boyfriend. This was as peaceful as I'd been in months. His fingertips lightly traced circles on my naked back, sending a pleasing shiver down my spine. I tilted my head up, resting my chin on his chest, and gazed on his chiseled face. His hair was tousled from our late night fun after the bar, and a morning shadow of stubble graced his chin. My leg hooked over his, and I was afraid to move it, knowing how sore my legs were from my night of bull riding and from the extracurricular activities before and after. His blue eyes sparkled in the morning light as he stared at the bare ceiling, his eyebrows creased in thought. I bit my lip in worry. He usually wasn't this oblivious when I woke up.

"Mornin', cowboy."

His stare never wavered, but he squeezed me tighter. I exhaled slowly as I reminded myself that Tom loved me, and that he was nothing like Ryan. I closed my eyes, trying to push the bad thoughts away. Tom made me a stronger person. With him by my side, I didn't have anything to fear. Ryan was far away, moving on with his life. I had to keep reminding myself of that.

"Hey. You okay?" I whispered as he squeezed me again, but he still didn't take his eyes off the ceiling. I moved my head off his chest to try to get him to look at me. He was freaking me out. "Tom?"

"Move in with me."

My heart stopped. My breathing stopped. Everything stopped except for the butterflies in my stomach. He finally turned his head, his eyes landing on mine. I exhaled the withheld breath.

"What did you ask me?"

His gentle smile brightened the room. His fingers caressed my cheeks and then threaded in my hair. "Would you move in with me?"

Tears pricked the back of my eyes. I wanted this. I wanted this so bad, but was it too soon? I wasn't wrong about Tom. I knew his heart. His eyes gazed on me with undoubted sincerity as he whispered, "It just doesn't feel like home unless you're there."

"Yes." I didn't need to question it any longer. He pulled my lips to his as a tear broke loose. This was so fast, but I couldn't worry about the past. I had to look to the future. Tom was my future. Our kiss ended and he pressed his forehead against mine as he sighed in relief. He pulled me tight against his chest, engulfing me in his arms.

"So, when does this happen? Like tomorrow? Next weekend?"

"Now." He scooted out of the bed. I propped myself up on both elbows with the sheet covering my chest as he rounded the bed.

"Now? It's Friday. You have to work."

My naked boyfriend opened my closet door, pulled out the empty suitcase and plopped it down on the foot end of the bed. I moved my feet out of the way before it hit me.

"Yep. Now. We've got plenty of time. Paul will cover for me." He went back to the closet and pulled a bundle of clothes from the rack, haphazardly tossing them into the suitcase.

"Tom, do you have any care for organization?" He laughed as he continued with the task at hand. "There's nothing wrong with seeing a naked cowboy, but do you want to put on clothes before you dismantle my suite?"

He dropped the last of my hanging clothes inside my suitcase and grinned from ear to ear. God, he was hot. I couldn't help biting my lip as I feasted over the man I was moving in with. He quirked his brow and hopped on top of me, wiggling himself in between my legs even with the sheet separating us. He kissed the tip of my nose, my cheeks, and ended on my lips.

"I'm gonna take the day off and spend it with you in bed. However, I would like to do that in *our* home where you can scream as loud as you want." My legs were suddenly not as sore and I wiggled underneath him. He smirked again, knowing full and well what I was doing. "Not until we're home, darlin'."

"Well, then put some damn clothes on."

He laughed as he scooted off me. I huffed a bit at having to wait, but he wouldn't allow me to be idle and pulled me out of the bed. Naked and all.

"OKAY, BABE. THAT'S all of it," Tom said as he set down the last bag of my belongings in his bedroom—our bedroom. Thankfully, I only had clothes and a few personal items. All Tom had to do was make some closet space for me. It turned out I needed a lot more closet space than I'd thought, one of downsides of having a friend who owned a boutique – not that I was complaining.

After we finished hanging my clothes, I went over to my bag of toiletries Tom had set on the bed to complete the move, but as I reached for it, he swatted the bag to the floor. I looked up at him, puzzled.

"What the hel—" I was interrupted when Tom crushed his lips against mine.

"We can deal with those later." That husky voice of his made me stop all movement until he pushed me on the bed. I propped up on my elbows, letting my legs hang open. He yanked his T-shirt over his head, messing up his hair. Damn, he was sexy.

He launched himself on top of me. I started to giggle at his forcefulness. While stripping off my shirt, he kissed my body, speaking in between kisses, "You." *Kiss.* "Are." *Kiss.* "Officially." *Kiss.* "Mine."

He ended on my lips, and I willingly opened to his lustful tongue expertly massaging mine.

"Forever, cowboy."

Holding himself up on one elbow, he caressed my face with his fingers, gliding them along my lips. My legs bent up around his waist, needing to feel the bulge inside of his jeans. He dragged his lips down my neck and to my chest, kneeling back on his heels. While I was drowning in his eyes, he unbuttoned my jeans and peeled them slowly down. He stood up beside the bed, pulling off my boots and removing my jeans. My heart pounded with anticipation as his eyes roamed over my nearly naked body, but it was my view of him that gave me the craving to be filled completely. The muscles in his chest rippled down to his sculpted abs. The button of his jeans hung open, beckoning me to release him.

"How am I lucky enough to have you?" he said, his voice husky with desire.

My heart jumped at his comment. How was *he* lucky? How was *I* lucky? I sat up on the bed, reaching out for the waistband of his jeans. As I grabbed a hold of them, I pulled him close to me and slowly unzipped the fly. I yanked them down and he sprang out before me. While gazing into his eyes, I massaged him, and he grew within my grip. My hand slid up and down, and just as I wrapped my lips around his tip, he hissed, running his hands through my hair. I took him slowly in my mouth, as far as I could, and showed him how I was the lucky one. He coddled my face, releasing myself from his grip.

"Lay down," he whispered. I scooted back onto the pillow, watching him intently as he pulled his jeans off. He knelt on the bed and slid his hands over my chest, unclasping my bra and tossing it on the floor. He scooted around, kneeling in between my legs, and hovered over me, taking my aching nipple into his mouth and sucking gently. He unlatched as he straddled me, gazing over me. He roamed his hands down my body, caressing every inch of me while my hands twitched to touch him. I wrapped my hands around him and began pumping. He attempted holding back a thrust, but he let go when I didn't give up.

Tom held my arms as he gently pulled himself out of my grasp and crawled down the bed. My breath was already erratic, and he hadn't even touched me. As soon as he did, my back arched off the bed. When his tongue replaced his finger, my hands fisted the sheets.

"I need you now. Now!" I begged with a yearning pain to be filled.

He wasted no time repositioning himself. I pulled his lips down to mine as he slowly nudged his head inside of me. Holding himself up, he hooked my knee over his other arm, spreading me wider and filling me deeper.

"I love you," he whispered against my lips. I wrapped my arms around him, squeezing his ass and urging him to push harder and deeper. He raised my hips higher as he leaned up slightly, thrusting deep. I clutched and clawed at his back, needing to come.

"I feel you, clenching around me." His eyes full of lust. "Shit, Jordan." Ecstasy built inside me, his back tensing under my hands. I screamed. I screamed loud as he grunted my name and poured into me. Our breath intertwined as Tom pressed gently on top of me.

"I love you. I love you. I love you," he whispered before I pulled his lips to mine, echoing my declaration of love for him.

He slowly pulled out and wrapped his arms around me from behind. Together we dozed away the afternoon. The sun brightened up the room. The warm sheets warded off the outside chill. After a while I managed to escape Tom's arms to finish unpacking.

The little things made my heart bloom, like putting my razor beside to his, placing my toothbrush next to his in the holder, hanging my robe by his behind the door. After everything I had been through, moving away to the middle of nowhere, I never thought I'd give anyone a chance again. I came back out of the bathroom to see Tom propped up on the pillows on *our* bed. He smiled at me as I jumped on the mattress and snuggled in his arms. I wonder if he had any idea how blissfully happy he made me.

"Welcome home, darlin," he whispered and kissed the top of my head. I was home… in his arms.

The afternoon sun began to set. My growling stomach interrupted our mood. He lifted his head from the pillow as a smirk rose up his cheeks.

"I guess I should feed you, huh." He winked and I wrinkled my nose at him.

"Food would be good, but I can go make us something." I started to push away from him and he pulled me back down.

"And what do you plan on cooking?"

I shrugged my shoulders and smiled. "Grilled cheese sandwiches."

"How about a steak?"

"I'm not good with anything other than grilled cheese sandwiches."

"That's why I love you." He leaned over and brushed his lips across mine. "We'll eat out on the deck. I'll go start the grill."

He pulled on his jeans and a long-sleeved shirt, and left the room. I decided to take a quick shower. It would save me time before we went out later. I bypassed his big tub and went into the standing shower, adjusting the spray to a warm temperature. Water dripped down the sides of my face, cleansing my whole body. I stared at the tiled ledge where my razor lay next to his, my shampoo next to his, my loofah next to his wash cloth. This was the right thing to do. I was certain of it.

After my cleansing pep talk, I padded downstairs in a pair of yoga pants and a long-sleeved T-shirt. As I glanced around the house, I couldn't believe I could call this home. It was almost surreal. I turned into the kitchen and watched my boyfriend at the grill through the screened back door. I pushed it open as the cool breeze chilled my wet hair.

"Hey, darlin'. You got a shower?" He pulled off the last steak and dropped it onto a platter. He walked to the table, putting the platter in the center. He'd even been thoughtful enough to have two glasses of red wine, poured and waiting for us.

"Yeah, I figured I'd start getting ready for later." I sat down at the table and took a whiff of the freshly cooked meat as he put the smaller steak on my plate. "This smells a lot better than grilled cheese."

"I thought we'd stay in tonight."

I paused mid-cut and glanced up at Tom.

"But it's Friday. We always go out on Friday."

He shrugged his shoulders, not looking up from his steak.

"I figured I'd keep you to myself tonight." After I didn't say anything for the span of two seconds, he looked up at me. "Is that okay?"

"Of course."

He grinned and went back to consuming his food. Well, it was a special day. I didn't mind him keeping me to himself for the night.

TOM

"So, I've found out that he has a Swiss bank account."

I had received a text from Caleb last night to call him first thing in the morning. He knew I didn't want Jordan to find out about Ryan.

"How are you able to find this out?" I asked into the phone.

"I'm pulling strings, and besides, this town is too boring. I've got idle hands."

"So, what about this bank account?"

"He's transferred five hundred thousand out of the account."

"To where?"

"It was all I could do to get that information. I don't know to where." He exhaled. "I'm sorry, Tom. That's all I've got."

"Thanks, man. Just keep me posted if you find out

anything else."

"I always do."

I closed my phone and stared out over the fog-covered foothills. I sipped from my coffee while the dawn lit up the farm. Hampton trotted up the stairs from the yard and laid down by the front door. It had been a couple of weeks since Jordan had moved in with me, and I had been keeping this secret about Ryan ever since. Before Jordan moved in, we were practically inseparable. I had hoped that since we now lived together, it wouldn't seem as noticeable that we never went out and did anything outside of the house.

After I put my coffee down on the railing, I rested my hands on either side of the mug and hung my head. The weight on my shoulders had become nearly unbearable, but I couldn't tell her about Ryan. I still didn't know if not telling her was the best idea, but seeing her trust me more and more each day convinced me that I was doing the right thing. She acted like she was finally content, and knowing I played a part in that meant everything to me. I couldn't let her live in constant worry. She needed to be free of that bastard.

Releasing an exhale, I lifted my head and grabbed my mug, ready to start my day with Jordan. As I turned to head inside, a familiar truck rolled up my driveway. I took a sip and waited for Lance to hop down from his truck and approach the steps.

"Hey, why are you here so early?"

Lance stuffed his hands into his pockets and leaned up against a front porch post. He dug the heel of his boot into the wooden porch as he stared down mindlessly. I put my mug down onto the flat railing and leaned against the neighboring post, folding my arms across my chest.

"You've been a really good friend to me and a really understanding boss with working around my school schedule, but…" He sighed as he looked out over the clearing fog, not yet meeting my eye. "But I don't think I can work here anymore."

I pushed myself off the post as my arms fell of their own accord. We had been friends since we were in kindergarten. He started working with me—never *for* me—in high school, just like Paul. And that was the reason he was going.

"Dude, you can't stay mad at Paul and Ellie. You let her go a long time ago."

His eyes finally met mine with a mix of regret and determination.

"It's not just that. If I take a full schedule next semester, I can graduate in May instead of next December. I want to make something of myself. You and I both know I'm not cut out to be a farmer. I'm not meant to stay in the country."

I raised my hand to stop him, giving him a second to settle down. I picked up my coffee and sat down on one of the rocking chairs on the front porch. Lance followed my lead and joined me on the chair next to mine. I took a sip of coffee before I spoke because it was still really early and I didn't like to have serious boss-like conversations before the first cup.

"I know this is partly because of Paul, but I'll overlook it since you brought up some good points. How 'bout you still handle the books for the farm? That would give you a little more of a push on your resume when you graduate. I can pay you the same."

"Tom, your books take like five minutes a day."

"I know."

"That's not much work for the pay."

"Are you negotiating a lower pay grade?" I glanced over at him.

He looked back at me like I was some kind of stupid prick and smirked, "No, sir."

I set down my coffee on the table separating us and extended my hand across to him.

"So, we have a deal then?"

He shook my hand, confirming our deal.

"You're a good friend, dude." I picked up my coffee, preparing to take a sip.

"I know."

I took a sip of my coffee as we stared out over the farm. Lance leaned up in his chair, rocking forward to a stop. I glanced over at my best friend as he turned his head back toward me.

"I want to thank you for being a good friend."

I set my mug back on the table and leaned up in my chair. "Paul is a good friend, too, ya know."

He leaned back in his chair as he shook his head.

"Come on, Lance," I persisted. "You can't punish them for this."

"I can't sit back and watch. That was my girl."

"*Was* your girl. You dumped her when we graduated high school. You can't dwell on the past." He glared back at me for not taking his side, but I continued. "And Paul is your friend whether you like it or not."

He shook his head as he pushed himself out of the rocking chair. "He's dead to me."

"Come on, Lance!" As he went down the stairs, I hollered, "He's been in love with her all along, ya know. He didn't go after her back then because he knew you liked her. He stepped aside because he valued your friendship more. You can't do this to him."

He hopped into his truck and hollered back at me, "I can right now, and it might always be this way."

The slam of the truck door confirmed that I wasn't going to get through to him. The sun crept up over the mountains in the distance as his truck sped away over the gravel. I rocked back in my chair and sipped my morning medicine, but before I could decide my next breath, another truck came roaring up the drive. This time, it was Paul. He hopped out of the truck and walked up the front steps.

"Where was Lance running off to?"

I drained my coffee and set the empty mug on the table, I stood up and folded my arms.

"He quit."

His eyes widened, and after a slight pause, he tipped up the brim on his hat. "What'd he go and do that for?"

"Well, we know the obvious, but he claims to want to be a full-time student this coming semester."

"He's never going to forgive me, is he." It wasn't a question, even though I did question it myself.

"He will, eventually."

Paul's shoulders hung down and his head dipped. He shuffled over and took the seat where Lance had been sitting. He leaned back in the chair and shook his head again as his knee bounced with a nervous twitch.

"What am I supposed to do? I love her."

"I know." I nodded, staring off into the hills. He turned his head toward me and away from the view.

"I can't just give her up."

I nodded in understanding. "I know."

"So, what am I supposed to do?" He leaned up in his chair, resting his elbows on his knees.

"I don't know."

He sighed as he leaned back in his chair. I reached for my mug, and realized it was empty. I put it back on the table.

"Leaving her is not an option."

I leaned forward to meet my best friend's eye.

"He'll get over it. It's just the way it has to be. In the back of his mind, he knew all along you had a thing for her. So, this shouldn't be new to him."

"Enough of this crap. I'm headed to the barn." He pushed himself up and trotted down the stairs.

"All right. I'll see you out there."

As he left for the weathered barn, I stood up and stretched, trying to rid myself of the morning's stress. I pulled out my phone and read the time. It was only 6:40… way too early for all of this shit. I headed inside and Hampton followed. As I shut the front door, I heard the shower running upstairs. A smile slid up my face as I imagined those curves under the shower's spray. I headed into the kitchen, dropping my mug down on the counter, and sprinted up the stairs, hoping to catch her in the middle of her scrub.

The bathroom door was cracked open as steam bellowed out. I peeked inside, and through the steam-covered shower door, I gazed on the love of my life. Her arms lifted up as she scrubbed the top of her head. Suds rolled down her chest, hugging the sides of her body. I wasted no time stripping off my T-shirt and jeans. Her tired morning eyes popped open as I stepped under the spray. I stared into them. They were always the bluest in the mornings. I coddled her face and gently pulled her lips to mine.

"Mornin', darlin'." Her smile widened as my hands replaced hers. She turned her back to me and I ran my fingers down her long brown locks. I began to massage her scalp and her head fell forward.

"You're going to put me back to sleep."

"No one says you have to wake up. It's Friday. You're off today."

"I wanted to go in and prepare an exam for next week."

"Do it from home."

"I just felt like getting out and about today."

My fingers slowed in her hair. I hated not telling her about Ryan, but I just couldn't do it. I wanted to get rid of the problem before she ever found out it existed.

"Stay home with me. There's not much to do around here. Paul can handle what there is."

She turned around as the suds rinsed from her hair.

"I kind of feel cooped up."

"Well, then why don't we go up into the mountains or something? It's a nice day."

She tilted her head and stared at me. I faked a smile, hoping to disguise my worry.

"There are a lot of towns in the mountains. Which one are you going to take me to?"

"Have you been to Spruce Pine?"

"Nope. What's there?"

"Antique shops and stuff."

"You're taking me shopping?"

"Yeah, why not."

THE DRIVE SOOTHED my nerves. My hand wrapped around Jordan's for the hour trek into the mountains. I glanced over at her as we wound up another curve. The drive did not soothe her stomach.

"I think I should have eaten."

"Then it might have come up."

"Are we almost there?"

"Yes, city girl, we're almost there."

The moment I parked the truck, Jordan hopped out and took a deep breath of cool mountain air. She leaned up against the side. I walked around, resting up against the truck with her.

"Think you could eat?"

"Maybe. Let's give it a try."

I scooped her hand in mine and we walked across a calm street just before eleven in the morning. As we approached a diner, I held open the door for her. A sign at the entrance read, *Seat Yourself.* We headed to a table that overlooked the downtown area, and when we sat, Jordan's face began to regain some color, though she still looked a little pale.

"You know, we have to go back down the mountain."

"Ugh… we do?"

I nodded. Her shoulders slumped as a waitress approached our table.

"Hey, y'all. What can I get for ya?"

"I don't know..." Jordan groaned. "Something bland... grits, maybe... with butter."

The waitress turned to me.

"Same," I said, "With a sweet tea."

Jordan reached out her hand to stop the waitress from leaving.

"Sweet tea also, please. Thank you." She propped her elbow on the table and rested her head on her hand.

"You really don't do mountains well, do you?"

She shook her head. "I think I'll go to the ladies and splash water on my face."

She scooted away from the table and walked behind a wall, down a short hallway and into the bathroom. The waitress brought over two Mason jars full of sweet tea. I took a sip and drowned in the sweet richness of summer, even though it was November. I set the jar back on the table and leaned back in my chair as I crossed my arms and looked out over the street. My heart stopped when I saw a man crouched down by the front tire of my truck. I shot up and ran out of the diner.

"Hey!" I charged, but the guy took off. He looked back over his shoulder and I stopped suddenly as Ryan's devil-smile blazed in the light of day. *Fuck!*

I turned around and ran back inside. As I walked in through the door, Jordan sat back down at the table. *Shit, what was I supposed to tell her?*

"Jordan, we have to go."

"Why? What's wrong?"

Her question stumped me. I stalled a second to pull out

my phone.

"Paul just called. The cattle are out. I need to go back and help him." I walked over to the counter of the diner just as two bowls of grits were placed on a tray. "Ma'am, could you put one of those in a container to go?" I turned back to Jordan. "Maybe eat slow. I'll drive down carefully. I promise."

She nodded with such a confused face.

Oh, God. She is going to hate me for lying.

I had to get Jordan out of this fucking town and I had to get her out, now.

Chapter Twenty-One

JORDAN

A chill filtered through the air as golden leaves littered across the ground. I inhaled the scent of baked pumpkin and roasted turkey. I turned from the view of the yard as I watched Tom frantically moving around the kitchen. Thanksgiving meant so much to me, but to Tom, it meant meeting my parents.

I was so glad that Tom could cook, because I sure as hell couldn't cook anything except a grilled cheese sandwich. He bounced around the kitchen, checking on the turkey, the stuffing, the collard greens, and the homemade yeast rolls. His nerves were shot from his perfectionism in the kitchen, and he just couldn't seem to settle down. I knew the official meeting of the parents was a big deal, but I assured him that Cal and Marie Hawthorne were no one to be worried about.

When the doorbell rang, I peered up at Tom, who wore

the deer-in-the-headlights look like no boyfriend I'd ever had before. I tried to withhold a giggle, but it was no use.

"It's okay, Tom. They'll love you as much as I do." I kissed his cheek, and turned toward the door. Hampton stood there with his tail wagging. The excitement thumped as I ran over to the door, throwing it open and jumping.

"Daddy!"

My big, burly father wrapped his arms around me, twirling me around like I was five again.

"Oh, my baby girl, I've missed you so much!" He set me down as he said, "Marie, look at our beautiful daughter."

As my tiny mother come in, she placed her hands on my shoulders, her eyes glazed over with happiness. I get my spunk from Dad and my emotions from Mom. She wrapped her arms around me.

"Jordan, you look beautiful." I blushed as she said in a hushed whisper, "It's the glow in your eyes, baby girl. You've never looked more beautiful."

My mother and I both laughed at our silly tears. I had attempted to keep walls up at one time, but a certain cowboy tore them down. A hand rested against the small of my back, and I turned toward the eyes of the love of my life.

"Mom, Dad… This is Tom," I said with a grin while I kept my eyes planted on him. He was doing his best to appear calm and reserved, but under the rugged exterior, I knew he was a fit of nerves.

My dad grinned like the usual jokester and offered his hand out to Tom as he said, "It's nice to meet you, son."

"It's nice to meet you too, sir." Tom shook my father's hand as a welcoming smile eased up his face, warming my heart.

He guided them into the living room, and as Tom began to walk toward the kitchen, he said, "Mr. and Mrs. Hawthorne, I hope you're hungry."

My dad stopped in his tracks, scowling. I stared at him in confusion and Tom stared at my dad like he was about to run out of his own house from fear. My dad raised a finger in the air, motioning everyone to pay attention.

"Let's get a couple of things straight here," he said, pointing his finger at Tom. Poor Tom's eyes grew wide. "Number one, it's Cal and Marie. Mr. and Mrs. Hawthorne are my dear parents... God rest their souls."

He paused a moment and made the sign of the cross.

"And number two," my dad held up two fingers this time. "I'm always hungry!" He let out a roar of laughter.

Tom's nerves deflated. My mother giggled, shaking her head at my father. I wrapped my arm around my father's waist, squeezing him tight.

"It's good to have you here, Dad."

Tom's nervousness eased up a bit as we continued with dinner. My dad could be scary if someone crossed him—he was such a tall, well-rounded guy—but he really was just a big teddy bear. My mother seemed frail because of her tiny frame, but she had a heart of gold with the bite of a beast.

"Tom, why don't you show me around your farm and let these lovely ladies do their duty and clean up." My mother gave a teasing gasp at my father's words and threw her napkin in his face.

"Aw, I love you, honey," he said as he rose and kissed the top of her head. I smiled, watching what a great relationship my parents still had after twenty-six years of marriage. I glanced over at Tom. He was already watching me with that love showing in his eyes. I always wanted what my parents had, but being in love with Tom was so much more than I could have ever dreamed. I still didn't know how I got so lucky.

"Let's go, Cal. I'll introduce you to a couple of heifers who might catch your eye," Tom said, standing up with a humorous grin.

"Ha! Cattle humor! I love this guy, Jordan!" Dad's laughter carried throughout the house as they went out through the front door. I shook my head and laughed. I loved my dad.

I brought the dirty dishes to the sink. I was about to turn toward the dishwasher when my mother's arms wrapped around me. She peered up at me and asked, "Jordan, can we give this a minute and talk?"

When I turned my head to look at her, she seemed a little worried. Did she not like Tom? Surely, my living with him wasn't an issue. What on earth could it be?

"Sure, Mama. Why don't we go into the living room and sit by the fire."

I sat down and took a deep breath, but I couldn't relax; my heart was pounding. My mother angled herself toward me and reached out for my hands, grasping them tight inside of hers. She released a breath and said, "Your father thought it was best that I told you since he can't keep it together sometimes."

Now, I started to get really scared. Was either of my

parents sick? "Mom, you're scaring me. What's wrong?"

Mom took a deep breath and started, "I asked Katherine not to tell you this because I know you two talk all of the time."

My breath caught when she said Katherine's name. Had something happened to Katherine? I had no idea what was going on.

"There's a warrant out for Ryan. They went to his apartment to arrest him, but… he wasn't there." She looked at me with tears in her eyes. I knew there was more.

"What else? You have to tell me."

The tears streamed down her face, rolling endlessly.

"Baby, they found pictures and notes and a map of the state hanging on a wall in his bedroom. Jordan, he's trying to find you. He has pictures of you and Tom together. I don't know if he took them or if he hired a private investigator, but…" She shook her head, and then finished. "There were so many pictures."

She started bawling with no sign of stopping. I sat there as she gripped my hands. I could barely breathe. Ryan had fled, and there was only one place he would go. He would go after what he wanted.

The back door flew open, slamming against the wall in fury. Tom ran toward me. My dad must have told him because Dad's face was a fiery red. Tom knelt in front of me and pressed his hands over my mother's grasp on mine.

"Baby, you're fine here. He won't harm you. I promise." He wrapped his arms around me as I glanced up at my dad. He seemed to cool down a little.

"Jordan," my dad started. "I just asked Tom, but I'm going

to ask you. Your mother and I would both like to move in for a while and be near you." He sighed and continued, "It would help both of our sanities, baby girl."

I looked up at him and nodded, but the truth was that it didn't matter if the military police guarded this house. If Ryan wanted me, he was going to get me.

Everyone settled down on the sofa. Tom kept my hands inside of his as he stared at me, his forehead wrinkling in worry. I shook my head. I didn't want him to have to deal with this. It would all work out okay.

"When Tom told us about Ryan being in town a few weeks ago, we couldn't keep still. Now, since the police don't know where he is, we wanted to come stay here."

The blood ran out of my face as I stared at my father.

"Cal." My mother's voice echoed, but I could only hear what my father had said. *Ryan being in town a few weeks ago...*

"What did you say?" My heart pounded an erratic beat. I pulled my hand from Tom's and lifted it to my chest in hopes of easing the racing, but it was no use. Everything that had happened before I moved here crashed down around me. I should have known better than to trust any man. I glanced at Tom, but he wouldn't look me in the eye. He kept his head down and his eyes closed.

"Is this true?"

"I'm sorry, Tom. I thought you had already told her."

Tom's only response was to shake his head, acknowledging what my father didn't know. Tom's face was riddled with worry. This was big. He'd lied to me, and this wasn't about something minor. This was pretty big.

"Look at me," I demanded.

His eyes flew up to me. My voice was full of the hurt I felt. It broke my heart to sound so hateful toward him, but this was something he should have told me.

"Is this true?"

His voice caught in his throat. He closed his eyes and nodded his answer. I slipped my other hand out of his grip and stood up from the couch. I walked in front of the lit fireplace and stared into the flames. I honestly didn't know what hurt more: Ryan stalking me or Tom lying to me.

"Cal, why don't you show me around the farm," my mother said as I kept my gaze on the fire, hoping that it would send some sort of warmth through my body. Two pairs of feet walked across the hardwood floor. The sound of the front door closing confirmed their departure. I closed my eyes, exhaling slowly into the tense quiet. I didn't know what to say. Tom had never hurt me before. I didn't know how to react.

"Darlin'?"

I raised my hand up toward him, hoping he would respect the tense quiet for a moment longer.

"I can explain." The leather shifted as he moved from the sofa. My blood ran cold as I recalled the last time I had heard that line, the last time I had trusted someone with my whole heart. Tears slowly bled down my face, the fire's flames blurring in front of me. His footsteps approached, and as soon as his hand touched my hip, I stepped away from the fire, crossing the distance over to the window, trying to focus on anything other than this situation.

"Jordan, please."

I turned around and my heart broke watching the tears fall from his eyes. I wanted to brush it off. I wanted to let it go, but this was a big deal. Ryan was here and Tom hadn't told me.

"You lied to me." My voice cracked as I tried withholding a sob.

"I did not lie to you, Jordan. I just didn't tell you."

"Whichever way you want to paint it, you know what you did." My shoulders shook as the sobs took over. "I just don't understand why."

"You had started to have more confidence in yourself. You weren't broken like you had been. You bottled it up real good in the beginning. It was hard to get through to you. I knew you had doubted me so much." He took a few steps toward me, but I didn't move away this time.

"Tom, this doesn't help." I shook my head. "That doesn't even make sense."

"I didn't want you to be scared. I didn't want you living in fear."

The walls closed in around me. I needed air.

"I have to get out of here." I made for the door as he hollered behind me.

"You can't go, Jordan."

I shook my head, not really caring what he said.

"I'll come back, Tom. I just need to breathe."

He grabbed my arm, keeping me from reaching the door.

"I won't let you go out the door!"

What the hell? I yanked my arm from his grip, glaring at him like he wasn't even Tom, because he wasn't acting like Tom.

"What? So, now you're going to lock me in here? I can't ever leave the house again?"

"I'm not going to have someone else taken from me!" My heart lurched from his desperate plea. He came within a foot of me and stopped, leaving me with the breathing room I needed. "My parents were killed in a car crash. My grandfather died soon after. My grandmother died when I was a teenager. My aunt and uncle are getting up there in age. You're all I have left." He took a breath, but the tears kept rolling down his face. "You're all I have left, Jordan. I'm not going to let some crazed psycho take you from me. And if that means you stay here and never leave again, then so be it, but I'm not losing you."

He pressed his lips to mine as if there was no tomorrow, and then he stepped away without a glance back toward me. He climbed up the stairs and closed himself off in our bedroom. In that moment, I had never felt so lost in my life.

Chapter Twenty-Two

JORDAN

"Ryan was there?" Katherine asked through the phone as I flipped the page of some random celebrity gossip magazine; not really paying attention, just busying myself while I hid away in the bedroom.

"Yep." I answered Katherine's question as I filled her in on what had been going on the past couple of weeks while she was up to her ears in work.

"In your town?"

"Yep." I closed the magazine and reclined back on the pillows. "Tom apparently had a beer with him, too."

I waited as she absorbed that piece of knowledge.

"Do what?"

"I… did… not… stutter."

"He had a beer with him?"

"Uh huh. He sure did."

"My mind is not comprehending."

"He didn't realize it was him. I mean, I can't fault him for that. I had just *assumed* that he would at least know what the guy looked like."

"You know what they say when you assume."

"Yep." I sighed along with her.

"So, are you doing okay?"

"I'm fine, really. I've been stuck inside the house. Unless the house burns down, I'll be just fine."

"Let's not give crazy Ryan any new ideas."

"I don't think he's coming within two thousand feet of this place." Until the cops found him, this was my life. "So, anyway, since it doesn't look like I'm going to Charlotte for Christmas, why don't you come here?"

"I can definitely do that, or maybe for New Year's."

A genuine smile crimped up my face. Sometimes the love of a best friend could make everything so much better.

When the initial shock of being literally hunted wore off, I had become raging mad. Not only did I fear what would happen when Ryan actually took me, but the constant coddling from everyone in my life became too much to deal with. I didn't need the military police to protect me. I had Mom, Dad, and, worst of all, Tom. It was either one of those three or Ellie and Paul, or Lance who were always with me. The only time I left that house after Thanksgiving break was to teach my classes. After finals were over, I was bored out of my mind.

The only problem with all of this was that I knew Ryan would find a way to get me. He was just waiting for me to be alone. I knew he was watching me. I could feel him. I was at the point where I had become fed up with everything. I was imprisoned in my own personal hell.

After reading the eighth book in same number of days, I got up from the recliner and went into the kitchen. I needed a drink that wasn't my mother's hot chocolate. Not caring that it was only eleven in the morning, I reached into the cabinet above the fridge and pulled down some good ol' whiskey. I got a glass from the cabinet next to the sink and began to pour without a shred of guilt. After pouring about three shots' worth in the glass, I threw it all back with a big glug. The burning sensation tore down my throat to the pit of my stomach. My eyes watered as I exhaled the fire from within. Steeling my nerves, I proceeded to repeat. The burning wasn't as harsh the second time. The whiskey began to work its numbing magic.

A *thump* echoed near the back door. I turned around to find Tom with tears in his eyes. My poor cowboy… he didn't deserve this. The glass crashed down to the floor as I started to crumble. His arms wrapped around me, holding me up while I sobbed.

"I can't do this anymore." I sobbed into his chest.

He picked me up and carried me up the stairs. As he laid me on the bed, he whispered, "Jordan, we can get through this. They're going to find him and it will be over. Just hang on, darlin.'"

"Can we just get out and do something today? Like meet everyone at Dixie's, and drink a beer, or go shopping for Christmas gifts?" The sobbing subsided, my childish antics embarrassing me. I just needed a break.

"Let's do both, huh? We'll go shopping today and go out to meet everyone tonight. And when we get home, we'll take a nice bubble bath together." Tom looked at me with a hopeful grin and I gripped my arms around him. He pressed sweet and tender kisses along my cheek and lips, and then rested his forehead against mine, trying to calm my breathing.

"I love you. I'm so sorry this is happening. I just want you to not stress over it, or hate me because of it, either."

I pulled back from his whisper and gazed into his worried eyes. I traced my fingertips down his shaven cheek, absorbing the feel of his skin. I shook my head at his words.

"I love you more than life itself. As much hell as I have gone through over the summer, I would take a thousand times worse if it meant I could be with you. I'm so sorry for getting mad at you. I understand you did this for me, for us."

He shook his head. "It was selfish of me. I won't ever do something like that again. You're my life. I want to share all of me with you."

I reached up and pecked his lips, melting in his words as his arms wrapped around me in a tight hug. For the first time in weeks, I felt okay.

"Come on, sexy. Go get dressed, and we'll get gifts for your parents and everyone else." He smacked my ass as I got up from the bed. I missed us. This whole ordeal and my childish antics during it had put a damper on our relationship. I hadn't been worried that we might be over, but the drama had pulled the spark out of us. Maybe today would be a good recovery day. Christmas spirited the air and I got to spend time with the people I loved.

After a trip to the mall in the next town, a trip to the market, and a quick stop by Ellie's to buy a new shirt for tonight, we came back home to make dinner for my parents. We decided to drag them out with us to Dixie's Tavern. It would give them the opportunity to get to know Ellie and Paul better. Tom even convinced Lance to come as well. He suckered him by saying that I wanted him there and guilting him with the fact that I hadn't gone out much over the course of a month. Lance and Paul seemed to be on better terms, but only when Ellie wasn't the topic of conversation.

After stowing the Christmas gifts in my closet, I went back downstairs to find my dad opening a bottle of wine. I glanced around the table at the three most important people in my life, and I hated myself for how ridiculous I had been acting. None of them deserved it.

"Hey, baby girl," my dad said as I arrived at the table. They all looked at me so lovingly. I sat down and let out a sigh of relief. It was the most content I'd felt all week.

"Hey y'all," I said to gain their attention. "I'm really sorry for the way I've been acting these past few weeks. I didn't really understand why all of this was happening and I think I lashed out at the ones around me, and unfortunately it was all of you." I wiped away the traitorous tear escaping, and continued, "But I hope that tonight we can at least try to forget about everything and enjoy the evening."

I looked up at Tom. He smiled and winked, which allowed me to exhale a withheld breath and smile back. I sniffed the steak Tom had grilled for us, and I finally felt at peace. I wanted to enjoy the night knowing that nothing would happen to Tom and me. Everything would be okay.

Ryan would be caught soon. I just had to have a little faith.

FREEDOM FINALLY ARRIVED. As I walked through the door of Dixie's Tavern, our little group called my name in unison. I grinned from ear to ear as Tom wrapped his arm around my waist tighter and led me and my parents to a table near the bar. Paul and Lance both shook hands with my father, but while Paul nodded curtly at my mother, Lance pulled her into a big Lance hug, which made her laugh like a hyena. She wasn't used to the ways of Lance yet. She would soon be immune to them, but it wouldn't happen tonight.

Paul ushered Ellie to sit down beside my mother before going to the bar to get two pitchers of beer for everyone. My mom and Ellie started talking clothes as the guys talked Panthers. I was going back and forth between the conversations since I loved both clothes and football equally. The talking grew louder as the third round of pitchers emptied. For one moment, I'd forgotten everything. All of the bad had been swept away under a rug as if it never happened. My life was here with Tom, and I owed every bit of my happiness to him.

Several pitchers of beer later, the whole group of us, parents included, started to play a drinking game. It was my dad's idea to play Quarters, which really wasn't that shocking. He liked revisiting his college days after he'd had a few beers. Mom would just laugh at everything. It was fun watching my parents get drunk like the rest of us.

Once Angela showed up at Dixie's, Lance became unavailable. Paul and Ellie moved away from us, but with the thick crowd in here, I couldn't tell where they went. My dad and Tom were still chatting as my mother rested her head on the table. It appeared as if she'd pretty much passed out.

"Hey, Jordan!"

I turned around to find a few students from my evening class. I assumed they were at least twenty-one, but I really wasn't sure.

Getting up from the table, I went over to the group at the bar and said, "Can y'all even be in here?"

They all laughed. One of my students drunkenly said, "Yep, we're all twenty-one."

I eyed them suspiciously, and said, "Fine, fine. If y'all say so."

Another one of my students turned around with a tray of shots and said, "Let's go, Jordan! Show us what you've got!"

I caved into the teenage peer pressure. We all grabbed a shot and held them out in the middle of our circle as the girls in unison chanted, "One! Two! Three! Shoot!"

And down the hatch it went. I didn't even know what we were shooting. Then another girl cheered and hollered, "One more! One more!"

Before I could even protest, there was another shot in my hand with a sugarcoated lemon on the rim. I assumed this meant vodka. The counting chant began, and the familiar burn scorched down my throat.

Two shots later, the room was fuzzy. The only member of our little group I could find was Tom, but his head was leaning against the wall as he slumped in his chair. Just as I was about to wake him, my stomach churned from the toxins I had consumed. I began to do the "beer before liquor, liquor before beer" rhyme in my head, but I couldn't remember which one got you sicker. I stormed down the hall into the bathroom and emptied all of the poison from my stomach.

After wiping my tears and my mouth with some toilet paper, I decided it was time to call a cab. As my stomach seemed to settle, I unlatched the stall door and pulled it open.

An intense pain struck my head. I saw nothing but stars, then total darkness.

Chapter Twenty-Three

TOM

"Tom?"

"Tom!"

A continuous nudge poked my shoulder, my name echoing over and over. I cracked open my eyes. They felt like sandpaper as I peered up at Mrs. Betty.

She sighed and said, "I called you a cab, Tom. It's three in the morning and the bar is closed."

I looked up at her, squinting from the light and confusion as I asked, "What?"

Where did everyone go? I sat up from my slouching position against the wall, and I winced due to a screaming headache. I shook my head a little trying to find some relief, but it didn't work. Betty helped me up from my seat. I staggered slightly, but composed myself. When I got my bearings, I knew something was wrong.

"Betty, where's Jordan?"

She blankly stared at me, and replied, "Tom, I don't know. I assumed she just took a cab back with her parents. Everyone seemed pretty messed up."

"Okay, Betty. Thanks again for the cab," I said and left the tavern.

I climbed into the back of the waiting cab and instructed the driver where to go. I distinctly remember Cal and Marie going home. He had to help her out of the bar. Why on earth would we have drunk so much? I guess we all needed a night to let go a little, but the uneasiness in the pit of my stomach wouldn't disappear. I couldn't figure out what all had happened. I knew Jordan wouldn't leave without me, and I couldn't remember her leaving. Impatience began to set in.

"Excuse me, sir. Could you go a little faster? I need to get home."

He nodded and sped up, curving around the mountain roads at a high speed, but I didn't care. I needed to see my girl.

He turned into the drive as I pulled out a twenty-dollar bill. I thanked him and handed him the money when he stopped in front of the house. I darted out of the car with my keys in hand. I fumbled at the door, my hands shaking from nerves. As soon as I got it unlocked, I barged up the stairs to our bedroom to find the bed still made. The shaking in my hands spread throughout my body as my blood turned cold. I went into the bathroom, finding it empty. I ran back downstairs to search the house, but it was dark and empty. I went to the back of the house, to the guest suite, and knocked on the door. I got no answer. I pounded harder this time, hoping to wake up Cal and Marie. Cal opened the door, a little groggy, and peered at me through half-closed lids. Then he became startled when he saw my face.

"Please say she's in here." My vision blurred as my eyes glazed over with tears. Marie appeared at the door with tears already coming down her face.

I turned around, grabbing the cell out of my pocket and dialed Jordan's number. The voicemail answered, "Hi, this is Jordan. Leave a message."

Choked up already, I spoke into the phone. "It's Tom. I don't know where you are but I'm here with your parents. We're worried about you. Please call me."

I hung up and called again immediately, hoping she would answer, that maybe she was sleeping at Ellie's or something. The voicemail answered again. I hung up, slamming my phone down on the kitchen island.

"Fuck!"

Cal and Marie hurried back into their room and changed out of their sleep attire as I grabbed my phone again. I dialed Ellie. Thankfully, she answered on the third ring.

"Please say she's with you?" I said before she even said hello.

"Shit," she muttered. "Tommy, is she not with you? Where did you last see her?" She sounded panicked.

I tried to think. As Cal and Marie joined me in the kitchen, I said, "I saw her taking a shot with some girls that she taught over at the community college." I was trying so hard to think through the drunken blur of the evening. "That's all I remember, Ellie! I can't remember anything else!"

I could hear her sniffles through the phone. "Tom, call

Lance just in case. I'll be over there in a few minutes, and I'll bring Paul."

The call ended. I dialed Lance.

"This better be good," he answered.

"Lance, have you seen Jordan?" I snarled.

"What? Jordan? I'm with Angela right now, and have been ever since we played quarters."

The line stilled.

"Tom? Do you think…"

He didn't continue and I heard movement in the background.

"Tom, I'll be there in a few."

The line went dead.

I looked at my love's parents. Marie was sobbing uncontrollably while Cal stared blankly at nothing. I held the phone in my hands, willing it to ring. I dialed Jordan's cell again to no avail.

That bastard took her. He took my girl.

In a fury, I grabbed the vase that was sitting on the countertop and threw it across the room. Of course, it was no cure for my mental anguish. I laid my palms flat against the cool granite as they continued to tremble. Cal came over to me and rested his hand on my shoulder.

"Son, you have to stay strong for her. She needs you to be strong," he said. Marie wiped her tears and started to make a pot of coffee. Cal continued, "I'm going to put a few logs on the fire. You call the police, Tom." A tear slipped from his eye, and his lip began to quiver. "We'll have to wait twenty-four hours to officially file a missing person's report, but we still need to call the police."

As I was about to dial 911, Paul and Ellie barged through the front door. "Tom," Paul began, "I called my brother. He's on his way over."

I nodded at him. A few moments later, Lance came in. He looked troubled.

"Lance? Are you okay?" Ellie asked, walking over to him. He buried his head inside of his hands, and his shoulders shook from sobs. Ellie wrapped her arms around him.

"I shouldn't have left with Angela," he said. "I shouldn't have left."

He looked over at me and left Ellie's arms. He moved to stand in front of me. His sobbing reduced to sniffling as he said, "Tom, I'm so sorry. I should have been watching out for her."

I shook my head and said, "Lance, she wasn't your responsibility. Don't put the blame on yourself."

He looked sullen as he walked to the sofa and plopped down. The room became silent as everyone stilled with nothing to do. I had nowhere to look. It was still dark out, being only 4:30 in the morning.

Everyone sipped their coffee as I paced near the front door, waiting for Caleb.

"And I'm to have nothing more to do with Angela," Lance blurted out.

Everyone looked at him, wondering why he would bring this up.

"Why is that, Lance?" Ellie asked.

"She had the nerve to claim that Jordan was faking and that nothing really happened to her." He shook his head and continued, "She never did like Jordan. We're aware of why, but I didn't think she would say something like that."

Ellie peered up at me from the other side of the room, "Tom, you don't think…"

"No. Angela's not smart enough to do something like that," I said with utter certainty.

Caleb finally arrived and questioned us each individually as to when we had last seen Jordan. Unfortunately, all of our thoughts were blurry.

"Officially, a missing person's report can't be filed until this evening," he said looking at Cal and Marie. He turned to me and added, "But unofficially, we're going over to Dixie's to look at the security film."

When it hit 8:00 in the morning, Cal said he was going into town to ask around for people who might have seen her and would also try the police department. Marie and Ellie decided to stay at the house in case Jordan ended up coming home. Lance, Paul, and I hopped into Caleb's cruiser and headed toward Dixie's. We arrived to a very tired looking Betty.

"Oh, Tom," she started, wrapping me in a hug, "I wish I was paying more attention. I had no idea anything like this was going on."

I pulled back from her and said, "You'll be doing a lot of help by allowing us to look at the security tapes."

"Y'all come back to the office and we'll see if we can find anything." She motioned all of us to follow her into the back of the bar. She opened up the door to her office, and immediately turned the monitor around for us to see. Logging into her computer, she said, "I have six cameras set up around the perimeter of the bar. These cover the cash register, the length of the bar, the front of the bathrooms, and both the front and back doors. There are also two cameras outside, one in the front and one in the back."

We all huddled around the security computer as she positioned the tape to where our table was in sight. My knee bounced as I crossed my arms, leaning my elbows on the desk. The monitor was directly in front of me because I wouldn't have it any other way. We watched the tape roll through the night as she fast-forwarded it through the dancing and drinking. We watched as Lance made off with Angela, and then Paul and Ellie slipped away. The table was left with the four of us—Cal, Marie, Jordan and myself. The tape showed Cal and me talking as Marie plopped her head down on top of her arms on the table. We watched as Jordan turned around to the group of girls drinking by the bar. This scene then shifted to another camera. Cal helped Marie up and they staggered out of the bar. At the same time Jordan was on shot number two. With a heavy heart, I saw myself sitting back admiring my girl as my eyes closed with a smile on my face.

On the video screen, the girls at the bar were chatting and took a couple more shots. Jordan staggered toward the table while I dozed in an alcoholic stupor. She stilled, clutching her stomach with one hand and covering her mouth with the other, and then ran toward the bathroom. We leaned in closer to the screen to see the hallway's dark camera footage. We saw the light from the bathroom as Jordan pushed the door open. A few moments later, the door opened again, but we couldn't see the face of the person walking in. My fisted hands pounded the table. I was only a few feet away and unaware of everything. Lance rested his hand on my shoulder in an attempt to keep me under control as I watched the dark figure emerge from the bathroom with Jordan thrown over his shoulder. He turned to the back door and exited. We looked at the next security shot and saw him throw her in the back seat of his car.

"Pause it!" The tape stopped at Caleb's command.

On the screen, the evil specimen of life stood turned toward the security cameras with his devil's grin. It was as if he knew he'd finally gotten away with it. He had known I was only ten feet away, and he had kidnapped my girl right from under my nose, my stupid drunken nose.

It was Ryan.

He'd declared victory.

My girl was gone.

Chapter Twenty-Four

JORDAN

A screeching *thump* continuously pounded the inside of my skull. My heart raced with every throb. A wincing pain shot through my body, the nerve endings screaming in agony. I tried to pull my arms around my stomach, but a thrashing pain scorched through my limbs. Darkness swallowed me as stars flew behind my lids, dancing around in the night sky.

Fireflies.

A dark field surrounded me. Everything in my sight hazed into a blur except for their shooting glow. I followed their flight as they scurried forward, flying away in fear. My heart pumped as goose bumps rose on my skin, the hair on my arms standing on end. I ran and ran until I was consumed by the fear-filled darkness. I succumbed to the lurking evil torment. I stopped running and exhaled into the night. I couldn't open my eyes. I feared the darkness, but the fear warned me of what was beyond the protection of my lids. I focused on my heart and the man it beat for. A piercing sting penetrated my skin as heat seared through my veins. The blood pumping through my body eased my discomfort as I slipped further into the gloom. My body floated in weightlessness. I couldn't tell if I was alive or dead. A groan bellowed through my chest as mumbled words echoed inside my distrusting ears. Fireflies reappeared, creeping inside my nightmare. I watched them as they swarmed around my being. I didn't move as they flew around, encircling me. My skin scorched from their fire. The pain dulled as the fireflies took their flight and left me once again in the darkness of my own personal hell.

MINUTES, HOURS, DAYS, months… I couldn't calculate the time as my eyes began to quiver behind my heavy lids. My body ached. I wanted to slip back into the dullness of black. A finger traced against my jaw. My eyes slowly fluttered open and then shut against the blaring light. I had been consumed by darkness for an unknown amount of time and I was content in the hell that I knew. I was scared of the light, scared of what I might see… of whom I might see. Words purred in my ear, but I couldn't understand what was being said. Lips kissed the crook of my neck, but my body knew it wasn't Tom's lips. I wanted to flee. I jerked at the touch.

"Jordan?"

My eyes flickered as I heard a voice whispering my name.

The pit of my stomach hollowed at the sound, bile rising up my throat. I turned my head away, trying to get as far from him as I could, but his hands held onto my face, forcing me to stay still within his grasp. His hand slapped me, my face thrown to the left with the sting burning my right cheek.

"Wake up, you little bitch!"

I kept my eyes closed, hoping I wouldn't have to see the demon. Fear crept over me as tears seeped from under my eyelids. The fear took over. His hand grabbed my jaw, shaking my head in fury. My heart froze as my blood pumped with ice. My eyes popped open to the snarling eyes of the grinning devil. I tried to turn away, but he back handed my other cheek. He pulled my jaw, forcing my head straight as he leered at me. An evil laugh escaped his throat.

"Hey, baby. It's good to see those pretty eyes of yours." He nuzzled his face into my neck, breathing deep. He cuddled next me. I tried to move within my restraints, but they wouldn't give. He sighed into my neck as his hand grazed down my naked chest. I cringed as I tried to steady my breathing. His arm wrapped around my bare torso, pulling my side against him. "It feels so good to have you in my arms again."

I couldn't help the whimper that escaped. I wanted Tom. My tears flowed as I prayed to get out of here. He pulled his arm away and grabbed my face, forcing me to look at him again. I couldn't stop the tears of terror.

"I told you… you are mine," he seethed into my ear. He got up and dug in a drawer next to the bed. He pulled out a syringe, and my body shook from fear. I shook my head as my mouth moved, but no words would come out. I begged with my eyes as I watched him pierce my skin. A sting spread through my arm and the drug raced into my body. I flinched from the instant pain searing in my blood. "But until you can come to grips with that, you won't be allowed out."

The drug pulled me under and I welcomed the darkness. My eyes fluttered closed as the fireflies danced again. They weren't bringing me into the depths of my mental hell; they were protecting me from my physical misery. They slowly surrounded me and danced me into the darkness again.

EMPTINESS ENGULFED ME as my lids slowly slid open. I blinked against the light. My eyes burned as if they wanted to remain swollen shut. I gently pulled my arms, but I was still bound to a bed. I forced my eyes to focus, to figure out where I was being held. The crisp light shone throughout a room made of wood. I was in a cabin. The vaulted ceiling with exposed beams assured me it was a cabin of luxury— only the best for Ryan Gordon. The dull, foggy glow from the outside windows told me it was around dawn, and as I peered out of the window, a slope of trees let me know I was in the mountains. I didn't know what day it was or how long I'd been bound to this bed. I just knew I ached and my face stung from the beaten bruises. After our breakup, I had come to learn that he was nothing but evil, yet to kidnap me, drug me and bind me to a bed for an endless amount of time—I didn't know evil could get so low.

The doorknob slowly clicked and turned. I flinched in pain as the door pushed open. He stuck his head through the cracked opening. Evil burned in his grin. I tried to move as far away as possible, but I could go nowhere. I exhaled slowly, knowing that trying to fight him was the wrong approach. I had to make him believe that he had won, but being appreciative of his kidnapping was easier said than done. He gloated, hovering over my face and watching my fear.

"Why, Ryan? Why?" I looked him straight in the eye as the only words I could manage croaked out from my cracked, parched throat. His finger swept along my jaw and across my bottom lip. The will to pull away was great, but I kept the image of Tom near. Tom was the only thing that could pull me through this. I had to get back to my heart.

"I told you, Jordan… You are mine, and you always will be."

I forced myself not to flinch. I had to get out of the restraints if I was going to have any chance of getting away. I knew I couldn't do him physical harm… yet. But I had to act like I trusted him. This was the only way. I forced my fear down, trying to look sad and hurt as I gazed lovingly into his eyes.

"Baby," I croaked, "I didn't know you really cared about me. I was upset. You picked someone else over me." I willed a tear to escape as I solemnly turned my face away from his. His grimy hand wiped away my tear.

"You disobeyed me, Jordan."

I looked up at him as my lips started to quiver. He rolled his eyes in annoyance. I sniffled for dramatic effect.

"Don't cry. I hate when you cry."

"Can you at least untie me so I can hug you?" I attempted to look sincere while trying to contain my gag reflex. I just didn't know how else to get out of here. "I missed you, Ryan. It was agony being apart from you."

He leaned over and gently brushed my lips, making me shake with fear and pain. He gazed longingly into my eyes.

"On one condition."

I looked up at him, allowing my bottom lip to quiver.

"Anything, Ryan. I'll do anything to get you to trust me again." *Oh God, I hope this works.* His evil eyes retreated as I saw the presence of the man I had once fallen in love with come to the front.

"Love me like you mean it."

My brow crinkled with confusion. I didn't understand how he had switched, but I now knew what he was truly capable of being.

"Of course I love you, Ryan. I don't know what to do to make you believe me."

He glared as the evil pulsed from him once again, and then slithered back inside.

"No, Jordan. Make love to me like you have before."

My blood ran cold, knowing what he intended.

"Ryan, I'm in so much pain. Please untie me and hold me," I begged, hoping he could see my actual pain.

"If I untie you, do you promise for tomorrow?" He was really fucked up.

"Please. Please! I feel so weak." I nodded an answer as he waited for the one I couldn't say. Tears rolled down my cheeks as I realized what I had just agreed to. I started to whimper. He let out a sigh and leaned over me, untying my right hand. The broken skin screamed in pain. He repeated the same with my left. I winced as I brought my arms around my stomach, trying to hold the ache.

I wasn't able to recover from the pain. He wrapped his arms underneath me and carried me across the room and through an open doorway. He stood me up as my eyes shed tears of pain. I crumbled to the ground in my weakened state, the cold tiles freezing my naked and battered body. I glanced up to hear the sound of running water. The room surrounding me had the same wooden walls as the bedroom, bare, with no accessories hanging on them. He stood in front of me as he stripped off his shirt and jeans, followed by his briefs. He picked me up again as he stepped into the tub. He crouched down, bringing his body behind mine. I cringed as I leaned back against his chest.

The wounds, from my sore muscles to my torn wrists, yelped as we soaked in the hot bath. I reached my hand up and slowly patted my matted hair, wincing again as I brushed my fingers across a lump on the back of my head, now covered with dried blood. He pulled my hand away and stroked the back of my head, causing the pain to worsen.

The only thing that could get me through this was the thought of Tom. *My loving cowboy.* I had to do everything I could to get back to him. It would take a few days to build up my strength again, but if Ryan trusted me, he might not hold me hostage to the bed. I would make him believe I was doing this of my own accord. The possibility of things I might have to do chilled me to the bone, but if it got me the fuck out of here and back into Tom's arms, I didn't care. I would dance with the devil. He nuzzled into my neck again, peppering kisses. I remained stoic and staring at the wooden walls as a fire burned through me.

"I'm so glad I have my Jordan back in my arms. Don't ever leave me again." His arms wrapped around me tighter, and my body ached from the abuse.

"I won't, baby. I'm yours forever." My whole body and soul deflated with those spoken words. I hoped Tom would forgive me for all that I would have to do.

Chapter Twenty-Five

TOM

The scent of lavender filled the room as I lay on our bed, hugging her pillow to my chest. Cal and Marie made me go to bed around midnight, but I just laid there, propped up against the headboard as I kept her scent close to me. I stared out of the window as the black of the night changed into a royal purple. As flecks of white drifted down from the sky, I prayed the misery would stop. It had been two days without her. I was losing my mind. Tears wanted to fall. They pricked the back of my eye, but tears would mean I'd lost hope. *I can't lose hope!* I took one last breath of her scent and laid the pillow back in its spot, waiting for her to return. I gave up on sleep and hoped a shower would refresh me.

When I walked into the bathroom, the first memory of her hit me like a ton of bricks, my water goddess staring at me, completely naked and completely in shock. I stared at our tub and remember the dozens of times we'd been together in a bath full of bubbles, Jordan falling asleep against my chest. I ached without her here. I knew I had loved her so much before… but I never realized exactly how much until now. I pulled myself out of the daze and showered off.

Hope.

I would find her and I would find her today.

After the shower, I tried my best to stay positive. I knew the lack of sleep would hinder my focus, but without Jordan, life was a blur in itself. I could battle through the haze to find her, and that was exactly what I intended to do. I headed down the stairs to start a pot of coffee for the day, but the smell of the roasted beans met me on the stairs. I expected to see Marie starting off the day before me, but curly gray hair and hot pink framed glasses welcomed me into the kitchen.

"Aunt Et, do you have any idea what time it is?"

She looked up at me over her glasses as she continued wiping down the countertop. Three catering pans covered with foil sat on the stove. A whiff of biscuits hit me as I walked deeper into the kitchen.

"Yep, a time of day when even farmers are still sleeping." She tossed the paper towel into the trash can at the end of the counter and looked back at me. "Why are you awake at this Godforsaken hour?"

She leaned her hip against the countertop of the island as I sat on the stool and looked at my aunt. I could still remember being a teenager, and all those times she used to come over in the morning and make me breakfast. I had spent one year of high school alone with no other family but my grandmother's sister, and I honestly didn't think I would have survived without her.

"I couldn't sleep." I shrugged as her parental eyes hovered on me.

She folded her arms; I knew which question was coming.

"When was the last time you did sleep?"

I sighed and waited and hoped that would be enough of an answer, but when she cocked her eyebrow, I knew I had to give her the details.

"When I passed out drunk at the bar while Jordan was being kidnapped right from under my nose." I tore my eyes away from her gaze and looked down at the bare countertop, tapping my fist.

"Tommy... You can't do this to yourself. The only person to blame is Ryan. He's the reason why Jordan is gone. But she will come back, dear."

I looked up at her, hoping to absorb her confidence.

"How can you be so sure?"

She raised her hands up with a nonchalant shrug. "Do I seem worried?"

"You're here, aren't you?"

She folded her arms again. "And what does that mean?"

"You only come here before breakfast when you're worried about me. You haven't done this since I was seventeen."

"I'm worried about *you*. I'm not worried about finding Jordan. I know she'll come home." She moved away from the counter and uncovered one of the catering pans. "Your uncle is trying something different." She carried the pan over to the counter and said, "Breakfast burritos! I think they're pretty tasty. Get your protein now. You've gotta get your girl back."

By the time the sun rose and the clock hit 7:00, the usual suspects filled my house. Lance and Paul inhaled the breakfast burritos while Ellie sipped coffee with Marie and Aunt Ethel in the living room in front of the fireplace. Cal stared out of the front window as he waited for his little girl to come home. I shared a spot next to him and we waited together. A cop car pulled up the gravel drive. Cal took a sip of coffee as he shifted from the window.

"It's go time." He turned away and walked into the kitchen. I sipped my last bit of coffee as I watched Caleb step out of his cruiser and pull a file box out of the trunk. He made his way to the door. I opened it as he reached the porch.

"What's all this?"

"This is a lot of missing pieces." He lifted up the box.

He walked into the kitchen, set the box on the island, and nudged Paul and Lance to move out of the way. The ladies joined us as Cal finished making himself another cup of coffee. I set my empty mug in the sink and stood next to Caleb by the counter. The front door opened again as two more police officers joined us, but they stayed just inside the doorway. Caleb began pulling out the files, stacking them on the counter. He opened the top file and pulled out an eight-by-ten black and white photo of a girl in her late teens or early twenties, probably college age. Her hair was dark and her eyes appeared either a shade of blue or green with slight dimples in her cheeks—very attractive.

"Meet Lexi Andrews. Age nineteen. English major at Auburn University; however, she never did graduate. In fact, after a Saturday night football game, she reportedly dumped her boyfriend of eight months at a bar. She was last seen leaving that bar and never seen again."

We all stared at Caleb as we tried to figure out where he was going with this. He pulled out another photo, but before he set it down, he said, "Let's meet the boyfriend."

He laid the eight-by-ten in front of me. Those same malicious eyes stared back at me from the night I shared a beer with him. My hands clenched and shook.

"Ryan Gordon? Ryan was the boyfriend?" Paul asked as Caleb pulled out a blown-up copy of a student identification card.

"Actually, his name was Randy Goodson, and Randy Goodson was never heard of again, nor is there any birth record of a Randy Goodson meeting this description."

"So, who the hell is Randy Goodson?" He pulled out a copy of a yearbook page, a name highlighted with a picture circled.

Ryder Gowin. I glanced back up to Caleb, who wore a proud smile on his face.

"Ryder Gowin hopped from foster home to foster home during his high school years. When he was fourteen, his mother was murdered... by his father, who has since been tried, convicted, and executed for her murder."

My heart plummeted before I even asked the question.

"Why did he kill her?"

"She wanted a divorce."

"What the hell are we dealing with?" Cal asked as I kept

my eyes glued on the picture of the devil.

"A seriously screwed-up dude," Lance's voice echoed from beside me.

The conversation continued between everyone in the room but me. I wanted to absorb as much hate as I possibly could for that man. I stared at the picture, the evil in his eyes, lurking years later. Never in my life had I ever dreamed of hurting someone, but the next time I saw those eyes, I swore, the barrel of my gun would be the last thing they saw.

In truth, though, Ryan loved her. In his crazy, fucked-up mind, he loved her and wanted to be with her, so he kidnapped her and locked her up. Jordan would do everything to get on his good side; I knew it. She would never sacrifice herself. I knew she would do whatever she could to come back home to me.

"She's going to be okay." My words quieted the kitchen. I didn't know why I'd said them out loud—possibly, to reassure myself. I looked up from the picture and glanced at everyone around. I nodded and continued, "He loves her. He won't do anything to her."

"Tom… that's not necessarily true."

I turned back to Caleb.

"Sure, it is. He wants her back," I reasoned.

"Unless she's fighting him off," Paul added, but I shook my head.

"I know Jordan. She'll do whatever she can."

"We just gotta get to her," Cal echoed behind me.

"We need to find her," I reaffirmed what he said. Caleb's cell rang at that moment and hope beat in my chest.

"Harris," he answered. We stared at him, hoping this was

a good lead. "Where at?"

My chest now ached. We were so close.

"How far from the interstate?" Caleb silenced, then ended the call and clipped the phone back on his belt.

"A man fitting Ryan's description checked into a motel the night before last about a mile outside of Morganton. They didn't know if he had someone else with him or not. He checked in alone."

"Let's go," I said as I pushed away from the counter.

He pressed his hand into my chest.

"Tom. I can't let you go."

"Then I'll follow you there, but I'm getting my girl back." I stared him down; I wasn't budging on this.

"Go get your coat, then." He held his stare a moment longer and I nodded in acknowledgment, reading between the lines.

I darted up the stairs and knelt down next to my bed, pulling out a case. I flipped it open and stared at my pistol. I popped the clip out, making sure it was fully loaded, and snapped it back into place. I stuffed it in the waistband of my jeans, turned back to my closet, and dug out my heavy coat. I ran back down the stairs. I didn't speak to anyone on my way out, I just followed Caleb to his car and hopped in the front seat. I latched my seat belt and we sped off onto the highway with the other patrol car following close behind us.

"Tom, if you shoot, you hand me the gun afterward."

"This doesn't have to be complicated. I see Ryan or Rylan or whatever the fuck his name is, and I kill him. We can deal with the consequences afterward. I'm killing that son of a bitch."

"First off, you need to calm the hell down or you're liable to shoot someone you're not supposed to."

"I can handle a gun."

"Not in this condition, you can't. Calm the hell down."

I nodded at his request and stared out into the dreary day. It looked like more snow would fall tonight, but I didn't care. I was getting my girl back.

AN OLD MOTEL came in sight. The adrenaline pumped through my veins. My knee bounced as I tried to picture Jordan's beautiful face. I had to believe he wouldn't hurt her. Caleb slammed on the brakes near the room where we thought Ryan was located. I pulled off my seatbelt, but before I could jump out of the car, Caleb grabbed my arm.

"Make sure we have an ID before doing anything. Shooting is a last resort. Got it?"

I nodded and jumped out of the car. I ran in step with Caleb and the other two officers. When they drew their weapons, I pulled out mine, pointing it down and away from everyone. We reached room twelve. I blew out one breath in an attempt to calm my nerves, but it was no use.

Caleb banged on the door while I kept my back against the wall next to it, flanking one officer while the other stood behind Caleb. When there was no answer, Caleb banged on the door again.

"Police! Open the door!" With no movement inside, Caleb took a step back and kicked the door open with one powerful motion. We all ran inside. My heart clenched at the sight. The pillows were stained with blood. The sheets were thrown around. All over the floor were crumpled towels sullied with blood.

"Don't touch anything," Caleb commanded.

I respected Caleb's order and did my best to not break down. I glanced around the room and noticed something blue peeking out from underneath the bed. I bent down to get a better look. Bile rose up my throat. It was the shirt I'd just bought her—the shirt she'd been wearing the last time I saw her at Dixie's – laid shredded to pieces on the floor in front of me.

Chapter Twenty - Six

JORDAN

oday was Christmas Eve.

It has been six days since I last saw Tom.

For the three days since my kidnapping, Ryan had kept me continuously drugged. Thankfully, I had no recollection of what he chose to do to me in that time. Lucky for me, I got my period the night after waking up. He wouldn't touch me after that. He never used to. Treated me like the plague during that time of the month, but due to the wonders of the birth control pill, he knew that my periods only lasted four days, which meant I had today left before he would be expecting something from me. He was absolutely unstable—the padded room kind.

This cabin I was being held hostage in was supposed to be my wedding gift from my ex-fiancé. If I had actually cared for the bastard, I might have been flattered, but I couldn't give a shit. It really was a lovely cabin. The house was suspended mid-air on the side of a mountain and anchored to it in order to stay in place. The front of the house was the only portion that was actually on land. I had always said I wished I had a mountain home where I could have little getaways. His sane side must have bought it for me. This reason alone was why he took me here. He assumed he could win me back with this lavish house and trying to show me what our lives would be like together again. That would never happen.

I'd treated Ryan like a prince since he stopped drugging me, only so I could be in his good graces. He'd even trusted me enough to leave me alone at the cabin when he went out a few times. Unfortunately, he locked the door from the outside, and I had no way of unlocking it from the inside. I suggested one time that I make him his favorite meal, like how I used to cook for him. I had never been that much of a cook, but I could make pasta. I pleaded with him to get me the ingredients to make dinner for him, to make up to him since I couldn't do anything else for him. He agreed.

Stupid fool.

During those few times, I calculated that it took him roughly an hour and a half to go into town. Within that time frame, I would work out and build up my strength again. Then I would shower before he came back, hiding the sweats I'd borrowed from him and replacing them with the lingerie he'd bought for me. They were the only clothes he let me have. I really didn't know how my once simple life as a teacher ended up like this.

I had to put my plan of escape into motion. Tomorrow was D-Day.

I waltzed into the kitchen wearing a black and white lingerie ensemble, sat on the kitchen stool to his right and threw my legs over him as he flipped through a magazine. I knew he would put his hands on my legs. I also knew he liked clean-shaven women.

"Jordan, *what* is this?"

I flicked through another magazine, acting like I didn't understand.

"What are you talking about, baby?" I tilted my head in question and played stupid.

"Why haven't you shaved your legs?" The harshness oozed from his voice. I restrained from flinching and I forced down the fear that wanted to arise.

"Oh, baby, you know I don't like those kinds of razors that you use," I said, batting my eyes. "They always give me razor burn, and it stings so much." The way I had to act toward him was disheartening, but I needed to do it to get out of here.

"Well, it should be good enough for you." He turned away, and I reached out and touched his arm.

"Sweetie, I have to shave… you know… down there," I said, pointing downward. "I can't have razor burn. I want to be perfect for you." I needed him out of the house one last time before tomorrow. "You know I only like those pink ones." I smiled at him seductively and leaned into his ear.

"Come on, big boy, please do one little thing for me so I can rock you all day tomorrow." Gag me. He grabbed my chin, yanking it toward him. I knew he would wiggle his slimy tongue in my mouth. I endured it. It was the price I had to pay in order to be free from him. He pulled his mouth away from mine as a grin slid up his face.

"Those pink ones with the flowers?"

I nodded and smiled.

"That's them." I winked in convincingly, but instead of leaving, he grazed his hand down my chest, squeezing my barely-covered breast.

"Tomorrow is going to be a very satisfying Christmas morning."

I nodded as I swallowed the anxiety rising up my stomach. He stood up from the stool and didn't give me a backward glance as he headed out the door. I exhaled as I tried to keep myself from shaking. I closed my eyes and pictured Tom. I pictured our future together. I pictured the life we would have when I found my way into his arms again.

Tom's love gave me the strength I needed to get off the stool and make sure I could be strong enough to get out of here. I didn't know where in the mountains we were, but I couldn't rely on the people I loved to find me. I had to take care of myself and stand up to the bastard who put me here. I started doing the workout routine I'd developed the past few days, willing myself to become as strong as possible. I focused on Tom. My love for him was my strength.

In gauging the time that had passed, I figured I had about twenty minutes left before he got back, and I headed toward the bathroom to shower, not worrying about washing my hair. I made myself as presentable as possible and put on the same black and white lingerie ensemble I had on before my work out. I didn't want him to get suspicious about my shower.

I heaved a breath as I left the bathroom and glanced out of the window. A plan tickled my brain. My desire to rid myself of this bastard brought me over to the large window in the master bedroom that we unfortunately had to share. I flicked a small latch on the inside of the window pane, allowing it to push open outward. After I made sure it would be easy to open again, I shut it, but left it ever so slightly ajar so as not to be noticeable.

The door to the bedroom creaked open and I cringed inwardly, pretending I was staring out over the view. Ryan's arms wrapped around me while his face nuzzled against my neck. I decided to play the game and wrapped my fingers around his as he pulled me close to him.

"Isn't the view here so perfect? I can't believe you bought this for us." Turning around to face him, I wrapped my arms around his neck and gazed into his eyes, hoping for any sign that I would get out of this.

I asked, "Do you promise to never hurt me again? We need to love each other. I want to be enough for you, so you don't have to go somewhere else to get it."

His evil grin appeared as he gripped my ass and crushed my body toward him. "If you give me what I want, I won't have to look somewhere else."

"I'll give you anything you want… tomorrow! You know I'm so crampy, baby," I whined as I rested my head on his chest. He grabbed my shoulders and pushed me away. My eyes popped open, the fear tumbling out. He grabbed my chin, pressing his lips to mine, and yanked it back.

"Well, you're still going to have to do something for me now." He pressed down on my shoulders and forced me on my knees. He unzipped his jeans and I bit my shaking lip. I did what I had to do and acted like I enjoyed it.

Before he could zip his jeans back up, I ran to the bathroom to brush my teeth and take a shower, again. I scrubbed the filth away, holding my tears back. I used the razor this time so he would go along with the idea that I would willingly have sex with him tomorrow. I didn't care what it took. I would not be in this God forsaken cabin after tomorrow. One of us would die, and by God, I would make sure that it wouldn't be me.

My plan had to work.

TODAY WAS THE day… it was D-Day, the day that I would storm the beaches of Normandy.

Kill or be killed.

It was the only way out. I loved Tom with all of my being, but after what I had done, I was afraid he might not ever love me again. I could only hope that he would take me back, but the only way I could get back to him was to kill the devil first. I hopped out of bed early to make him a lavish breakfast with eggs, grits, and bacon. While I stood at the stove, he wrapped his arms around me as his revolting arousal nudged my lower back.

"Merry Christmas, sweetheart."

I wiggled out of his arms and turned around, pointing a spatula in his face.

"Nuh-uh-uh… not until breakfast, mister." I wished I could slap his face with the spatula, but instead I leaned up to kiss his lips and whispered, "Eat your breakfast while I take a shower to get ready for you. Don't come up until I call you."

He swatted my ass as I turned away. I glared as I continued my walk into the bedroom.

He would suffer for that.

I gave myself a really fast scrub in the shower and put on a very revealing two-piece ensemble. I lit candles throughout the room for effect. It was a cloudy cold day this Christmas morning, and I hoped to be in Tom's arms by the day's end. I set down the lighter and pulled open the drawer on his night side table. Adrenaline began to flood my system as I grabbed a little something that put me through hell the first few days. I nestled the end of the syringe inside the waistband of my thong with the needle sticking out, being careful not to poke myself in the stomach.

I faced the window, waiting for him to walk in behind me. My eyes held a murderous stare over the vast mountain side. My heart pounded inside my chest as my hands fisted with hatred. I clenched my teeth.

It was now or never.

Either he dies or I die.

"Ryan," I yelled as I glared across the peaks of Mount Mitchell. "Come and get me!"

The door slowly crept open. I held my stare over the bare mountain as my blood turned cold, seething ice through my veins. One hand rested on the window sill as the other kept a death grip locked around the syringe. The floor creaked with each of his steps; only five steps away from freedom, either from walking out of the door or the end of my existence. Whichever way the pendulum swung, I accepted my fate. This was D-Day. The day someone would die.

I counted each of his steps.

Five. I inhaled deep.

Four. I emptied my lungs in a silent exhale.

Three. My heart pounded and I readied myself.

Two. The breath caught in my throat.

One. My heart stopped.

In a swift crouch, I threw my leg back in a kick, aiming directly for his groin. My heel struck his erection in a full blow. He staggered backward, groaning from the hit. I threw my arm around, gripping the syringe and impaling it deep into his bicep. As he hunched over at the waist yelping in pain, I swung my leg around and side swiped his face. A sharp pain shot through my ankle, but I ignored it as I focused on keeping myself from tumbling. He fell toward the floor, but caught himself and pulled to his knees. I backed toward the window again. He swayed as the drugs entered his system, and I clenched my fists for whatever came next. His eyes glassed over, but the devil fire still bled through. This was the moment where God decided who lived and who died.

He charged at me in three drugged steps. I crouched low as his flailing body careened toward me. As soon as his body hovered over my crouch, I pushed up against his charging momentum. Using all the strength I had, I launched him through the unlatched window. I held onto its ledge as gravity began to carry me over with him. I released him. By instinct, he grabbed onto the window's ledge to keep from falling. His legs dangled, hanging above the earth.

"You fucking bitch! I am going to kill you." He slurred his words. His eyes turned wicked as his adrenaline surged, overpowering the drugs. My death stare locked with his as realization shocked his face. His eyes followed my hand as

I gripped the handle of the open window. I sneered back at him, mimicking the evil he'd admonished upon me.

"Rot. In. Hell."

I pulled the window down with every bit of my strength, slamming it brutally on his fingers. He released a yelp as one hand fell away. My grip tightened on the handle, and with every muscle in my body, I slammed it down again, shattering the window. Shards of glass flew outward, raining over the devil. He released a gasp as his hand slipped from my view. I bent over to watch through the broken window. A gut-wrenching scream echoed into nothing. His flailing body slammed onto a rock. The silence proved his death. Silence was the sound of freedom. The fear and anxiety poured out of me as I fell to the wooden floor, tears streaming down my face. I had killed Ryan. I had killed my ex-fiancé. I could go home.

Chapter Twenty-Seven

TOM

The constant ache continued to burn a hole through my heart. As the days dwindled, I slowly sank deeper into the depression that had become my life. The first and only woman I had ever loved was gone, and I couldn't do a damn thing about it except continue the endless search. I had searched for days upon days with no hope. The fire that once flickered in my eyes had been extinguished. It would never light until I was with Jordan again. It had been a week since I last saw my darling. I didn't know if I could survive much longer without her.

Five o'clock on a cold and dreary Christmas morning. My house had been serving as the operation center in the search for Jordan. Since it was Christmas, there wouldn't be as many volunteers and officers today, although at this point, I was praying for the hand of God to give us a miracle. The realization of what might be the end result was too much to bear. She had to be alive. I had to keep going.

Caleb Harris and a few police officers studied a map around the desk in my office; they were already discussing the search area for today. We had no leads or witnesses since the hotel incident. We'd had nothing to go on until yesterday evening when we received a tip from the owner of local drug store near Mount Mitchell in Yancey County. They had a customer fitting the description of Ryan. I wanted to head up there that evening, but due to the declining sun and the impending snow, my request was denied.

I waved to a passing officer and pulled out the ground coffee to start a fresh pot, seeing that another would have to be made shortly due to the number of people staying in the house. Cal and Marie were still in the downstairs suite. Paul and Ellie had taken over the second bedroom upstairs while Lance and I had been taking turns sleeping in my room. He seemed unable to sleep much either. Aunt Ethel and Uncle Al had been over every day. Uncle Al had made sure that everyone was well fed. Everyone had a home to go to, and I was thankful they all stayed here. I had lived by myself since high school, but this was one time when I just couldn't stand to be alone. As soon as I pushed the button to brew, someone's steps echoed down the stairs.

"Hey, Tom."

I glanced over to the gruff, tired voice of Lance; the bags under his eyes were as large and as dark as mine.

"Couldn't sleep, either?"

Lance shook his head as he plopped down on of the stools around the island.

"Doesn't feel too much like Christmas, does it?"

He hung his head while I glanced around the house at Jordan's Christmas decorations. I had never seen the house look like this, with all of the wreaths and garlands with little white lights strung throughout. The biggest Christmas tree that would fit in the living room was laced from top to bottom with ribbons, lights, and ornaments. I remembered Jordan begging me a few weeks ago to go out into the woods near the farm to cut down our own. Of course, I happily obliged. I would do anything for her.

"Nope, it sure doesn't," I said glumly. It was Christmas. I needed my girl.

Just as the coffee finished brewing, there was a quiet knock on the front door. Lance and I looked at each other, both of our faces scrunched in confusion. I glanced back at the clock on the microwave. It read only twenty minutes after five. I darted around the counter as he hopped off the bar stool. We both hurried to the door alongside Caleb and the two officers with him. I reached it first and hurled it open.

"Whoa, is this the Jordan Hawthorne search party welcome committee?"

"Katherine." I exhaled as I reached out to hug my new friend, and she gripped back. Her eyes filled with tears as I ushered her into the house and closed the door behind her.

"So, is this *the* Katherine?" asked Lance, who seemed to have lost movement in his eyes. They were glued to Katherine. Figured.

"Yep, that's me," she said, ignoring his stare as she turned back to me and dropped her bags. She must have heard about Lance already, because she completely blew him off. That never happened with Lance.

"I'm so sorry for coming this early in the morning. I've been in London all week, and for some reason my phone wasn't working well. I flew over as soon as I heard about Jordan. My flight landed about three hours ago in Charlotte and I came straight here."

With no delay, Lance picked up her bags. Katherine and I both turned to watch him. He was unbelievable.

"You must be exhausted. Let me show you to Tom's room. Sleep a little bit and you can catch up with Cal and Marie when you wake up."

Katherine nodded. She gave me another hug, and then followed Lance up the stairs. I shook my head after him as he departed, the goofiest grin spreading across his face as he walked up the stairs behind her. I turned back toward Caleb as I pointed at the map on my desk.

"Now, let's go find my girl."

EVERYONE GATHERED AROUND the map of Yancey County spread out on the desk in my office. We were about to be assigned to the areas we would be searching today. Everyone would be involved in today's search except Marie, Aunt Ethel, and Uncle Al. We didn't get any volunteer help today so the search team consisted of Caleb and two additional officers, Paul, Ellie, Lance, Katherine, Cal, and me.

"Okay team," Caleb begun. "We have two four-wheelers available to go through the denser forest areas around Mount Mitchell. I would like Paul and Ellie to go on one and Lance and Katherine to take the other."

"Really?" Katherine asked as she rolled her eyes.

"What's wrong with that?" Lance asked as he draped his arm over her shoulder and said, "Seriously, I don't bite... hard."

Katherine snorted.

"Fine! I'm doing this for Jordan anyway. Not you," she said, nudging Lance in his stomach with her elbow. Lance smiled at her response. It was the first genuine smile I had seen out of him in a week.

"Well, I'm glad we've got that sorted out... moving on," Caleb said as he turned his attention back to the map. "Cal, I'd like you and Tom to take his truck through the rural roads around the perimeter, and these two officers and I will take each of our cruisers around the major and non-major highways near the town of Burnsville. There's a snow storm coming through again tonight, so we will have to abort the search at sunset. We can't have anyone getting stuck out in the dark. We don't have the men to search for y'all as well."

His focus switched to me as he emphasized the part about stopping before dark. I knew he wanted me to agree, but if I was close enough to get my girl, I'd be damned if I would listen to some cop telling me to stop. We all retreated to our points of interest. Cal and I hopped into my truck; the four-wheelers we were to use were to be dropped off by the officers in their respective search locations. Uncle Al packed each team a few sandwiches and thermoses of stew to keep the chill off. Paul, Ellie, Lance, and Katherine covered themselves from head to toe in winter hiking attire in order to keep as warm as possible in the cold elements.

Today would be the day I would find my girl.

As the growing darkness crept into the sky, Cal forced me to head back home. With the looming clouds, we were sure for another night of snowfall. Tonight's storm looked like it would be harsher than yesterday's. The gloom wedged its way inside my soul. I feared the worst now. I was afraid all hope was lost. We hadn't made any headway, and the snow-covered mountain made maneuvering very difficult in my truck, even with the four-wheel drive. The roads hadn't become iced over as of yet. Due to the expected snow fall tonight, I was afraid that our search efforts would be quite limited tomorrow. The agony pierced through my body. *Please God, bring her back to me.*

The truck was eerily silent. Cal and I were both going through our own personal torment. I searched for any shred of hope inside of me, but there wasn't anything left. If I couldn't find my girl on Christmas, when would I find her?

"Cal?" The lump in my throat dared the tears to come rolling down. I swallowed as best I could. Cowboys didn't cry. I was her cowboy. He turned to look in my direction as I continued to drive down the highway.

"I'm going to marry your daughter when we find her." A tear slid out of my eye. Maybe cowboys didn't cry, but a man who lost his heart did. The truck remained silent. I had hoped he would give me his blessing, but I didn't care if he did or if he didn't. I was going to marry his daughter, and no one was going to stop me.

"I wouldn't expect anything less, son."

A small smile curved my lips as the tears glazed my sight. I held back a sob. I would not lose hope. I would put my grandmother's ring on her finger, or I would die with her.

We all made it back to the farm around 7:30 that night. Paul, Ellie, Lance, and Katherine all huddled around the fire, eating more of Uncle Al's stew. I wasn't hungry in the least. I headed into the kitchen and grabbed my bottle of whiskey. With a deep breath, I poured myself a hefty glass and fed the inevitable doom, the only thing I could think to do. After taking my third shot, a hand touched my shoulder. I turned to look into the tired eyes of my best friend. Paul gripped me in a strong hug as the tears poured out of me.

"Paul," I muttered. "What if we never find her? What if she's… Oh God, Paul. What am I going to do?" I started to sob. It was the first time I had let the emotions fully take me over. It wasn't the fact that she had been kidnapped. It was the fact that I was afraid she was dead.

Paul led me over to the sofa in front of the fire as Ellie wrapped a blanket around my shoulders. She hugged me as I continued sobbing, and she cried with me. This was the first time I actually doubted we would ever find her. I knew she wouldn't give in to Ryan easily. I knew how his mind worked, but after all this time, there was no sign of Jordan. I started to believe that my darling… my sweet Jordan… was gone forever.

Everyone had tears in their eyes. Katherine's head rested on Lance's shoulder as he consoled her. Cal and Marie had retreated to their room to mourn in their own private peace. Paul seemed to need some privacy of his own to let himself cry. He was never one to show any sort of emotion unless Ellie was involved.

"I'm going to call my brother and see what our next course of action is," Paul said.

We all nodded. I looked up at him and saw his lips begin to quiver. My sobbing began again in earnest.

I heard the unlatching of the door as Paul left the house. I stared into the fire and prayed over and over.

Of all things Holy, please let her be alive.

I held my head in of my hands, closing my eyes. Her beautiful smile came through the darkness, her eyes shining bright. Her words of love echoed in my mind. This couldn't be it. God wouldn't take someone else that I loved away from me. I couldn't lose someone else. She had to be alive. My heart drummed in peace. I knew she was alive. She had to be.

The door swung open and crashed against the wall, breaking our somber disposition. We all turned to look as Paul ran in.

"Tom! Get up! Help!"

I sprinted over to the open door and ran outside. I saw what he was running to, and I ran faster. The tears poured down my face as fast as my legs would move. She crumbled to the ground just steps away.

"Oh my God! Jordan!… Jordan!"

Chapter Twenty-Eight

JORDAN

The mysterious field surrounded me, but the fear I once felt in this field vanished. It was replaced by hope. One simple word was so hard to grasp, but as the fireflies danced around me I knew that all of the evils were gone. They flew about the dark sky, directing me toward a glimmer of light. As we arrived closer, a welcoming buzz pulsated, drawing me like a moth to a light. I began to walk closer into this light. I turned around to look for my friends as they scattered into the night. Their protection over me was complete. I had to walk into this light alone.

My eyes flickered open to an echoing beep, constant and repetitive. Unable to get my bearings, I closed my eyes, looking for my protectors. There was only darkness again. The smell wasn't of my field; it was of bleach, sanitizer, and a scent so welcoming… the scent of sunshine and leather.

My eyes flickered open once again as I looked around my dimly lit surroundings. My neck ached as I turned my head to the left. Darkness lurked behind the curtained window with no sign of morning yet. I winced as I turned my head to the right. The most beautiful face slept in a chair next to my bed. His head rested on the mattress while his hand held mine in a loose grip. I reached over with my left hand and brushed the hair away from his brow. I trailed my thumb underneath his eye. The dark circles grabbed my heart. It ached for what he had gone through. I caressed his cheek with the back of my hand, the stubble brushing against my knuckles. I could be with this man for as long as he would have me, and I didn't have to hide from anyone. I was finally free.

Tom let out a little groan as I pulled my right hand from his grasp. He blinked his eyes open, still half asleep. A smile rose up my cheeks as I gazed at my loving cowboy. His eyes blinked again, finally catching my gaze.

"Darlin'?"

He raised his head and a tear dripped from his eye. I wiped it away with my thumb as another one fell. He sat on the edge of the bed and wrapped his arms around me. I cried into the crook of his neck as he wept against my hair. He pulled back to look at me, still keeping his arms around me.

"I thought you were taken from me forever." He sobbed as he leaned toward my face, kissing my tears away. I held his face in my hand and we looked into each other's eyes, revealing all the love we had for each other. Wasting no more time, I leaned up and kissed his beautiful lips.

"I'm yours, forever."

His thumb traced my jaw line, memorizing my face.

"You are mine, darlin'… always."

A FEW HOURS later I woke up again to a bright, dawning room. I turned around in Tom's arms to look into his face. His arms squeezed me tight as his morning grin brightened his face, and for one single moment, it was as if no time had passed and nothing had happened. I didn't know if I would ever forget what happened, but I knew I was strong enough with Tom by my side to move on. I would never let Ryan drag me down again.

"Good morning, darlin'."

I pressed my lips to his, so thankful for what I had.

"Good morning, cowboy."

The door popped open as my father's voice echoed throughout the quiet room.

"Why don't y'all scoot over and make room for your big ol' daddy."

I sat up as Mom and Dad came over to my side of the hospital bed. They both grabbed me into the normal parental bear hugs. I still couldn't help the tears. I thought I had lost everyone. I had been so close to death. I could have lost all of this. But what life would it have been had I not been able to be with the people I loved?

"We're so glad you're back safe." Mom refused to let me go and kept her arms tight around me long after Dad stepped away. I pried her off me as I tried my best to lighten the mood. I pulled back to look at my loving parents, holding both of their hands as Tom kept his arm wrapped around me. I didn't think he would let me out of his hold.

"In all seriousness, I need to know something very important," I asked.

They glanced at each other with the same perplexed face and then looked back me.

"What is it, Jordan?" Mom asked as I took a deep breath.

"Did the Panthers beat the Saints? I just have to know."

Dad chuckled and shook his head no. Tom laughed and kissed the side of my head. I added, "Well, it was an important game."

A knock rapped on the door.

"Can we come in?" Ellie poked her head through the open door. I spread out my arms for my friend, and she ran to me with tears in her eyes. She squeezed me tight and said, "I thought I had lost my model."

"I'm too stubborn for that."

Paul and Lance came in, finally looking like the friends they had always been. I greeted them with huge smiles.

"Jordan, I have one little surprise for you," Lance said as he held open the door.

"Katherine!"

She ran over to the bed, jumping on top of me and holding on for dear life. The welcoming tears resumed as we leaned back and smiled at each other. She playfully grabbed me and shook me.

"Don't ever do that to me again."

I pulled her back into a tight hug.

"Don't worry. Nothing bad will happen to me again," I whispered, thanking God that I knew I was right.

All of the most important people in my life were this

room. One of my hands was firmly in Katherine's grasp and the other was firmly in Tom's. This was how life should be... complete and happy. Another knock came from the door as a doctor and a nurse entered the room.

"Good morning, Jordan," the male doctor stated. "I'm Doctor Folse, and this is Nurse Taylor. We would like to go over a few things with you and also check your vitals. So, if the family would kindly depart for a moment."

Tom leaned over to kiss my forehead and I grabbed his hand. He gave me a confused look as I shook my head.

"Stay... please."

"Darlin', I don't know if I want to be here for this," he said as he eased into the chair next to me.

"I need you. Please stay. I can't do this without you."

He nodded and settled, albeit a little uncomfortably. I glanced up at Doctor Folse and said, "I'd like my boyfriend to stay."

"Jordan, we would like to go over a few things as to what happened. A female police officer will be in shortly to take your statement. Most patients do this alone."

I shook my head. I could not go through this without Tom.

"No, I need him here."

Tom looked at me and I reassured him this was what I wanted. He squeezed my hand and kept his eyes locked on me for the entire examination.

When the examination had been completed, Doctor Folse assured me that I had not been assaulted while I was unconscious. By the end of the exam, Tom's head pressed into my hand as he clenched it with both of his. It probably was a little too much to ask of him, but he was my only form of strength. I needed him like I needed air to breathe.

As the doctor and nurse left, a lady arrived at the door dressed in business casual attire, but I was pretty sure she was all business.

"Hello, Jordan," she said as she walked over to me and shook my hand, "I'm Detective Jan Holdings. Please call me Jan."

"Thank you, Jan. I want this over and done with." I swallowed hard as I looked at Tom. I didn't want to tell him the things that had happened, but he had to know. If I repulsed him after he knew, then it was better that I find out now rather than later.

"So Jordan, can you tell us where Rylan Gowin is now?"

My eyes narrowed in confusion as she looked up from her notepad, waiting for some sort of answer.

"I'm sorry. You must have the wrong patient."

Tom squeezed my hand and brought it up to his lips, pressing a kiss to my knuckle.

"Ryan has done this sort of thing before."

My jaw slacked as my blood ran cold.

"Do what?"

Tom turned back to the detective.

"Can you give us one minute? I need to fill her in on a few things." He held my hand as we waited for the door to close behind the detective. He turned back around as I searched his eyes.

"What is going on?" I asked. "Who is Rylan Gowin?"

He took a deep breath.

"Rylan Gowin was a foster home kid who witnessed his mother being murdered by his father. Rylan Gowin then became Randy Goodson. Randy Goodson's girlfriend dumped him in college. She then vanished, as did he. They never found the body or Randy Goodson."

I turned away from the new information as I stared off into space.

"He would have killed me."

"Do you think he would have?"

I turned back toward him and nodded.

"It was either him or me."

He tilted his head to the side as his eyes questioned my statement.

"Let her back in."

He nodded, stood up from the chair and opened the door to the detective. She joined Tom by my bedside.

"Jordan, can you tell us where Rylan Gowin is now?" She readied her notepad to resume questioning. I was ready to finally put this all behind me. Hopefully, Tom would still be by my side when it was all over.

"Yes, I do know where Rylan or Ryan or whatever his name is."

Tom leaned forward in his chair.

"Where is he, darlin'?"

I gazed up at him and took a calming breath. I had to do this. He had to know what I did.

"At the bottom of Mount Mitchell."

His hand slacked in mine as he fell back into the chair.

AFTER GOING THROUGH the whole episode of being knocked out and drugged, I felt exhausted. Tom shook with anger. I gripped his hand until all police and doctors left my room, which wasn't until sometime later. As soon as the door slammed, he let go of my hand and walked around the bed to the window. He folded his arms across his chest and I couldn't stop the tears from pouring out of me. I shrugged to myself. After all of this… after all I had been through to get him back… I had lost him.

"Tom? Please don't be angry with me. I did what I thought was best, but please don't leave me because of my poor planning. I just had to get out of there." I buried my face in my hands and sobbed. Not once after all that I had been through did I think I would truly lose him, not until this moment. Tom tugged my hands away from my face and pulled me into his chest.

"No, Jordan. I could never be mad at you." His voice cracked as his body trembled underneath my hands. "I thought I had lost you. I can't believe you had to go through that. *I* should have killed him. I wanted to kill him. I'm just glad that he's dead. I'm glad that he is rotting in hell and can never hurt you again."

"It's over, Tom. He can't hurt me anymore."

He leaned over and kissed me.

It was finally over.

Chapter Twenty-Nine

JORDAN

t was New Year's Eve when they finally released me from the hospital. My hand never left Tom's as he navigated the winding roads. I tried to pull my hand away a few times, but he squeezed it tighter. We drove up to our beautiful farm house that I now called home. As I reached for the handle on Tom's truck to get out, he motioned me to wait as he ran around to open the door for me. I smiled at his adorableness. I would never tire of him.

"You're always the gentleman, aren't you?"

He took my hand to help me down.

"Well, of course, Ms. Hawthorne."

He looped my arm through his, his eyes beaming in the moonlight. I was so glad the hospital let me go home to spend my New Year's. The only medicine I needed was Tom. Ryan and everything he represented was finally behind me. I knew that Tom was all I would ever need, and I couldn't help the smile that eased up my cheeks while we approached the front door.

He unlocked it and pushed the door open, allowing me to walk through. I gasped at the sight before my eyes. Lined from the entryway to the back door were dozens upon dozens of daisies and votive candles. Tom pressed his lips to my cheek.

"Welcome home, darlin.'"

I took his face in my hands and kissed him passionately. As my hands rediscovered his body, he kicked the door shut and pressed me against it. I hitched one leg around his hip as he leaned against me. I broke free as he kissed down my neck. I needed him. I needed to feel whole again.

"Come. I have something for you."

I nodded as I followed the magical walkway through the house. As we approached the back door, he turned to me with a sexy grin and said, "Do you trust me?"

I smiled, remembering the first time he had a surprise for me. I whispered, "Always."

"Close your eyes, darlin.'" He kissed my lips, and with a case of déjà vu, I closed my eyes. He hooked one arm under my knees and the other around my back, carrying me out the back door in true bridal fashion. I honored my word, keeping my eyes closed as I tucked my face into his neck, breathing in his scent and cherishing the fact that I had him for as long as he'd keep me. He set me on my feet and held my arm to make sure I was steady.

"Don't open your eyes yet."

I nodded, biting my lip. He shifted and I could feel him

standing in front of me. He gently cupped my cheek as his lips moved close to mine. He grazed over my lips for a moment and then pulled away.

"I loved you the first moment I saw you. It was just the better that you were naked," he said, and we both laughed.

"My first feeling of love was physical. I wanted every part of you, and I wouldn't stop until I got you." He let out a small breath. "Then I was lucky enough to realize that my water goddess was the most amazing woman in the whole world. That she wanted to give me a chance. She allowed me into her heart, as she was already in mine."

A tear escaped as my heart drummed a beat of pure happiness at his whispering words.

"Open your eyes, darling."

The tears streamed down my face the instant my eyes settled upon the view. He had reincarnated our first meal on the farm the best way he could. He had strung thousands of twinkling Christmas lights throughout the open field. Being surrounded by the fiery lights that led me to peace, my heart danced. The deck mimicked the inside of the house with dozens of daisies and candles, making my home welcoming even more special. I looked into the eyes of the man I loved as I smiled a teary smile.

"Darlin', I know that I could never survive without you. I felt hollow when you weren't here to fill my heart." A tear dripped from his eye. I wiped it away with my thumb, caressing his cheek. A smile broke through the tears. He grabbed my hand in his and continued, "I believe with all of my heart that I was put here in this world to make you happy for the rest of our lives. Forever."

My heart started to beat rapidly as he lowered down to one knee and opened up a small, square box. Per a woman's instinct, I covered my open mouth with my hand as I gazed on my cowboy in awe.

"Jordan… my sweet darling… would you allow me to try to make you the happiest woman alive? Would you allow me to show you how much happiness you give me by just waking up in my arms every day?"

My eyes filled with tears as he let out a breath, preparing himself for the biggest question of our lives.

"Jordan, will you marry me?"

All I could do was to stare at Tom as the happiest of tears rolled down my face. I couldn't believe he wanted me forever. How was I so lucky? I gripped his hand to stand him up, and as I gazed in the eyes of my future husband, I answered the best question any girl could ever be asked.

"Yes."

He slipped an antique ring on my finger and I saw four small diamonds set in the center with a platinum band around. It was so simple and beautiful.

"It was my grandmother's, and I know she would want you to have it."

I wrapped my arms around his neck, kissing him deeply. Not breaking the kiss, I jumped up and wrapped my legs around him. My eyes filled with lust as I looked back into his. With a sexy smile, I purred, "Take me to bed, cowboy."

He carried me up the stairway into our bedroom. If my eyes weren't solely on him, I might have noticed the flowers and candles strewn throughout the room, but my eyes were glued to his. My fiancé.

He put me down as we both knelt upon the bed. He slowly pulled my shirt over my head and started kissing down my neck and to my chest, unhooking my bra. He looked at my body as he had the first time… full of both love and lust.

I reached for the hem of his shirt and pulled it up and over his head. I reclined onto the bed with his pressing body pressed above me as he kissed from my neck down to my breasts, paying special attention to each nipple, which budded immediately under his touch. His hands roamed down my body as he unbuttoned my jeans, pushing them down along with my panties. I did the same with his pants and boxers. I needed him. I needed this.

His hand grazed over my chest, across my stomach, and down to my core. My body pulsated with the same yearning that erupted whenever he was near. He looked at me and our eyes were both heavy with want.

"I love you forever, Jordan."

"I love you, cowboy."

He licked my bottom lip, allowing me access to his perfect tongue. Never breaking the kiss, his hand returned to where I needed him the most. He slipped one finger inside me, slowly pumping and milking me, which had me begging for more. I gasped inside his mouth as he slipped a second finger inside. I couldn't help thrusting into his fingers. I needed him so much. He kept a steady rhythm as he flicked with his thumb. I jerked with the intensity of my impending orgasm, and broke away from his kiss as I continued to moan. He kissed down my neck to my nipples again. I began to pant. I hadn't felt this in so long. I missed his love.

He kissed down my body and nuzzled his mouth to

my core. He used his tongue with such precision, my body arched off the bed. I began to come. He didn't break free as every molecule in my body exploded in delight.

When my body started to descend, he slipped inside of me and thrust gently, allowing me to ride the wave. We looked into each other's eyes with every thrust and never broke contact as we continued to make love.

"I love you, Jordan."

"I love you."

Feeling me nearing orgasm again, he lifted my hips and lunged inside me repeatedly. I screamed out his name, and he covered my mouth with a kiss. He moaned inside of my mouth as he poured inside of me.

With him still on top of me, we continued to kiss lazily, willing our breathing back to normal. He caressed my check as I wrapped my arms and legs around him.

"You are the most beautiful woman to have ever lived, and I'm so blessed to have the chance to marry you."

He still made my heart melt. I shook my head and said, "We're both blessed. No one could ever be as happy as I am right now."

For the rest of the night, we remained naked and cuddled together. The only thing I refused to take off was my engagement ring.

I was going to be Mrs. McCloud, and it was the happiest day of my life.

NORMAL TWENTY-SOMETHINGS WOULD spend New Year's

Eve at a bar, ringing the New Year in together with friends, but due to the circumstances of a little stay in a hospital, we postponed our celebration until New Year's Day. We still went to our local watering hole, and as Tom opened up the door for me, we saw we weren't the only ones planning on continuing the New Year's celebration. College bowl games were littered across the televisions, and I peeked at a few when we passed by. Tom glanced back at me when I slowed my steps.

"What?" I grinned. "It's football. You should be lucky that your bride-to-be is obsessed with football."

"Oh, I am. I completely am." He placed a chaste kiss on my lips as we headed back to the same table where we'd all sat not too long ago. Tom paused as we approached it. I wanted to prove the point that I had moved on, so I pulled out my own chair and sat down. I grinned at my fiancé and he smiled back before heading to the bar for a couple of pitchers. I sat back and tilted my head, watching him walk to the bar. I was marrying that. I was the luckiest girl alive.

"Jordan!"

I glanced away from my fiancé's ass toward my best friend's voice.

"It is so awesome to see you in this little town," I said as she hugged me tight and then sat across from me.

"Where is everybody else?" Katherine glanced around the bar.

"Are you wondering where Ellie is, or are you wondering where Lance is?"

"Lance, what?"

Lance joined our conversation and sat right next to Katherine. She smiled instantly, and he whispered, "Hi."

Her nose crinkled and I knew exactly what she was doing. It was going to take some time, but Lance would get her if he didn't let up. Tom came back and filled a pint for the four of us.

"Seriously, where's Ellie?" Katherine asked as she tossed her hair back over her shoulder, trying to avoid Lance… or make him believe she was avoiding him. She turned her head.

"Hey, y'all made it! Ellie, come and sit right here."

Katherine patted the chair next to her. Paul went to get a second pitcher. As Katherine and Ellie talked, I noticed Lance couldn't stop looking at Katherine. As long as he didn't screw her over, I was okay with it.

Tom wrapped his arm around me, pulling me close to him. "When are you going to tell everyone?"

"Soon. I just wanted to wait until everyone was settled."

He pressed his lips to my forehead as Katherine's voice pulled us away from our moment.

"Lance!" She groaned and turned to Ellie. "You really dated him for four years?"

"Yep, you get used to it." Ellie grinned at Lance. I was just thankful that everyone seemed on better terms. I watched as Lance got Katherine's attention again. The blush rose up her cheeks and I couldn't help but smile.

He whispered something in her ear again, and she pushed him away, groaning. "I should have never kissed you."

Everyone at the table gasped.

"That's it," Tom said. "It's over."

"What? What's it?" Katherine asked as she glanced around the table and met Ellie's eyes.

"He's a goner," Ellie said.

Katherine gasped as she shook her head, yet she seemed to be smiling. Lance leaned back in his chair and crossed his arms with a smirk across his face. When the table fell silent, I looked at Tom and bit my lip to contain the smile. He nodded for me to let everyone in on our news.

"So, we have an announcement."

Chapter Thirty

JORDAN & TOM

6 months later...

I gazed at my reflection in the mirror as I sat applying the finishing touches of my makeup. I had never seen myself so happy. I never thought the day would come when all of the dreams I had ever wished for would come true. This would be my last few moments to myself as a single woman. I studied myself in the mirror... I would soon be Mrs. Thomas McCloud.

The smile radiated from my face as my mother and my two best friends walked in, all wearing shades of blue. Mom stood behind me, setting her hands on my shoulders. She looked at my reflection in the mirror.

"You are absolutely beautiful, baby girl. I'm so happy for you." I smiled lovingly back at my mother as she continued, "Now, you can work on those grandbabies for me."

I just laughed… if only she knew.

Ellie and Katherine came in wearing one of Ellie's designs. The dresses each were peacock blue and strapless, tailored to the waist then flared into an A-line at the hip, reaching their knees. A white ribbon fit around their waists.

"Okay, Jordan," Ellie said as her aura glowed. "It's time for your dress."

I was so excited! Ellie had made this dress specifically for me, and it was absolutely perfect. It was a knee-length white satin gown with a lace overlay. It had a ribbon tied around the waist, matching the bridesmaids' color of peacock blue.

I stood up and took my robe off as Ellie said, "Girl, I'm glad you finally made a switch from those granny panties you used to wear."

I blushed. I wasn't wearing anything overly lavish, only a matching set of white lace… simple, yet elegant. Besides, it was June. I didn't want to be hot all day. Katherine and Ellie held open the dress to allow me to step into it. They pulled it up over my hips, and Ellie zipped up the back.

I turned around to look at myself in the mirror. I hoped Tom would love it. I pulled my hair half up, leaving cascading curls hanging down my back. He always loved my long brown hair. I wanted to please him, although I had to deny his suggestion of the girls wearing cowboy boots.

Katherine looped her arm through mine and said, "Yeah, I have hot friends." I giggled as she whispered, "Jordan, I think I'm as nervous as you are."

I shook my head and said, "Don't worry. Everything is going to turn out fine."

There was a knock on the door as my daddy entered with

his hand held over his eyes. "Man in the room! Man in the room! Put some clothes on."

"Daddy, the coast is clear."

He peeked through his fingers, still joking around, but his hand fell as he looked upon me. His face radiated a gentle sadness, but also a sense of accomplishment.

He reached out for me and pulled me into a bear hug as he whispered, "I'm so proud of you, Jordan." I smiled as he continued, "I couldn't have asked for a better daughter."

And the blasted tears rolled, messing up my mascara.

The door opened again as Lance walked in and suddenly stopped, not looking at me, but at Katherine. Her face turned a deep blush. Well, this should be interesting.

"I, uh, came to, uh… are y'all ready yet?" he babbled.

I nodded and said, "Okay, it's show time!"

Today I would become Mrs. Thomas Everett McCloud!

Tom, you lucky bastard. You got her to marry you. I stood anxiously at the end of the makeshift aisle in my back field. I wouldn't let Jordan peek outside, as this was my wedding gift to her. It was hard keeping her from snooping, but Katherine and her parents had been good distractions. I tried to turn the outside area into what I hoped would be her dream wedding. Wooden logs lined each side of the aisle on a diagonal since we had a small number of people attending. A white aisle runner led from the back door to the edge of a wooden platform, where I stood with the preacher. The aisle was lined with daisies and glass hurricane lanterns with candles nestled inside, the same way I had done for my proposal. White paper lanterns hung from the trees overhead, casting a flickering light as the sun set on us. If my timing was right, the fireflies would come out when I kissed my bride.

Paul and Lance stood down the few stairs from the deck. Once Marie was seated, Ellie appeared at the back door. She smiled at Paul as she stepped down from the deck. He wrapped her hand around his arm, and he could barely take his eyes off her. After all they had been through, I smiled for them. I glanced over at Lance and his face beamed for them as well. His eyes widened as his face slacked. I looked back toward the door as Katherine appeared. He stood in awe for a second too long and then snapped out of it. She stepped off the deck as he carefully looped her arm through his. When they reached the front, they separated. He winked at me. I chuckled as I shook my head. Always the player.

The violinist segued into the next song as I gazed up at the doorway, my heart thumping with happiness. Cal stepped out and then turned back, holding out his hand. My eyes started to glaze over as my beautiful water goddess, my darling, my Jordan, smiled at me as she stepped into sight. She stopped in awe, taking it all in, and beamed at me. I covered my heart with my hand, feeling all the love I'd ever experience pumping inside me. All I ever wanted to do in life was make her happy. Her eyes were as teary as mine by the time she and Cal met me at the end of the aisle. He kissed her cheek and placed her hand into mine.

I stared into the eyes of my love and mouthed, "I love you."

She smiled and mouthed back, "I love you."

The preacher began, "Dearly beloved, we are gathered together here in the sight of God, and in the face of this company, to join together this man and this woman in Holy Matrimony..."

I LOOKED UP at Tom while we held each other's hands, smiling the giddiest grin a girl could ever smile as the preacher said, "By the power vested in me by the state of North Carolina, I now pronounce you man and wife. Tom, you may kiss your bride."

We smiled at each other as he wrapped his arms around me, pulling me against him. He greedily kissed my lips. I could hear the applause erupting as Tom picked me up by my waist and swung me around. We broke apart, giggling, and he rested his forehead against mine. My eyes flickered to the evening sky as my fiery friends blessed our wedding with their magical light. For always and forever, I would be with the man I loved, and we would spend the rest of our lives watching fireflies.

"I love you, Mrs. McCloud."

"I love you, cowboy."

After the introductions and greetings, the DJ introduced us as Mr. and Mrs. Thomas Everett McCloud, and we walked onto the dance floor for our first dance. I looped my arms around his neck as he held me tight around my back. Together we swayed, gazing into each other's eyes.

"There's just one more thing to make this the best day, cowboy."

He leaned in and pecked my lips, "What's that one thing, darlin'?"

I smiled as I leaned up to his ear and whispered, "Letting you know that you're going to be a daddy."

I looked back and smiled as his face blanked.

He stopped moving.

"Tom?"

He stared in my eyes with no expression on his face.

"Tom?"

"I'm going to be a daddy?" he whispered.

"Yes."

"Wait, wait, wait," he said a little louder. "I'm going to be a daddy?"

The crowd had quieted now as they all trained their eyes on us. I nodded and said, "Yes," again.

He picked me up and spun me around as he yelled, "I'm going to be a dad!"

The wedding attendants cheered, and we were soon drowning in congratulatory hugs from Paul, Ellie, Lance, and Katherine. We danced with the light of the fireflies around us. Tom's lips found mine, his hand grazing over my stomach.

My cheeks hurt from smiling, but I couldn't stop. Wrapped in the arms of the man I loved, I was finally home.

The End

Acknowledgments

I never expected to get to this point. I never thought that my words would be read, and I would acknowledge people after a story. If it weren't for these people, Watching Fireflies would have never flown.

Where to begin … and will it ever end …

To my awesome parents: Thank you for your undying support and sending me to LSU. Geaux Tigers!

To my sister: Thank you for lending me a book that will go unnamed here. After reading unnamed book, I decided that I could write. So, I did.

To my hubster: Thank you for the endless supply of coffee and helping me make this dream possible. I know I suck as a wife sometimes, but I hope this makes up for being locked away in the writing cave.

To my besties: Even though we don't see each other every day like we used to years ago, I'm thankful for y'all every single day of my life.

To my girls in accounting: Thank you for listening to me for over two years about these damn bugs!

To Alex Rosa and Len Webster: Watching you both achieve your dream of publishing helped inspire me to follow in those footsteps. Maybe I should thank Jane Austen. If it weren't for her, our trio might have never been.

To Maja Skvorc: May our love of cowboys and dragons never die.

To Laura Perry: Thank you for pointing and saying, "This! Fix this!"

To Jaycee's Army: There's no better support than a Street Team! Keep on Buzzin'!

To Josh Vitalie: I would have never guessed that my biggest help in writing a romance novel would be from a dude. Thank you for analyzing this cowboy and helping me restructure this into a story that I am now actually proud of. I don't think it's shit anymore. Thank you for assuring me that it isn't shit. I think I owe you a donut.

www.ingramcontent.com/pod-product-compliance
Lightning Source LLC
Chambersburg PA
CBHW020246180626
46810CB00006B/2382